DOUBLE NEGATIVE

NOVELS BY DAVID CARKEET

Double Negative

The Greatest Slump of All Time

I Been There Before

The Full Catastrophe

The Error of Our Ways

From Away

FOR YOUNGER READERS

The Silent Treatment

Quiver River

DOUBLE NEGATIVE

DAVID CARKEET

THE OVERLOOK PRESS
NEW YORK

This edition first published in paperback in the United States in 2010 by

The Overlook Press, Peter Mayer Publishers, Inc.
141 Wooster Street
New York, NY 10012

Cataloging-in-Publication Data is available from the Library of Congress

Book design and typeformatting by Bernard Schleifer
Manufactured in the United States of America
FIRST EDITION
2 4 6 8 10 9 7 5 3 1
ISBN 978-1-59020-300-2

For Barbara

CHAPTER ONE

"JUST WHAT DO YOU DO with these babies, anyway?" Cook paused at the open door of Wach's office when he heard this question, just out of sight of the two men who were talking inside. He smiled as he listened for the reply. This was exactly the kind of question that made his boss rise to his full, contemptible glory.

"I'm certainly not unwilling to answer that question." Cook could imagine the quick, empty smile. "A number of complex variables intersect in any serious attempt to establish a direction of inquiry, a program thrust, a, an, ah, Jeremy, there you are." Cook had stepped forward. It was too painful to go on listening in helpless silence. "I want you to meet the good reporter from New York, who is writing for . . . for . . . ?"

"For nobody in particular. I'm doing this freelance. Philpot."

This last was directed to Cook, and it must have been a name, but how much of one? As with Chinese names, one didn't know right off where to put the "Mr."

"Jeremy Cook," he said, shaking hands with the rather short man.

"Call me Henry."

Cook was glad to have that little question cleared up. Wach said, "Jeremy here knows all there is to know about this place. And about some other things too, right, Jeremy?" He chuckled coldly. "If you'll be so good as to take Mr. Philpot to the nursery, Jeremy, and to the gym, and some of the other units, and introduce him around—let him meet Woeps and Stiph and Milke and the others—and just have a good time, you two, then later we'll all have lunch together." He looked down at his desk and cleared his throat.

Cook looked at him. Wach was best behind that desk, alone, free of human contact. Why did he pretend to be friendly? The place would run just as well, or better, if he gave it up. And why was he giving these directions? Hadn't he already taken up the preceding afternoon preparing him for this visitor, outlining in unnecessary detail the tour that would most favorably impress Philpot? Wach's superfluous instructions made sense, though, in light of Wach Rule Six: appear to be spontaneous except where the appearance of deliberation is called for.

Cook nodded. "Fine, Walter. We'll be back at twelve." He looked at the freelancing Philpot. "Would you like some coffee? I know I would, and Walter here never has any in his office."

"Never touch the stuff," said Wach, almost shouting.

"I'd love some," said Philpot.

"I've got a pot brewing in my office. We can talk there for a while before I show you around."

Wach yelled out something falsely jovial as Cook led Philpot through the small outer office used by Wach's secretary, who was in her accustomed position—filing her nails, a telephone pressed by one shoulder into her hair. She was fairly new to the place. Cook's final opinion of her after two months was that she was too dumb to have a consistent personality.

"Oh, I hate him all right, but for a different reason," she said into the phone as Cook and Philpot passed her desk. Cook swallowed hard. Her comment disturbed him almost as much as the one he had overheard in the elevator that morning. Two young mothers were delivering their children for the day and were talking on the ground floor as they waited for the elevator. When Cook walked up, they fell silent and remained so as the three of them rode up in the elevator. Just as they reached the seventh floor, one whispered: "That's what happens to people when they live alone for too long." All that morning, as he tried to work in his office, images of deviant solitary behavior danced in his head.

"I can't get a handle on that guy," Philpot said, jerking a thumb over his shoulder.

Cook blinked. "Yeah. He's like that. He's not important, though. He just runs the place."

"That's partly right," Cook said to Philpot. He sipped his coffee and put his feet on his desk. "We're concerned with language acquisition in the earliest stages, up to age five. We combine daycare with close observation, audiotaping, videotaping, and some simple experiments. The kids—I think there are about seventy-five now—range from six months to five years in age. They receive the typical care that any child receives in a daycare center. The only difference is that there are seven linguists here lurking in the halls and in the playrooms and beside the changing tables and under the cribs, listening for verb suffixes and glottalization and such things. It's a strange place—none exactly like it in the country. But after you've been here awhile it seems normal enough."

"Why here? Why southern Indiana?"

"It *is* a bit out of the way. The Wabash Institute was originally a center for primate studies. The old buildings are in back of me on the other side of the little river down there, which is called the Baby Wabash, by the way. It feeds into the larger, better-known one." He gestured to the window behind him, which opened out to a road seven stories below and, beyond it, a narrow river, a field, and a few wooden buildings. "Part of what they did was study language acquisition in chimps, using ASL—American Sign Language, used by the deaf—and that grew and became what they mainly did. At the same time, on this side of the river, a sizeable daycare center developed out of a defunct boys' reformatory, serving a variety of folks—Otis Elevator ten miles to the north, Busby Baptist College six miles to the east, and the town of Kinsey just to the south. There was nothing like the number of kids here now, but there were enough to suggest to the primate people—among them Wach, who was second in command—that the daycare part of it could be secondary and the language study part primary, and then the place would be one big lab for research on language acquisition in different species.

"Grant money poured in. This was in the sixties, when the Department of Defense for reasons mysterious to me showed hot interest in linguistics. The reformatory was further remodeled, and the Wabash Institute began to take its present form. Since then the primate center has virtually folded. There are still two or three people over there, but they've got just a few chimps and they confine themselves to studying how red their fannies get and things like that. We've taken over the language area completely." He paused. "It's nice how the movement of language across the river parallels the course of evolution. In fact people here call the wooden footbridge over it Scopes Bridge."

Philpot laughed. "I can use that."

"But you aren't writing anything down."

"No. I don't need to. It'll come back to me tonight in my room. What do *you* do, exactly?"

Cook squirmed slightly in his seat. When he was asked this by neighbors or by townies in Kinsey, the answers he heard himself give were sheepish and apologetic. What could he say? That he was the "resident genius"? That was what his friend Ed had once called him. Cook had his own research, but he liked to help others too. He could see the virtue of imaginative projects and make them better, and he could spy unpromising work well in advance and discourage it at the outset. Every publication coming out of the Institute since he had joined the staff five years earlier had thanked him by name. But it was hard to hang a simple job description on his work. There were slack days and hours when he sat nearly idle, or just read, matched by hectic days of inspired labor. Maybe it was like freelance writing in that respect.

"My job is a bit like freelance writing," he said to Philpot, and as he went on to describe it he realized with one part of his mind that he had just practiced Wach Rule Fourteen, even though the situation didn't call for it: before you manipulate people or lie to them, point out how similar you are to them. He had been around Wach too long. "It varies a lot from day to day. I'm somewhat unfit for specialization, and I say that unboastfully since I consider it a limitation of sorts."

"What are you working on now?"

"Something that doesn't really have my boss's blessing, but I try to keep him ignorant of it. I'm studying what I call 'idiophenomena.' These are linguistic devices that children develop on their own, with no basis in the adult model. They can range from simple utterances with fixed meanings, like a toddler's *buh* for 'I want the toy duck,' to highly original intonation contours."

Philpot frowned and fingered a pen in his shirt pocket as if to withdraw it, but then he just scratched his chin.

"Parents miss a lot of this. They tend to view language acquisition as a straightforward process of gradual accretion highlighted by comical blunders. But a lot more than that goes on. You have to be able to distance yourself from the steady drivel that comes out of children's mouths to find the rules, and that's the main point of the Wabash Institute. What we do is what a good many linguists have done with their own children—observe them and tape them and analyze the result—only we do it better. From what I've heard, it's hard for a person to be both parent and naturalist at the same time. You can ask Ed Woeps about that." Cook nodded to his left. "A colleague with a sixteen-month-old son here at Wabash. I've observed Ed's son, at least linguistically, much more than he has. It was his son, by the way, who actually used *buh* in the way I indicated."

"Do you have any children of your own here?"

"No," said Cook. "I'm not married."

"Can you tell me about the other linguists here?"

"Let's go meet them," said Cook. "Words would not do them justice."

As the two men stood up a strange and loud laugh was easily heard from the office to Cook's right. Because no other sound preceded the laughter, it was as if they were being watched by a silent eavesdropper who found the sight of *Homo sapiens* rising out of a chair hilarious. But Cook knew better. It was only Orffmann. Orffmann liked to laugh, especially when he was alone. Cook would often be working at his desk with his door closed and his mind engaged, when peals of Orffmann's mirth would crash around him. Many a noble, science-advancing thought had thereby been assassinated. Philpot was frowning uneasily at the wall, but Orffmann was one of those that Wach had left off Philpot's visiting list, and Cook figured the less said about him the better.

The same for Aaskhugh, who, standing as he was just outside the door of Cook's office as he and Philpot stepped into the hall, was less avoidable.

"Who's your friend, Jay?" said Aaskhugh, looking at Cook and then at Philpot. Cook performed the introductions, though he was irrationally tempted to lie. Aaskhugh was unique in having this effect on Cook, not a regular liar and in fact normally a very bad one. It was Aaskhugh's attitude toward information that did it. He traded in it. He collected it and dispensed it, without hesitation or discrimination. His fund of knowledge was great, and to keep it that way he asked questions, forever reminding Cook of the unfortunate fact of life that people were out there ready to think about you if you gave them the chance.

Over the years Cook had developed two evasion tactics. One served most handily when he felt mentally dull, say, after drinking or before his morning coffee: he would ask Aaskhugh a question first. Of course, this brought a great deal of useless information into his brain and made him mentally duller still. The second tactic was more challenging: Cook would raise a general philosophical point, one having no direct connection with his or anyone's life, and he would hold to it with maniacal fervor, always being careful not to let his personality slip through. This ploy guaranteed that, short of resorting to hypnosis, Aaskhugh would never learn anything about Cook beyond what he could squeeze from others, and also that Aaskhugh would never be able to charge Cook publicly with being dull—in the sense of being not talkative, at least.

"How long are you going to be here?" Aaskhugh said to Philpot.

Philpot answered, saying several days, perhaps a week. Where was he staying? Philpot named a motel just outside of Kinsey. Whom was the article for? Philpot explained. What had he written that Aaskhugh might have read? Philpot named some pieces, looking to Cook imploringly.

Cook roused himself and broke in with tactic one. "Adam, perhaps you could tell us what you're doing here. Mr. Philpot might be interested."

By "here" Cook meant the observation window facing into a playroom directly across the hall from Cook's office door. But Aaskhugh looked at Cook as if he had said something very silly indeed. "I'm not doing anything here, Jay."

Cook frowned. "But you were standing right outside my door. Weren't you?"

"No, no, no, Jay. I was passing *by* your door. Passing *by*." Aaskhugh's tone implied that Cook would never understand anything until he mastered his prepositions. "See?" By way of demonstration, he began slowly walking away from Cook and Philpot, looking back over his shoulder with a foolish grin.

The curve of the hall finally took him out of their view. Cook turned to Philpot, who stared down the hall in wonder.

"Why does he call you 'Jay'? Isn't your name Jeremy?"

Cook smiled. This was the second thing wrong with Aaskhugh. Or maybe the third. It was hard to keep track. Shunning stale custom, Aaskhugh often ignored the names optimistically given people by their parents in favor of his own inventions. Cook was "Jay" to him. Now and then Ed Woeps was "Daisy" for reasons neither Cook nor Woeps understood. Wach's secretary, Mary—in Cook's mind simply Mary the Secretary—was "Mary, Mary," and Wach's name, which was pronounced like "watch" by its bearer and everyone else at Wabash, occasionally became more Germanic in Aaskhugh's "Wachtmeister." Cook looked forward to the day when he retaliated and rechristened Aaskhugh, perhaps, since the man's first name was Adam, giving him "A" for "Jay," or maybe even "Fucking A."

Cook explained all of this to Philpot as best he could. Then, seeking an antidote to Aaskhugh, he said, "Let me introduce you to Ed," and directed Philpot to Woeps's office next door. Woeps was by far the sanest person on the staff. Though fifteen years his senior, he was the only male friend Cook had. Their having offices next to each other helped, for Cook believed that two people could never become good friends unless they were in daily contact. Of course rollicking Orffmann on the other side proved this was not a sufficient condition.

Woeps was on the phone. Cook heard him say, "Is it bad?" and he suspected his friend was talking to his wife about yet another domestic calamity. Woeps's only serious fault—and it could hardly be called a fault—was his Odyssean attraction for bad luck.

Cook mouthed, "I'll be back." Woeps nodded distractedly and Cook closed the door. "He's busy at the moment," he explained to Philpot, who was still looking wonderingly up the hall.

"I don't understand the shape of this building," said the writer. "And where's the men's bathroom?"

"I'll explain as I show you." He pointed up the hall in the direction Aaskhugh had gone and they began walking. "This building is a circle, in case you didn't notice."

"I'm beginning to."

"It's a seven-story cylinder, actually. It was built for the harder core of the boys in the reformatory. Around the edges of the circle were the cells, expanded and remodeled into offices for us, with the bars removed from the windows. Except in the bathroom, for some reason—you'll see them. Then, working inward to the center of the circle, there is this hall, formerly the catwalk outside the cells. Then there's a central core to our left divided into playrooms, an eating area, a little gymnasium, and so on. The hall goes all the way around it, almost. Wach's office gets in the way. He had it built in such a way that it extends from his window clear to the central core, so the hall ends at each of his walls. We just passed Orffmann's office on the right. You'll meet him later, of course. Here's Miss Pristam's office. She's out of town. Stairs and elevator." He gestured to the right. "There's another wing there, on a tangent with our building, but it's not used now. Neither are the lower floors of the building, except for part of the floor immediately below, where Sally Good's office is. She's the head teacher who runs the daycare side of things. I'll take you down there later. And here is Arthur Stiph's office."

"Whose?"

"Sorry. I'm used to lowering my voice around him. Maybe you'll see why." Cook peeked into the half-open door of Stiph's office and saw what he expected. At a desk in the middle of an office cluttered well beyond the limits of tasteful eccentricity sat Arthur Stiph.

Stiph was asleep. He was often asleep, here in his office, or outside on the shaded lawn gently sloping down to the Baby Wabash, or in a playroom corner, quite oblivious to his crawling, vocalizing, peeing informants. Now, as always, he gave the appearance of being at peace not just with the world, but with all known forces of darkness.

Suddenly Stiph snorted and smacked his lips open and shut, causing his old swivel chair to squeak once before settling back into silence. Reflexively the two men at his door split apart and hid out of sight, like commandos about to pitch grenades.

"That's Arthur Stiph," whispered Cook. "We can catch him another time. The bathrooms are just ahead at the end of the hall. The men's is on the left." He led Philpot away from the door.

"It's eleven in the morning," Philpot whispered. "What's he doing?"

Cook shrugged. "He's old. He works some, but he sleeps too. About as much as a cat. He's fairly new here."

Philpot muttered something and went into the bathroom. As he reached the door Aaskhugh stepped out. He smiled at Philpot as if the bond between them were tighter than that between most mortals, then did the same to Cook. With that same smile on his face he looked in at Stiph as he passed by his office and whispered, loudly enough for Cook to hear but not necessarily for his benefit, "Lazy turd." Cook recoiled. He stepped to the door and looked in at Stiph again. He sat tranquilly, his gray-topped head cocked sharply to one side. He looked almost like a heavy-headed newborn asleep in an infant chair. A small beam of sunlight streaming through a dent in his metal window blinds illuminated his shoulders, where a few leaves—dry, dead leaves—clung to a gray sweater. Cook found the man utterly free of his capacity for censure—something he could say about few other people. He suddenly wished he knew him better. Their contacts had been too brief, too professional. Stiph looked so personable, so approachable—a potential friend, despite the extreme difference in their ages. They could teach each other things.

Cook suddenly heard a scream. It came from the central core—long and high-pitched. He opened the door leading into the core and ran in. A young teacher was stumbling out of the nap room with a baby pressed to her chest. Sally, the head teacher, was with her, trying to get at the baby.

"My God," said the younger woman. The way she said it told Cook she was the one who had screamed.

"But he's all right," said Sally.

"My God," she said again.

"Look. He's all right." Sally pried the baby away from the girl's chest. He squirmed and began to cry. The girl looked at him in amazement.

"I thought—"

"Is everything all right?" asked Cook.

"What's going on here?" asked Wach, approaching from the other direction. "I demand an explanation."

Sally rocked the baby in her arms and looked at Wach. "Just a minute, Walter," she said. "I'm going to put him back down." She opened the door to the nap room. One or two of the other babies inside had been awakened by the noise and were crying. She stepped inside and closed the door behind her.

"I'm sorry, Dr. Wach," said the girl, bringing a hand to her forehead. "I thought . . . it was foolish of me, but I thought it was another crib death."

"Another?" Wach exclaimed. "*Another?* There has never been a death at this Institute during my administration."

"I think she means before, Walter," offered Cook, feeling both compassion for the girl in her awkwardness and shock from those screams. "You know, before you came there was—"

"That doesn't concern me," Wach said loudly, speaking to Cook without looking at him. His eyes remained fixed on the girl. "Just what happened? What's your name?"

"Phyllis, Dr. Wach. I'm sorry. Some of us were talking about crib deaths this morning, so it was on my mind, and the way he was lying there was, well, I felt his chest to see if it was moving, and it wasn't, or I didn't think it was, and I couldn't hear him breathe, and when I picked him up he seemed so limp—"

Sally opened the door from the nap room and stepped into the hall, her index finger to her lips. "Let's step away from the door," she said, herding the group down the hall. "Back to work, everyone," she said to three teachers who had joined the group. Cook saw that Aaskhugh was among them too, his eyebrows dancing with unspoken questions. "Everything's all right," Sally said. "False alarm. Are you okay now, Phyllis?" She put an arm around her as they walked down the hall.

Cook had turned to go in the other direction, back into the main hall, when Wach called out to him.

"Jeremy, I don't want that reporter getting wind of this. If he heard the ruckus, tell him it was a joke or something. Tell him nothing if he didn't. Is that clear?"

"Yes," said Cook. As he opened the door to the main hall he heard Wach speak again:

"You, whatever your name is . . . you come to my office."

Cook closed the door behind him and saw Philpot emerge from the bathroom with a quizzical smile on his face. "I got a little surprise in there," he said to Cook as he joined him. Cook glanced at Stiph, who slept on undisturbed, and began to walk with the writer back up the hall, wondering what he meant. Then he understood. That had to be it. The timing was right, too. Wach must have been responding to the screams, taking a short cut.

"I know," said Cook. "He really ought to knock."

An architectural oddity lay behind Philpot's little surprise. The men's bathroom on this floor was adjacent to Wach's office, and a special small door connected the two. This door was the subject of some controversy at Wabash, for it opened directly into the only toilet stall in the men's bathroom. Despite repeated hints and requests, and even despite a parliamentarily proper motion made by Cook at a recent meeting and instantly seconded by Woeps but then ruled out of order, Wach chose not to knock. Usually he withdrew with apologies. Sometimes he passed boldly through, taking a short cut to the stairs or elevator. One of Cook's revenge fantasies featured the entire staff storming the stall when it was occupied by Wach. Beyond this the fantasy became obscure; it was the initial image that was appealing.

Woeps was hurrying down the hall toward them, pulling a sweater over his head without bothering to remove his glasses. The crew neck of the sweater caught the frame and threw his glasses to the floor at Cook's feet. Cook picked them up, relieved for his friend's sake to see that they were undamaged. He handed them to Woeps and gestured to Philpot.

"Ed, this is—"

"I can't talk, Jeremy. Amy's fallen down and bumped her head hard. I'm meeting Helen at the hospital."

"Is it serious?"

"Going for X rays." He opened the door to the stairwell and was gone.

"That's the one you like?" asked Philpot.

"Yes," said Cook without thinking. Then he saw the implication. It struck him as remarkable that Philpot could have sensed his dislike of the others so easily. "It's sad. His daughter Amy has a muscular problem of some sort."

"And his son, the one who stays here during the day?"

"Wally? He's fine. A healthy kid." He gestured to his right. "Shall we go into the central core? We could see some kids and meet some of the teachers."

They backtracked a few steps and entered through the north door, the one Cook had used when he heard the screams. (Two other doors, one at the east and one at the south, opened into the core from the hall. A fourth door connected Wach's office directly with the core; like the bathroom door, this one was always locked from the inside, public access to Wach from the hall being limited to the route through Mary the Secretary's office.) The door to the nap room was closed and all was quiet. Farther along they paused at an open door.

"This is the playroom for the toddlers," explained Cook. "Nine to twenty-four months."

They looked down upon a frenzy of antisocial activity. Each child was playing with a toy, or his hands, or a piece of dust, as if alone on the moon. Cook greeted Jane, one of the teachers, and introduced her to Philpot, noticing in her eyes the glazed look he often saw at Wabash—the result of long hours spent in baby care. The same thing happened to him when observing. He missed a great deal of data for that reason, no doubt.

"A lotta kids," said Philpot, looking down at the dozen or so children on the floor.

Cook thought he detected a note of distaste. Could Philpot, like Wach, be a kid hater?

"Makes me miss my own," Philpot added.

"How many do you have?" asked Jane.

"Two. Eleven months—a boy—and a girl of three. I'm missing her birthday tomorrow." Philpot sighed. "Couldn't be helped."

Cook suppressed an impulse to put a consoling arm around Philpot's shoulders. There was that much pathos and regret in his voice. Jane, the teacher, looked as if she felt the same way, but then the teachers were a generally sentimental lot. Cook watched another on the floor playing patty-cake with a responsive, rotund lad. She was new as of two days ago. Paula, her name was. Very nice looking. A graduate student at U.C.L.A. and here just for the summer. Very handy, that. It was awkward when they stayed after things with him fizzled out. He watched her reach up with both hands and smooth her long hair away from her forehead. He would have to meet her soon. Why didn't Wach do the right thing and introduce people around when they came instead of letting them drift? If he ran things he would do it that way.

Paula sat with her back to the two men, deeply engaged in her game.

One of the children began crying and Jane excused herself and hurried to her. Cook stepped back into the hall with Philpot, and at the same time two boys from the four-year-old group came running down the hall, giggling loudly.

"Shhh," said Cook, pointing up the hall to the nap room. "You kids are supposed to be in the gym." The youngest, easily intimidated, turned to go, but the other pointed into the playroom.

"I wanna show Bobby the baby in there that says 'buck-a-buck.'" The boys giggled again. "All she says is 'buck-a-buck.' What's the matter with her? Is she *stu*pid?"

"She's just young. Go on, now."

"Who's *that*?" the same one said, pointing to Philpot as if he had antlers and a light bulb for a nose.

Cook sighed. "He's a policeman and a fireman and a cowboy and he'll be in the gym in a few minutes to tell you how to be one, so get going."

The boys looked at Cook as if they knew he was a fraud, but since he was a fraud with authority, they obeyed.

"Up ahead," said Cook, continuing the tour, "is the staff lounge. Next to it is an eating area for the kids. We call it McDonald's just to make them happy, though the older ones, like those two, know it's a lie." Cook led him through this room to the other playrooms, and the story-time and crafts rooms. In the last of these, Emory Milke, a large, bearded colleague of Cook's, an excellent linguist and a formidable sexual rival, was setting up a video tape recorder and consulting with a technician.

Cook approved of Milke but didn't like him much. The women at Wabash were always talking about how charming he was. Cook had tried to pin this down on a number of occasions, but all he ever got was some nonsense about his voice and the way he looked at you. But Cook, if pressed, would have admitted there was something commanding about Milke's eyes, surrounded as they were by shaggy black hair atop his head and all over his face. And he was smart, the bastard. It was, in other words, harder to dislike Milke than others—the inquisitive Aaskhugh, say, or orffing Orffmann—but Cook worked hard at it. Milke's name helped, and so Cook thought about it a good deal. It had a slippery quality. For half of the Wabash community it was homonymous with the white liquid; for the other half it was disyllabic, like the cognate adjective. Cook deplored this public confusion and removed himself from it by never referring to the man in conversation. This meant that properly introducing Milke to Philpot was going to be tricky. But as it turned out he was saved from compromising his principles on this point.

"Goddammit, man, no wonder it's not working," Milke shouted at the technician. All conversation in the room stopped, and most of the children looked up from their finger painting expectantly.

The technician mumbled something by way of explanation.

"What do you mean 'no more batteries'? For Christ's sake."

The technician mumbled again.

"That tightwad prick!" shouted Milke. He moved toward Cook and Philpot at the door, as if bent on searching them roughly for hidden batteries in their pockets. They parted and Milke brushed by them. Cook thought he smelled liquor in the air, but it might have been deodorant or cologne. Milke disappeared through the east door into the encircling hall on his way to Wach's office, which was no more than twelve feet from where Cook and Philpot stood if only access through the west door were allowed. Cook turned and looked at it. The thin metal blinds over the window, always closed, were open at one of the slats at eye level, and this popped closed just as Cook's gaze reached it. Wach would not be surprised by his visitor.

As Cook and Philpot passed through McDonald's—Philpot having expressed a desire to return to Cook's office in pursuit of linguistic questions, to which Cook had eagerly consented—Cook reflected on the number of interesting sentences he had overheard so far that day. He was so absorbed with his thoughts that it took him a moment to notice that the new girl, Paula, was standing with Jane at the coffeepot. Their backs were to the room. Cook and Philpot were going to pass by quite close to them. Cook's first "hello" to her, which he hoped would be deep-voiced, as he knew Milke's would be (or had been already?), was well beyond the planning stages when he heard her utter a sentence. The sentence consisted of an arrangement of American English vowels and consonants that could have been random, generated by one of six million monkeys at six million typewriters. Yes, it could have been random, but it probably was not.

"This fellow Cook is supposed to be a complete asshole."

Philpot, leading the way, turned and gave Cook a mournful, mouth-open look of sympathy, while Cook stared straight ahead into the middle distance, where there was nothing but air. With an uncomfortable half-smile fixed on his face, he gave the appearance, but only the appearance, of amused self-confidence.

CHAPTER TWO

COOK'S HALF-SMILE remained fixed in place as he walked with Philpot back to his office, asked him to take a seat, and said he would return shortly. He hoped his face suggested inner tranquility—first to Philpot, then to Orffmann, who looked up frowningly through his open door as Cook passed by, perhaps wondering why his neighbor, if he was truly amused at some private joke, was not laughing outright after his own fashion. After checking to be sure he was alone, Cook walked up to the bathroom mirror, relaxed his face, and watched himself turn into an aphasic middle line-backer.

"Gnnarnghrackagh goddammit grack oh jesus ghorki," he yelled. He kicked the large metal trash can and sent it rolling into a corner. It made such a violent noise that fear of discovery suddenly calmed him, or at least stopped him from making more noise. He leaned forward on the sink, bringing his face close to the mirror, and looked into his eyes. Yes, it was easy to imagine. Someone had been showing her around, pointing out the rooms and toys and things, telling her about the people she was meeting and the people she would soon meet, among them one Jeremy Cook, who, by the way, was a real asshole. No—*complete* asshole. Or the original utterance could have been "a real asshole," incorrectly remembered by Paula as "a complete asshole." Or maybe the original was just "somewhat of an asshole," or "a slight asshole," or "not too much of an asshole," or even "not an asshole like the other people here." No, that was going too far. In fact, there was no dodging it at all. In someone's mind he was a complete (or real, total, consummate, etc.) asshole, and this person talked about it, so in other people's minds he was *supposed to be* a complete (or real, etc.) asshole.

"Supposed to be." The classic mark of a secondhand report. Wasn't there some American Indian language that made a distinction in its verb forms between knowledge acquired firsthand and knowledge acquired secondhand? Hopi? Navaho? Well, English had an equivalent device, Cook now realized. It was less integral to English structure, but it still told you how things stood: "supposed to be."

But was it really "supposed to *be*"? Hadn't he read somewhere that in some languages *be* and *have* were the same verb? And didn't English *have* replace the perfect auxiliary *be* in the nineteenth century, when "He is arrived" became "He has arrived"? Could he have misheard what she said, or could she have missaid it? "This fellow Cook is supposed to *have* a complete asshole." No. This couldn't save him either. He was upset. His reasoning was all wrong.

"Supposed to be." She didn't necessarily believe it. She had only heard it. From someone. Not from Jane, with whom she had been talking at the coffeepot—one doesn't give information back to one's source. That left the entire adult speaking population of Wabash. A lot of people. Seven linguists, an administrator, a secretary, fifteen or so teachers, an audiovisual man, and some janitors. Mary the Secretary didn't seem to like him much, and she would be likely to speak with newcomers to Wabash and poison them against Cook. Or maybe that horse-faced teacher, Dorothy Plough. She always seemed a bit standoffish. Yes, there were lots of possibilities. Not just at Wabash, either. Paula was from U.C.L.A. In the course of his career had Cook offended some teacher there in an article or review, who had then conveyed these tidings to Paula as a kind of travel tip? If so, or even if not, it was going to be a tough search.

That it was Paula in particular who had been told this nonsense bothered him some, but not greatly. To be sure, there was now a certain obstacle to overcome in his maneuvers, but that was minor. It could even be seen as an advantage, something that made him mysterious. Wasn't it true that people who were initially threatening, on proving to be just moderately pleasant, appeared to be about the most pleasant people on earth? And after Paula met him she would always be looking beyond his winning charm to that essential asshole fundament, until one day she would decide that he had been unjustly vilified. She would reject her source. And reveal it then too? Ah! *That* was the investigative line to pursue. But he would have to move cautiously. Cautiously in that respect, but with lusty dispatch in the other.

He turned on the tap and splashed cold water on his face. As he dried his hands he became aware of loud but unintelligible voices coming from the other side of the wall. Wach and Milke discussing the budget. The thought of this made him smile, but he felt it as a mean, low smile. Did being called a complete asshole make you enjoy such things? He would have to watch himself.

Philpot was not in his office. Cook went into the gym in search of him, assuming he had gone exploring on his own. Jane, the teacher who had been with Paula, walked over to him, and he was suddenly self-conscious. Had she risen to his defense, insisting that he was a complete sweetie? Had she hesitated and withheld comment? Had she said with a sneer, "There's no *supposed to be* about it"? Not knowing, he felt he could not talk to her. He turned away.

"Dr. Cook?" she called out. He turned around and faced her. "Dr. Wach wants to see you. Mary was asking for you."

Cook thanked her in a way that he thought was incompatible with being a complete asshole and left the gym. That's right, Wach, he thought as he walked down the hall. Don't look for people yourself. Send someone after them, and then make sure they come to you.

Mary the Secretary looked up from her desk, where she had been unbending a paper clip. "He's expecting you," she said as if she were important.

Wach stood up from his desk when Cook entered. He circled around the desk and closed the door behind Cook. He pointed to a chair facing his desk. Cook had sat in it many times before. He knew that it was permanently positioned just far enough away from Wach's to make conversation uncomfortable. He sat down, wondering why he had been summoned. Wach never gave one verbal preliminaries to suggest the tone of a visit.

"Where did you leave the reporter?" Wach asked.

"I don't know," said Cook. "I mean in my office, but he's not there now."

"Where is he?"

"I don't know. I was looking for him."

Wach looked at Cook with the impatience of a father whose children had all been unwelcome accidents. "Jeremy, we can't have that man just wandering around here all alone."

Cook shifted in his seat. "I didn't intend for him to, Walter. Anyway, I see no harm in it."

Wach waved his hand back and forth in front of him, as if to bat aside each word as it reached him. "I'm taking you off this case, Jeremy."

Had he really said that? And seriously? "What do you mean?"

Wach pursed his lips a moment and studied Cook. "I don't want you showing Philpot around anymore. Besides, we've got a grant deadline Friday and I need someone to work on it. Ed was going over the draft but he had to leave for the day. I need someone to take over."

Three questions struck Cook simultaneously. The first—why couldn't Wach take over Woeps's job—was unaskable. Wach would see the question as a challenge. The second could be asked, but the answer would probably be maddening.

"Who wrote the draft?"

"Clyde."

It was. Orffmann's general worthlessness extended to, included, and was symbolized by, his prose style. The third question was dangerous, but Cook had to ask it.

"You said 'besides,' Walter. What other reason do you have for taking charge of Philpot?"

Wach's frown approached a scowl. One of his rules, to which Cook had not yet assigned a number because it hadn't yet become fully articulated in his mind, was that between administrators and underlings overt hostilities should never be verbalized.

"Let's just say I think I can do a good job," Wach said.

"'Let's just say'?" asked Cook. "Instead of what?"

"Well you *have* made a bit of a mess of it, haven't you?" Wach spoke quickly now, his words escaping uncensored. "You let me stumble upon him in the bathroom—rather awkward for both of us, I must say—and then you let him see Emory blow up and stalk out of the playroom. What kind of place must he think this is? And now you don't even know where he is."

Cook laughed. It was either that or leap over the desk and twist the fool's ears off.

"It's more serious than you think, Jeremy. This reporter might well place his article in a magazine with national circulation, and there we are, open to inspection by everyone."

"But there's nothing to hide here, Walter. If you just let him have a good look around, I don't see—"

"You don't understand these things at all, Jeremy. Now you had better get to work on that proposal. I want it on my desk with your revisions at eight tomorrow morning. It's in Ed's office. You can get Mary to open it for you."

"And thanks for pitching in like this, Jeremy. Good of you, especially since it will mean quite a long day and all." Cook supplied these words silently as he stood up, and he found them heartening. When he opened the door he saw Philpot sitting in Mary's office. He gave Cook a friendly smile.

"Dr. Wach will see you now," Mary said dully.

Cook expressed sincere regrets to Philpot that he would not be able to be with him the rest of the day (perhaps even the rest of his visit to Wabash, he thought). Philpot suggested they get together for a drink later that night. Cook wondered if Wach would approve, then hated himself for wondering it and agreed, saying he would call Philpot at his motel when he finished his work.

"It may be quite late, though. Eleven or twelve?"

"No problem," said Philpot. "Have a nice day. And don't let these things get you down."

Cook asked Mary for the master key, and, contrary to policy, she gave it to him instead of walking with him to Woeps's office, unlocking it for him, observing him, and then locking it again. This was fine with Cook. Disobedience on this small point, though motivated by pure laziness, meant that Mary might be counted on when the revolution came.

And what about good old Philpot? "These things." There was the complete asshole business, but since he used the plural he must have sensed other things, like maybe Wach calling him on the carpet. He was sharp, and this meant that Wach couldn't possibly hide anything from him and would only get himself into trouble if he tried.

Whistling and stepping jauntily now, Cook took the draft of the proposal to his office and returned the master key to Mary. On his way back to his office he decided to get away for a few hours to clear his mind. One nice thing, perhaps the only one, about Wach's administration of Wabash was the complete freedom of schedule he allowed the linguists. Wach too had once been committed to the life of the mind, and he knew that professional thinkers did their best thinking when they felt like thinking. Cook would go home, eat, have a beer, and return with a fresh sense of purpose, as if working on the proposal were entirely his own idea.

He took his coat from his office and locked the door. On his way to the elevator he spied an awake Arthur Stiph in one of the playrooms. He paused at the observation window. Stiph was leaning against a wall studying two children playing on the floor with an orange tennis ball. Stiph's sport coat was draped over his shoulders without his arms being in the sleeves. The kids must have just done something funny, because Stiph was gently laughing and his eyes were sparkling as he stood there, armless, against the wall.

Cook moved on, thinking that seeing this had been the nicest thing that had happened to him all day.

Cook's house was in the country. In some circles this would be a mark of prestige, but in Kinsey County it was a normal thing. Unless one wanted to live elbow-to-elbow with the twanging Kinseyans in town, one lived in the country. His was a two-story wooden frame house set well back from a little-used country road, with five acres of unruly meadow and oaks in the back. Here he slept, worked, entertained guests—usually one at a time—and ate Grunt Meals.

Cook's philosophy toward eating was starkly realistic. Hunger was a pain that interfered with important things like doing linguistics. Food ended that pain. Food allowed you to get on with it. The most popular item on his menu was the Grunt Meal. This consisted of a single dish, casserole-style, with ground beef as the central ingredient; the dish was enhanced, or at least made bigger, by rice or noodles, with tomatoes or chili or condensed soup added to give the illusion of savoriness. For Cook's purposes, the outstanding virtue of a Grunt Meal was not that it made him grunt (though there must have been some connection or he wouldn't have given it such a name), but rather that it ensured that he would not want to eat right away again. If ever.

When he arrived home, Cook dialed Woeps's number to inquire about Amy, but there was no answer. He considered phoning the hospital but decided it would be too hard to get through to Woeps. He went into the kitchen and prepared a Grunt Meal, or rather he reheated the remnants of two previous Grunt Meals, and he dug into the dish with speed, if not relish. When sizzling hot on the plate, Grunt Meals were merely sustaining, neither good nor bad. When warmish or cold they were an offense to God's Green Earth. The two beers he took with the meal made it a little easier. After grunting a bit he poured himself a cup of coffee, put on a pullover sweater, and shuffled out into his backyard, where a moderately maintained lawn gradually shaded into the riotous meadow in the distance. He pulled up a lawn chair and slumped down in it, setting his coffee mug on the brick patio. He leaned back in the chair, put his hands behind his head, and closed his eyes. The wind picked up slightly and blew his hair across his forehead. He wondered if it was going to rain.

When he woke, it was after three o'clock. He jumped from the chair and hurried into the house. Knowing what he knew about grants and Orffmann, there was a good deal of work ahead of him. He drove the six miles back to the Institute. He parked his car, a dull corpse-white Plymouth Valiant, beside a Kinsey County Road Department truck, and wondered vaguely what it was doing there. Then he spied two orange-helmeted engineers, or people of some kind, walking around the far side of the building. He was pleased to see Aaskhugh leaving. One potential distraction from work would be gone for the day.

Outside the elevator he bumped into Sally, who informed him that Phyllis, the screaming teacher, had been fired by Wach. Although he had hardly known the girl, Cook found himself immoderately angered by this news. He swore under his breath.

Sally nodded. "I know," she said grimly. She then asked him if he had met Philpot. He said yes without offering details of his ignominious demotion.

"Walter brought him downstairs to my office," she said. "He seems very nice. I just hope he doesn't get a bad impression of the place."

"Why do you say that?"

"Well, Walter is sticking to him like flypaper. It's obviously making the guy uncomfortable."

Cook smiled. He asked her if she had been watching any of the children he was studying.

"Just Wally Woeps."

"Hear any *m-bwee* from him?"

"No. Just some *fffff* and *n-duh.* I think you're right about the distinction."

"Really? What were the contexts?"

She explained. Cook took mental notes, which he planned to make physical as soon as he was in his office.

"Did you go home and forget something?" she asked.

"No. Pressing work," he said obscurely. "I'm going to be here until the wee hours, I'm afraid." He began to move to the elevator but immediately bumped into someone who proved to be Arthur Stiph, just stepping out on his way home. "Sorry, Arthur," said Cook. He had bumped him quite hard.

"No problem, Jeremy," said Stiph, smiling somewhat sadly and brushing his gray hair back with one hand. "The wee hours, eh?" he said. "Busy boy." He clapped Cook on the shoulder and moved on.

"I'll think of you when I'm on my second martini, Jeremy," said Sally as she waved goodbye. This was a joke in that (a) Sally was a notorious teetotaler at Wabash, and (b) she had once dumbfounded Cook by asking him if he ever worried because he drank so much. Cook waved back and jumped into the elevator just before the doors closed.

The heavy traffic period at Wabash was beginning. Between three-thirty and six every afternoon, the Institute was in a transitional phase. Parents came one after another for their children, hoping to find them still intact after yet another day of linguistic scrutiny. In Kinsey County there was persistent uneasiness about Wabash, and for this reason a tiny fraction of Wach's abundant paranoia was justified. People felt uncomfortable about the disciplined eavesdropping their children were daily subjected to. This discomfort was rarely verbalized, but from many chats with neighbors and other townspeople about his work, Cook knew it was widespread. Luckily the low cost of Wabash daycare was sufficient enticement to keep the data coming in.

The bustle outside Cook's door in the late-afternoon hours never bothered him. He worked well either with steady noise or total silence. It was only intermittent noise, like Orffmann's disembodied laughter, that annoyed him. So he worked well until six, when Wabash closed and the building emptied, and he continued to labor happily in the following silence. He added Sally's information to his file on Wally Woeps and thought about it a bit. Then he went to work on the proposal. Oh, how he hated grant proposals. The hollow promises; the vaunting celebration of past success; the self-advertising emphasis on *importance* and *significance*; the absence of understatement; the omnipresence of exaggeration; the servile allegiance to tradition, formula, and established procedure; the utter predictability of every other sentence; the implicit greed of the genre—these were truly horrible things, and they were at their worst when penned by Orffmann. But Cook worked hard and productively into the evening hours, his brain continually nourished by what he knew was the protein-carbohydrate mixture that constituted the beauty of the Grunt Meal.

At eight o'clock he paused and went down the hall to the bathroom to clean his coffee pot and fill it with water. Back in his office, the perking sound was cheering. He took off his sweater and opened a window slightly. It was cloudy outside, quite dark, and the air was thick with moisture, giving a hint of the humid summer that was just beginning. He gazed for a moment at his books lined along the wall of his office, and then he resumed work. By now he had actually begun to believe in Orffmann's proposal, and he wrote and revised effortlessly.

When he was finished, he slammed his pen down with relief, leaned back in his chair, stretched his arms, and groaned loudly. He rubbed the bridge of his nose under his glasses, sighing with the contentment of the honest toiler. He looked at his watch: eleven-fifteen. He looked up the number of Philpot's motel and dialed it, looking forward to a nightcap or two with the writer. It would be fun talking with him about Wach.

But Philpot wasn't in his room. Nor was he in the bar, according to the clerk at the desk. Cook left his number with a message for Philpot to call when he returned. Leaning back in his chair, he let his mind wander. He thought about Woeps and kicked himself for not remembering to call him again to find out if Amy was all right. She probably was (Woeps tended to be overly fearful about small accidents), and it was too late to call. Married people with kids, he knew, went to bed at unbelievable hours like ten or eleven. Then he thought a bit about the new girl, Paula, her long hair and soft features, and hoped she wouldn't flee in terror when he presented himself. And if she did? Well, there was that young mother he had seen and greeted last week, who, judging from her smile, must have been divorced. Woeps had seen her too and had shared Cook's enthusiasm for the way she looked, though in his case, because he was married, it was necessarily academic. Perhaps that was why Woeps always whistled mournful tunes.

Someone was skidding. Loudly. Brakes had been slammed on hard, and it was a long skid. Cook froze at his desk in anticipation of a crash, but none came. It was suddenly peaceful outside, quiet again, as if nothing had happened. All he heard was the rustle of a paper on his desk from the gentle breeze blowing in the window, and after he placed his hand on the paper there was only the slight stirring of the trees outside.

The skid had been quite near. He stood up, raised the window all the way and leaned out. The road was seven stories below him, running from a small rise to his right down a hill to his left, some fifty yards or so from the building. It was a small road, used much less often than the main road on the other side of the building. He could see its outline in the dark, but down to the left it was obscured from view by the adjoining wing jutting out on a tangent with his own building. The skidding sound seemed to have come from behind the wing, not from the part of the road directly below him. He listened and heard only the soft wind blowing listlessly, struggling against the air heavy with moisture.

He called out, "Everything all right?"

There was a long pause and only silence. He listened, waiting. His voice had seemed weak and puny in the night air, but anyone down there beyond the wing of the building would have heard him.

"Are you all right?"

A long silence. Nothing. The hopeless sound of his own voice caused a sorrow to well up in his chest. He pulled his head in and sat down, rubbing his forehead and trying to shake the feeling. He sat still for a while, silent, hoping to hear something to let him know what had happened.

After a while he began to clean up his desk, gathering the pages of the grant proposal and arranging them in proper order. He evened the edges and set the papers neatly on his desk. Again he paused and listened.

A car door slammed. An engine started. Then the hasty squeal of tires. Cook jumped to his feet and looked out the window. Nothing. He ran out of his office and down the hall to the flight of stairs that led to the other wing of the building, the corner of which had blocked his view. He raced down the seven flights of stairs to the ground floor, taking the steps two and three at a time, and he ran along another hall until he reached the exit at the far end. He opened the door and looked up and down the road.

He walked down a sloping stretch of grass that separated the road from the building and saw nothing at all. Perhaps the whole thing had been a fancy of his bleared, linguistics-riddled mind. Then he saw it—a long skid mark, barely visible in the dark, running a distance of thirty or forty feet. But no glass, no metal, no sign of a crash. He walked up and down the length of the skid mark, examining the road closely, and both shoulders of the road as well. He stood for a moment between the skid marks, thinking.

He shrugged. The driver had seen something and slammed on his brakes. A dog, maybe. Or a cat. The wind came up and chilled him. He rubbed his bare arms, wishing he had brought his sweater down with him from the office, and walked slowly back up the hill toward the building. The darkness seemed to move with him. He fumbled with the door for some time before remembering that his key worked only in the main entrance on the opposite side of the building. He shivered, thought a moment, then turned and began to walk to the parking lot. He was done with his work, and there was no need to return to his office. It seemed important that he leave now, that he get away from the building. He ran the last hundred feet to his car.

But instead of leaving by the exit he normally used, he drove from the parking lot up onto the little road and stopped just short of the skid marks, his motor running and lights on. With an odd sense of urgency prodding him, he again examined the road and shoulders. They were skid marks—not a great deal could be said about them beyond that. As he stood in the middle of the road with his arms folded he became aware of the night sounds. He heard crickets on all sides of him, stretching out in every direction, as if he were standing at the very center of their population. And, far up the hill, he thought he heard an owl scream.

He rubbed his bare arms and hurried back to his car. A dog, a cat, a squirrel. Like Phyllis's screaming, a false alarm. A simple thing. He drove on up the road. When he cleared the wing of the building that jutted out he looked up and saw a lighted office on the seventh floor. It took him a moment to recognize it as his own. He slowed the car down, then stopped. He could see his bookshelves and a picture on a wall. On another wall was a calendar. As he stared up at the window he almost felt as if he hadn't really left his office, as if he were still up there working alone. And yet at the same time he was here, outside in his car, watching from afar—allowed by some freak of nature the rare and horrible privilege of spying on himself.

He had never felt quite so mortal.

CHAPTER THREE

"MARY, I overslept. There's a grant proposal on my desk that Walter wanted to see at eight this morning. Can you go get it and take it to him? Tell him I'll be there as soon as I can. Can you do that for me?" Cook ran his hand through his knotted hair and groaned softly. His voice was raw and his eyes were thick with the night's crust.

"Sure, Dr. Cook," said Mary the Secretary. "I'll go right down there and get it. Dr. Wach is in, and it's almost nine o'clock now, but he hasn't said anything about a proposal." She paused, then added, with a smile probably playing at her red lips, "Rough night?"

Cook imagined a Prussian boot surprising her secretarial fanny.

"Yes, Mary. Now if you could, it's quite important—"

"All right, Dr. Cook. I'm on my way. And I'll tell Dr. Wach that you're on yours." She giggled. "How do you like the linguistics of that?"

Cook laughed, hung up, and cursed. He dressed, combed his hair, decided to forgo a shave, and hurried out to his car. It was a day dark with clouds, and the air was so heavy with suspended moisture that he felt he could possibly drown if he breathed too heavily. He drove to Wabash, catching more amber lights than green ones, hoping that Wach was in a good mood.

Outside the elevator on the seventh floor he ran into Woeps. His friend seemed even more stooped than normal, and his face carried a sad, bewildered look.

"Jeremy," he said, his face brightening when he saw Cook, without, however, becoming any more cheerful. "Thank God you're here." He whipped his head back and forth, a motion Cook had never seen him perform before. "Jeremy, we found Arthur Stiph in your office this morning."

Cook hesitated, then burst into laughter. "Asleep? Do you mean he—"

"No," Woeps said impatiently. "He's dead. He's dead and in your office."

Cook reached out to lean against the wall, but it was too far away, so he walked two steps backward and leaned against it. Stiph was old and old people died. This was to be expected. But not in his office. Not in his office.

"What . . . I . . . what did he die of?"

Woeps reached out with both hands and held Cook by the shoulders. "Take it easy, Jeremy." He released his grip on him, slowly. "I don't know," he said. "Mary just found him this morning when she opened your office. Screamed like hell."

"But what's he doing *in there*?"

"I don't know. I just don't know."

"I mean . . . did he just wander in there to die?"

"I don't know. I don't understand it. It's all very sad."

"Christ," said Cook under his breath. "I left my door wide open last night. That's how he got in. He must have been walking around and seen the light on and the door open, and he must have just wandered right in. There was this skidding sound outside, so I ran out without closing the door behind me. I was afraid someone got hurt—" His knees felt weak again and he reached for the wall. "Oh Jesus. Jesus."

"What is it?"

Cook didn't answer. He hurried down the hall and forced his way through the throng of people outside his office, all hovering at the threshold as if it were a holy place.

Arthur Stiph sat calmly at Cook's desk. Cook took a few steps forward and stopped, eyeing the body suspiciously, as if fearful that it might suddenly do something indelicate. It was stretched out awkwardly on Cook's chair, straight and rigid, looking as out of place as a solitary mannequin on a Ferris wheel. And yet Stiph, though he was barely balanced on a chair about to slip away from him, reminded Cook of himself in his own favorite office sleeping position: eyes closed, legs extended, neck gouged by the sharp back of the chair (which in turn beneficially retarded blood flow to the brain), the curve of the buttocks against the edge of the seat the only means of support. So there was a naturalness to Stiph's position. But something else about him took away from this.

He had no hair.

The man's shaggy gray crop was missing, and this fact made Cook look even more closely at the body to make certain that it did actually belong to Stiph. But there was no mistaking that form. There he was, poised at last in the achievement of what perhaps had been a secret goal all along.

Cook moved forward, barely hearing the murmur of the people in the crowd at his back, none of whom had yet chosen to join him inside the office. He looked on the floor for Stiph's wig, guessing that Stiph had worn one and had somehow lost it in the course of his journey into the other world. He found nothing. He examined the head and saw patchy spots of stubble here and there and tender streaks of redness, as if the corpse had managed to shave itself. Cook backed off a step. Here indeed, he thought, was a man who followed the beat of a different drummer. He shaves his head, wanders into a strange office, and then gives up the ghost. Perhaps. But there was the skid, the skid, the sadness of that sound in the heavy night air.

"Excuse me, sir, but I want you out of here."

Cook spun around. Just inside the door stood a freckled, fat-faced man, overweight and puffing very loudly.

"Sorry," said Cook. "Are you—"

The man heaved his torso forward at the waist to pull a

wallet from his rear pocket. He flashed some sort of credentials by Cook's face in a swift, sweeping motion.

"Lieutenant Leaf," the man explained as he stuffed his wallet back into his pocket. "We got a call. Do you know this man? Is he a friend of yours?"

Cook looked at Stiph's pallid face. "His name is Arthur Stiph. He's a linguist. I don't really know him. I mean not well." He looked at the Lieutenant, who returned his look with a quizzical stare. "My name's Jeremy Cook and this is my office," he quickly added.

"Ah," said Leaf. "Do you know anything about this?"

"No. I just got here. I overslept this morning and I—"

"You don't know how he got here or how he died?"

"No. I just—"

"Okay," said Leaf. "I'd like to sniff around in here. Alone. I would like you to stay close by for a while. Not in here, but close. I'll be wanting to talk to you some more, Mr. . . . Mr. Crook, is it? Har, har, har." The man actually did laugh "har, har, har," and Cook found it mildly disturbing.

"It's Cook."

"All right, Mr. Cook. Thank you." Leaf moved toward Stiph's rigid figure and leaned over the body, bringing his face right up to Stiph's peaceful countenance, and Cook backed out of his office, watching the two of them—the one thin and gaunt and dead, the other roundish and bustling. It was then that Cook realized, in some sense for the very first time, that Arthur Stiph had died. His eyes suddenly welled up with tears and his throat constricted. He forced his way through the crowd in the hall, past a blur of inquisitive and concerned faces, until he finally broke free at the edge of the crowd and found Woeps waiting for him.

"What's going on, Jeremy?"

Cook sighed. "Some detective is in there looking at him. Let's take a walk, Ed. Get away from this." They walked down the hall to the elevator and talked as they rode down to the ground floor and walked out the front door to the grass in front of the building. Cook trod lightly, remembering that it was one of Arthur's favorite napping places. They sat down on a small bench that faced the river. Woeps summarized the events of the morning for Cook. He explained how he had been working at his desk when he heard through his half-open door what he naturally thought was Cook entering his office next door. But instead of hearing the soft groan that so often accompanied Cook's entry into his den of labor, he heard a scream that sent his pen scribbling reflexively across the page. In the hall he found Mary shaking at Cook's door. He reached out to calm her and a spastically swinging elbow caught him on the chin, causing him to bite his tongue painfully. (He showed Cook the welt; it was a large one.) Then he, too, saw Stiph. He examined the body and groped for a pulse—feeling stupid, he said, as he looked for signs of life from a wrist already rigid from death. Then he steered Mary down the hall to a couch in the staff lounge and called the police.

"You noticed his head?" asked Cook.

"Yes." Woeps stared straight ahead for a moment. "It made his whole body look funny. Surprised-like." He turned to Cook. "You were saying something about last night, Jeremy. What happened?"

Cook sighed. "Yes. Last night." He explained what he had heard and what he had done, recreating the events of the night before in some detail—for his own benefit as much as for Woeps's.

"So I left the door wide open and the light on." He paused. "Which suggests . . . well . . . a couple of possibilities, I guess."

"One of them," said Woeps, "is that Arthur was taking a late-night walk and saw the light up there and decided to explore. Or take a nap."

"After shaving his head," added Cook.

"Yes. There is that."

"What I think," said Cook, "is that some sonofabitch ran into him and killed him and thought it would be a neat idea to plant the body in my office."

"After shaving his head," Woeps pointed out.

"Yeah. There is that, isn't there?"

"And that part really bothers me, Jeremy. It suggests a certain craziness, a sickness." Woeps shook his head.

"He was so harmless, so benign," said Cook. "He never said a bad word about anybody. The teachers really loved him. One of the girls in the crowd up there was crying loudly—I mean really sobbing. I heard it while I was in the office looking at him."

"Yes. I heard it too."

The two men sat for a while and stared at the muddy river below them. The spring rains had caused it to rise, and it rushed by noisily. Cook rose to his feet and sighed. "We'd better get back up there. That detective wanted to talk to me."

"Was he the fat, freckled one?"

"Yeah. A weird duck."

Another such approached the two men as they walked back to the front entrance to the building. It was Aaskhugh, apparently just arriving for work. He looked dapper in a seersucker suit and whistled as he walked, as if he were celebrating something.

"Hello, Jay. Hello, Daisy. Hello to the two of you. What's brewing?"

Woeps turned to Cook, giving him the floor. After all, it was in Cook's office that the body had been found. Besides, Woeps didn't talk to Aaskhugh much. Cook's eyes gleamed hard as he framed a response.

"Personally, Adam, I think a storm is brewing. The air has been awfully thick the last few days. Have you ever wondered at the inaccuracy of weather reports in the Midwest? Do you know why they're like that?" Cook noticed Woeps staring at him from the side, his brow creased with wonder at this irrelevance.

"No, Jeremy," said Aaskhugh, faltering a bit, his eyes beginning to dart back and forth.

"Neither do I, Adam. Neither do I. Besides, Arthur Stiph was found dead in my office this morning. Freshly tonsured, too."

Aaskhugh registered surprise, to be sure, but probably less at the fact of Stiph's death than at the fact that Cook, after years of fruitless interrogation, was finally bringing forth news of some substance. He inquired into the matter, showing a true zealot's concern for detail, and, if any were to be found, parties that could conceivably be held responsible. Aaskhugh's inquiries normally went in this direction anyway, so the questions tripped easily from his tongue.

Woeps nudged Cook. "Here comes the ambulance crew, Jeremy." Cook watched two white-coated men roll a stretcher up the sidewalk and through the doors. Accompanying the men were three more policemen.

"I wonder what the autopsy will show," Cook mumbled to no one besides himself.

Aaskhugh heard it. "Do you have reason to believe it will show anything unusual?"

Cook said no and made sure that his tone implied unequivocally that he was hiding something.

"I'd like to see those skid marks, Jeremy," said Woeps with an indiscretion that made Cook want to yell at him.

"What skid marks?" asked Aaskhugh, forever Johnny-on-the-spot.

"The brown skid marks on the inside of your underwear," Cook wanted very much to say. "I'll explain it to you later, Adam," he said, lying for the first time that day.

The threesome walked to the building. As they waited for the elevator, Aaskhugh rocked silently back and forth on his heels, clucking his tongue. He finally spoke.

"Stiph was an odd case. Worked hard before coming here, then tapered off. I found his work in the year or so he was here to be no more than ordinary, though I never said so, at least not to him. But these things have to be said now."

Do they? thought Cook.

"Slept a lot, didn't he?" Aaskhugh continued. "I never could make much sense of that. Shame he had to go though. But perhaps it's for the best."

They stepped into the elevator. Cook wanted to say something, but he was stumped by Aaskhugh's idiocy. Woeps, too, remained silent as the elevator rose, while Aaskhugh continued to rock back and forth on his heels, musing.

"I think I'll just run down and take a little peek," Aaskhugh said as he stepped out of the elevator on the seventh floor and bustled down the hall.

"What an ass!" said Woeps, hissing. "What an utter ass he is."

"I've been telling you that for years, Ed. That was some thumbnail biography, wasn't it? Come on. Let's go get some coffee."

They opened the door into the central core and walked down the hallway. The eating area was crowded with linguists, teachers, and a few parents. Milke and Orffmann were talking to a young mother who appeared to be quite upset. By some quirk, Paula was again standing at the coffeepot and talking, this time to Wach. Cook noticed a redness in her eyes and a puffy look about her. Then he saw the same look on the faces of many of the teachers. Paula turned away from Wach and moved toward Cook and Woeps and then past them into the hall without looking at them. Wach beckoned to Cook, who wondered deeply what his boss was going to say.

"This is a sad day for Wabash," said Wach. Although this was a bit funereal and too public for Cook's taste, it at least suggested that some blood coursed through the man's body. He hadn't, after all, begun by asking Cook why he had been late with the grant proposal. "Wabash will miss Arthur Stiph. We will all miss him." He looked around the immediate area for support. "Do you know anything about this, Jeremy?"

"No." On saying this Cook realized he did know something, so he told Wach what he had told Woeps.

"But you didn't see anything?" asked Wach.

"No."

"Pity." Wach cleared his throat. "I had better get back out to the hall. I want to get the police out of here as soon as possible. This is all very awkward for Wabash, besides being tragic. Very awkward."

As Wach hurried away Cook spied a supine figure on a couch in the corner. It was Mary the Secretary, recovering from her encounter with the Grim Reaper. Cook hesitated a moment, then walked over to the couch to console her.

"How are you doing, Mary?" he asked.

She was lying on her back with one arm raised, sheltering her eyes. At the sound of Cook's voice she pulled her arm away and her eyes popped open. The one action seemed to follow from the other. She reminded Cook of a toy doll that would do interesting things if you moved her limbs just right.

"You!" she said loudly, startling him. She raised her head. "You knew he was in there. You sent me there just to torture me. You *knew* it."

"Don't be silly, Mary," Cook protested gently. "I had no idea—"

"You knew it, you cocksucker!" she screamed, causing all conversations in the room to terminate in mid-syllable. Heads turned. "You cocksucker! You're nothing but a big cocksucker, Dr. Cook!" She gave the word careful articulation, as if she were not used to pronouncing it regularly.

Cook allowed himself to be tugged away by Woeps, thankful indeed that his friend was doing it so that he could get away from this crazed banshee. He smiled awkwardly at the faces that blurred by. At the same time he became aware of crying from the playrooms. The infants and children were crying much more than usual, as if sensing and giving voice to the grief in the building. He heard the voices of the teachers vainly trying to calm them. He began to feel responsible for it all. It was almost as if Mary's accusations were justified. He shook his head at the thought. It was crazy.

The stretcher bearing the draped body of Arthur Stiph rolled past, wheeled by two clean-shaven young men who gave off no odor whatsoever.

"Let's go to my office, Jeremy," said Woeps. "It'll be quiet there." On the way, they were stopped by a uniformed policeman, who finally let them pass after Woeps explained they were going to his office, not to Cook's. Cook glanced into it as they passed by and saw several men in there, among them Lieutenant Leaf, who appeared to be in the act of smelling his fingers.

Leaf spied Cook and called out, "Dr. Cook? I would like to have those few words with you now."

Cook stopped and backed up two steps.

"Where can we talk?" asked Leaf, approaching him and wiping his hands on a handkerchief.

"You can use my office," volunteered Woeps. "It's right next door."

"Ah," said Leaf with a large smile as he turned his attention to Woeps. "That's very handy. Have you been in your office already today, sir?"

"Yes. There's nothing unusual about it. No bodies."

"No bodies, har, har, har. So you were in your office before the deceased was found this morning?"

"Before and during. I heard the secretary scream and I ran out and saw him sitting there at Jeremy's desk. I checked his pulse and called the police."

"Ah. Yes. I'll be wanting to talk to you a little later, Mr. . . . "

"Woeps. Ed Woeps."

"Mr. Woeps. Or should it be *Dr.* Woeps? I can never—"

"It doesn't matter."

Leaf frowned at this. "Very well. The secretary, too. I'll be wanting to talk to her."

"You can find me in the lounge. The secretary should be there, too." Woeps unlocked his door for the two men. He turned to Cook. "I'll see you later, Jeremy. Sit down and take it easy." Cook nodded.

Lieutenant Leaf gestured for Cook to enter the office. He complied, a little nervous, and sat down in Woeps's chair. The desk was littered with medical insurance papers. Leaf leaned against the door, his arms folded across his large torso. He looked at Cook.

"So. Let's begin at the beginning."

Some time later a weary Cook led the detective down the hall past milling policemen, linguists, teachers, and one escaped toddler who shouldn't have been out in the hall. One of the teachers scooped the child into her arms and took him back into the gym. Cook preceded Leaf down the same stairs he had descended so quickly the night before, then along the hall leading to the back entrance of the building, which opened out onto the road. They were going to look at the skid marks, which Leaf had enthusiastically seized on during Cook's narrative, without, however, indicating to Cook exactly why they interested him so much.

Cook opened the back entrance for Leaf, trying to be obliging in all ways. Leaf grunted his thanks. A strong smell of tar greeted the two men. Cook heard a loud burp from the road, where several county road workers were sprawled on the grass eating lunch. Out of a small trailer-like machine at the edge of the road a thin wisp of black smoke was rising, fouling the air. The road lay in shambles. Jackhammers—Cook suddenly remembered having heard them as he bent over Stiph's body, as he and Woeps sat and talked farther up the road around the corner of the building, and as Leaf interrogated him in Woeps's office.

Leaf turned to Cook after surveying the scene below them. "This is the road?" he asked.

Cook nodded.

"The skid marks were on the part of the road that has been torn up?"

Cook nodded again, biting his lip.

"The skid marks now sit in those two dump trucks over there? They're nothing but little crumbs of asphalt now?"

"I'm afraid so, Lieutenant."

"Mr. Cook," said the detective, raising his hands in front of him, outstretched, palms upward, presenting the scene below them for Cook's consideration, "Mr. Cook, this is a sonofabitch."

Cook looked at Leaf. "Lieutenant, you believe what I told you, don't you?"

Leaf laughed—a brief, impatient chuckle this time, far from his accustomed belly laugh. "Mr. Cook, spare me your selfish fears. I believe everything until I run into things that force me to change my beliefs. That hasn't happened yet." He stared at the workers below them, then stuffed his hands in his pockets and kicked at a pebble on the sidewalk. "I hate coincidences," he said bitterly.

"If ever there was one, this is it," offered Cook.

"And you oversleeping is another," Leaf said quickly.

Cook frowned. "I suppose it is. But not unrelated. In a way I overslept because of the skidding, as I explained earlier."

"Which you coincidentally overheard because you coincidentally were working late in your office, your coincidental window being coincidentally open. Just how often do you work that late at night in your office?"

"Once or twice a month," Cook answered truthfully.

"I'm glad I'm not a statistician," said Leaf. "If I were I'd lock you up on sheer improbability."

Umbrage, said Cook to himself, trying to focus his thoughts. Take umbrage. You have the right. "Now just a minute, Lieutenant," he said with some warmth. "You are in no position legally to make that sort of threat."

"Cook," said Leaf, his bulk suddenly looming larger, "don't disappoint me. I spend far too much time as it is dealing with the mental dregs of Kinsey County, which has plenty, let me tell you. There are more crazy Hoosiers out there than you would ever think possible. Now you are probably an intelligent man. I definitely am. Let's meet each other on that basis and save the butter for our potatoes. I'm a policeman who wants to find out who killed that guy up there. If you didn't do it you can help me find out who did. Whatever happens, don't pretend to be stupid and normal and don't for Christ's sake pull rank on me as a civilian. I'll honor that by not being stupid and normal and by not pulling rank on you as the law. Do I make myself clear?"

Cook hesitated an instant. "Perfectly, Lieutenant. I appreciate your . . . your—"

"Good," Leaf said crisply.

Cook cleared his throat. "You think someone killed him then?"

Leaf smiled. "My preliminary examination showed that the man received a blow to the back of his head so severe that it could have been self-inflicted only if he (a) dropped from a great height and landed only on his head, or (b) ran backward into a brick wall at a speed of say twenty miles per hour."

"Both being rather unlikely, given his presence in my office," said Cook, wanting to contribute.

"Right," said Leaf, smiling slightly. "Right."

"Lieutenant, if someone did kill Stiph, and if he killed him out here by running over him, why wasn't the body mangled? And why was his head shaved?"

"I don't know," Leaf said thoughtfully, "but here's a first approximation. When people . . ." He paused and looked closely at Cook. "What are you smiling at?"

Cook raised a hand, half in self-defense, half in apology. "Sorry. That's a favorite phrase in linguistic research, when a linguist is formulating a rough hypothesis: 'a first approximation.'"

"Well," said Leaf, appearing more pleased than Cook would have expected, "as I was saying, when people are hit by a car, the major injury is usually sustained as a result of a secondary blow—landing on a pavement, against a tree, against another car. Very often—and this answers your question about his hair, or at least it attempts to answer it—very often the body flies up, the center of gravity being above the bumper in an adult body of normal—"

"Excuse me, Lieutenant," Cook heard from the building in back of them.

Leaf turned to the door. A uniformed policeman held it open for him. "The woman upstairs, Lieutenant, the one who found the body . . . she's giving us a little trouble. Says she wants to go home, and that whoever is supposed to be asking her questions had better do it soon. That's what she said. Stolewicz is trying to calm her down, but she slapped him, and—"

"I'll be right up," said Leaf. He let out a soft string of curse words, then turned to Cook. "Can you stop by my office later this afternoon? About four? It's in the basement of City Hall. I'd like to get a more detailed account of what happened last night—times, skid marks, all that. Try to think of anything else that might help." He headed for the door.

"Suspects, too?" Cook called after him.

Leaf looked back at him. "Hell yes, suspects," he said gruffly. "I want to catch this guy and skewer him."

Cook remained outside for some time, leaning against the building and gazing down at the road now barren of clues. He wondered how much, exactly, a trained eye could have determined from the skid marks. He filed the question away for his next talk with Leaf. Suspects. The body in the office. Key to the office? No, it was unlocked, the door open. Key to the building? Yes. It was always locked at that hour. He realized with dismay that the killer could well be among the other linguists on the staff. None of the teachers had keys to the building, nor did Mary the Secretary. Cook, Woeps, Wach, Aaskhugh, Milke, Orffmann, and Miss Pristam. She was out of town—had been for a month and would be for another two. And unless he was insane, he, Cook, was not a suspect.

Woeps. Wach. Aaskhugh. Milke. Orffmann. That would make day-to-day life somewhat awkward.

He looked down at the road below. One of the workers had stolen an orange from the lunch box of another worker, and a group of them were throwing it around, playing keep-away. The wind came up and the sky blackened. The workers gathered their things together and scrambled for cover, and the heavy rain that had threatened for so long finally made good on the threat. Cook stood close to the building, sheltered, and watched the rain come down.

CHAPTER FOUR

"HELLO?"

"Hello," Cook said into the phone in a voice very different from his normal one. What he aimed for was the crackerjack, fast-talking, wide-lapeled wiseacre who was the newspaper reporter in every American film made in the thirties and forties. High-pitched, like Dan Duryea, with a bit of the owl-faced guy from *Citizen Kane* thrown in. Being a sensitive phonetician, this and other imitations came easily to him. "Is this Miss Dorothy Plough?"

"Yes, it is."

"Philpot here, Dorothy. Henry Philpot." Cook read from a prepared text so that he could concentrate on being sufficiently bumptious. "Haven't got you out of bed, have I?"

"No, not at all. I just finished breakfast. What did you say your—"

"Philpot's the name, writing's the game. I'm doing a little magazine piece on a cozy place down the road known locally as Baby Heaven but a.k.a. the Wabash Institute. Perhaps you've seen me roaming and combing the halls."

"Oh, yes, I've heard of you. In fact—"

"Did we meet?" Cook asked nervously, feeling himself slip out of character as he departed from his text. "I've met so many of you lovely girls I can hardly keep you all straight."

"No, we haven't met. But—"

"Good. Or what I mean is, it's good to be talking to you, Dorothy." He bit his lip and pressed on quickly. "The reason

I'm calling is that I like to make a practice of getting in touch with the nuts-and-bolts people in an organization and bellying up to them and feeling them up and down to get a real sense of a place, you know what I mean?"

"Yes," she said uncertainly. "I think so."

"I do it telephonically," he said. "The telephone is the investigative reporter's chief tool of the trade, you know. Somebody said that once, good old what's-his-name. Ha! I'd like some of your impressions of Wabash—the work, the kids, the people there. Straight from the shoulder. The straight dope from the Pope. For example, what do you have to say about this fellow Cook?"

"Dr. Cook?"

"Yes. This fellow Cook." He heard a pause and a sigh. He strained every muscle as he listened. His eyes were popped open at their widest.

"I'm not sure . . ."

"Yes?"

"I'm not sure what you want me to say. What do I think of him?"

"Yes. That."

"Apart from wanting to go to bed with him?" She laughed, boldly.

By way of response Cook coughed and gagged in confusion.

"Seriously, though, he's wonderful. He's just a wonderful man. Friendly, energetic, devoted to his work. He makes that place go. And he never pulls rank on anybody, the way some of the others do. Everyone I know at Wabash is really fond of him."

Fond? Fond?

"Now Dr. Orffmann is a different kettle of fish." As she went on to fry this particular fish, Cook scowled in disappointment. He wanted to get this business out of the way, and here was Dorothy Plough, a prime suspect on the basis of a sneer he thought he had seen from her once, letting him down and in fact talking like someone who would never call him even a marginal asshole.

". . . and Dr. Milke, despite his considerable charm, is a bit overbearing at times . . ."

Cook hardly listened. He didn't care about these people. He had one question he wanted answered. But he couldn't very well call up all fifteen or so teachers at Wabash and run through this Philpot routine with them. And his original plan of getting the information out of Paula seemed ill-conceived too. In fact it was a sudden loss of faith in that plan over breakfast that had prompted this call. Paula probably wouldn't even speak to him, at least not civilly. And she was so good-looking. Buxom, too, as they used to say. Why did they stop saying that? He clenched his fist angrily.

". . . and Dr. Aaskhugh is just a *total* twit . . ."

It was hopeless. He was doomed to wander the halls of Wabash in ridiculous ignorance, a "Complete Asshole" sign taped to his back. With some impatience he interrupted her and said he had an urgent call to make. Fearing he had been a bit abrupt, he added a word of thanks.

"Before you go," she said hurriedly, "I wanted to tell you that Dr. Wach has been asking for you. You haven't been to Wabash for a couple days, have you?"

It took Cook a moment to realize Wach had been looking for Philpot, not himself. "Well, no. Actually, I've been pretty busy here at the . . . at the motel."

She laughed. "Must be some kind of motel."

Cook chuckled nervously. How could he know where Philpot was? He was tired of being asked that question. "Tell him that I'll be in later today. After the Stiph funeral. And thanks again for your help. It really put some things in perspective for me."

"Anytime, Phil."

As he hung up he wondered if Philpot actually was going

to the funeral. He hoped this call didn't create any trouble for him. He felt a twinge of guilt about it. The hypothetical baboon he had impersonated had nothing to do with the mild-mannered Philpot. He glanced at his watch and went into the bedroom, and after rummaging around in the dark recesses of his closet he finally found a plain black suit, severely out of both fashion and season. He was surprised that he owned such a thing, and, upon trying it on, that it still fit him.

Arthur Stiph would be pleased. The elderly linguist was scheduled to be laid to rest in one hour, and Cook had decided, after prolonged internal debate, that yes, it would be proper for him to attend the funeral. It had taken him some time to quash the arguments he could raise against his going. After all, he hadn't been very close to Stiph, and he always thought it in bad taste for tangential people to intrude on intimate ceremonies. Also, his name had become connected with Stiph's death in a most uncomfortable way. Since Wednesday morning he had been interviewed more times than he could remember. In each instance he had offered a thorough, businesslike narrative of the events of Tuesday night and carefully declined to speculate when prodded to do so—or to "extrapolate," as he was asked to do by one skinny reporter. But no matter how professionally Cook had spoken, the body had definitely been found sitting at his desk. He became something of a suspect in the public eye, or "a figure linked to the crime," or something. Whatever it was, he didn't like it.

Despite these arguments, Cook had decided to go to the funeral. There were some good arguments for it, of course. It had been two days since Stiph's body was found, and Cook hadn't left the house in all that time. He had called in sick and stayed home, working a bit in his study and puttering around the house. Wabash seemed like a good place to be away from for a few days. Especially his office and desk and chair. It made sense to return to worldly activity via Stiph's funeral. There was a nice unity and completeness to that approach.

Besides, he genuinely wanted to have a silent last word with Arthur, and this was sufficient reason for going.

His little holiday at home had been healthy and constructive. He hadn't drunk too much, for example. Also, he had mowed the lawn, painted the back porch railing, and started his small annual garden. But he made a point of not washing his car. It would have been difficult to respond politely to some passer-by's joking query as to whether he had gotten all the blood off. Such a query certainly was possible. The skid marks, brief though their existence was, were public knowledge. Stiph had been run over. This was Leaf's opinion, as Cook had learned in the course of his Wednesday afternoon reunion with the detective, and it was the medical examiner's opinion, as Cook had learned, wincing with every utterance of his own name, from the Wednesday night news. That afternoon Leaf was able to finish making the point he had started to make earlier in the day, namely that the normal human body, having a center of gravity at roughly waist level, upon being struck by the bumper of a car is often thrown into the air in a snapping fashion, causing the head to resound fatally against some portion of the hood near the windshield, if not against the windshield itself. Stiph presumably had struck some car with his head, and Leaf had declared to Cook, "Show me a car with a dent in the hood and you've shown me the weapon." (It was no coincidence that the detective accompanied Cook out to the parking lot near the police station for a casual look at his old Valiant. Leaf found nothing incriminating, but he did say that the car was a rather dull one for a distinguished scholar like Cook to be driving.)

Stiph's head had been shaved, Leaf surmised, so there would be no traces of paint clinging to his hair that might lead an assiduous investigator (such as himself, he added) to the killing vehicle. "We're dealing with a clever fellow," Leaf said to him. "He's taken care of the whole boiling." Cook, amazed at the way Leaf repeatedly taxed his decoding skills, interpreted this to mean that the killer had allowed for all conceivable contingencies. There were, however, traces of the car on Stiph's person that had been overlooked by the driver: a hint of chrome on his pants leg and a bit of windshield wiper rubber embedded in his left ear. Not a great deal, but something.

There was also a trace of the killer in Cook's office—again nothing great, but something. It was a small puddle on the floor made up of bourbon and vanilla ice cream. This fact, stonily reported without elaboration on the Thursday night news, must have baffled all of Kinsey's population with the exception of Cook and the police, for Lieutenant Leaf had briefed Cook on just this point the preceding afternoon. Without mincing any words.

"We figure the guy puked in your office," he announced. "From overexertion, from anxiety, from nausea at hauling a corpse around . . . it's hard to say." When Cook asked if this was an important lead, Leaf shrugged. "Ice cream's ice cream," he said. "Fuck me if I can make anything out of it." Cook nodded uncomfortably at this, not sure of the semantic thrust of the imperative apodosis.

Leaf concluded with a final point, just as Cook was leaving the police station: the building at Wabash had been broken into. Cook smiled warmly at the news, for while it confounded the case, it cleared—or held promise of clearing—his colleagues. There was no point in breaking into a building you had a key to. But Cook's heart sank when Leaf went on to say that he felt "uneasy about the nature of the break-in"—a broken basement window—that something "wasn't quite right" about it, that he had a "funny feeling" about it, and that he just didn't feel "right." These remarks remained obscure and unelaborated, so Cook left the Lieutenant's office with ineffably "funny" feelings about just about everything in the whole case—the whole boiling, in other words.

Cook leaned toward the mirror and straightened his tie. Not a bad dark suit, he thought. Not a very good one either.

Warm, too, and it was going to be a hot day. He looked in his closet at some more stylish alternatives. More stylish, to be sure, but all of them inappropriate for a funeral. He closed the closet door. With this suit he would be properly bland and unnoticeable, just part of the background.

He looked at his watch. "Damn!" It had obviously stopped some time ago. He gathered his keys and wallet, ran out to his car, and drove off. The cemetery was on the other side of town. When he reached Kinsey he weaved from lane to lane and swore at the red lights until they turned green. He hoped his tardiness wouldn't be conspicuous. Somehow it seemed in terribly bad taste to be late for a funeral.

He stopped his car at the cemetery gate and looked in. A narrow road ran through the gate and then climbed for a short distance before dropping down into the area where the headstones stretched out. This little hill prevented Cook from seeing any sign of a funeral below, but the cars parked along the narrow road and then spilling out of the gate along the main road in both directions attested to a sizeable crowd down there at Stiph's grave. He backed his car down the main road and parked it at the tail end of the line of cars. Then he trotted back to the gate and up over the little knoll.

A large crowd was gathered at one of the gravesites several hundred feet below him. Cook walked down the gentle slope, recognizing first Woeps's prematurely stooped figure, then, as he came nearer, Orffmann's large neck, Milke's beard and pipe, Wach's plumb-line posture, Paula's long hair, and other people's attributes. A few heads turned as he approached—a solitary figure dressed in black slowly working his way down the green hillside. Then it seemed that a few more gazes settled on him. He moved on resolutely, cursing his luck. That portion of the group that hadn't yet noticed Cook—all those with their backs completely to him—suddenly looked up. En masse they swung their stares in his direction. What had attracted their attention was the mournful sound of taps being played by a bugler perched some distance in back of him at the top of the hill. The naturally curious eyes that rose solemnly from the grave in search of the bugler landed easily on Cook and remained fixed there.

Cook continued on after glancing over his shoulder to locate the bugler and then recommend him to perdition. Then he slowed down. Should he be walking? Shouldn't he stop? Yes. He should stop for the playing of taps. That was why they were all looking at him. He stopped and folded his hands in front of him. A few eyes left him, but not enough. He stood rooted in embarrassment alone on the side of the hill while the clear notes sounded in the air. As the melancholy tune came to an end, the eyes slowly left Cook and returned to Stiph's grave. Cook moved forward again, quickly, and as he arrived at the edge of the crowd he heard someone say "Amen," and a small sigh arose from the crowd. There began a general milling about. Cook sighed, wanting to share at least that much with the crowd. Amid soft murmurs, people began to walk back up the hill. Cook nudged his way through the crowd, fighting against the general flow, trying to get closer to the coffin sitting aboveground beside the open grave. He noticed uneasily that there was a spirited festiveness of color in the dresses and suits on all sides of him—a sharp contrast to his own lugubrious, blackish hue. Didn't people wear black to funerals anymore? He felt stupidly uninformed.

Someone was tugging at his sleeve. For an instant he thought it might be some kind of usher demanding to see his ticket. But, thankfully, it was Woeps. His face carried a look of worry and dread—just the kind of face that was right for a funeral, except that it was more or less his permanent face.

"What happened, Jeremy?"

Cook looked at him and shrugged. "I was late," he said.

"I know you were late, but . . . " Woeps smiled sadly. "Sorry. I see what you're saying. You're saying—"

"I'm saying," Cook whispered hotly to him, "that I was

late, and if the killer hadn't stuck the body in my office and if the funeral director hadn't put that stupid trumpeter up on the hill, no one would give a sweet goddamn about it."

Woeps frowned. "Look, Jeremy, don't take it out—"

"Oh I'm not mad at you, Ed," he said. He took his glasses off and rubbed the bridge of his nose. "Jesus, what a rotten time I've been having."

Woeps reached out and squeezed his arm near the shoulder. "You shouldn't let this get to you, Jeremy. None of it's your fault. Come on, I'll buy you a cup of coffee or something."

Cook shook his head. "I'd like to stay here a minute or two, Ed. I didn't come here just to be stared at." He looked at the coffin. Woeps followed his eyes.

"All right, Jeremy. I'll wait for you up by my car."

"Don't wait, Ed." Cook turned to him. "I'll see you back at work." His friend hesitated a moment, then nodded and moved off with the last of the crowd. Cook watched the clusters of people moving up the hillside before he turned back to the gravesite. The coffin lying beside the open grave looked thick, dark, and expensive. Cook began to stare at it, for that's what people were supposed to do at funerals. It was a privilege the living had over the dead. He began to feel better. It was right for him to be alone with Stiph now.

But he was not quite alone. A solitary figure stood directly on the other side of the coffin, an old woman in black. The widow? Not likely, thought Cook. People didn't leave widows alone like that at funerals. A sister? An old, secret lover? She was looking at Cook. Then she was speaking to him.

"Why are you still here?" she called out across the coffin. She hadn't stressed *you*, so she hadn't singled Cook out and questioned, in particular, *his* being there. Her voice was the voice of an old woman, but it was as clear as the notes of the bugle that had sounded just minutes before.

Cook shrugged and put his hands in his pockets. "I was late," he said across the coffin.

She began to move toward him, circling in a wide arc around the coffin. "I noticed," she said. "Who are you?"

"My name's Jeremy Cook. I work at the Wabash Institute."

She cocked her head a bit to one side, coming still closer, moving slowly. When she reached him she turned and faced the coffin and said, "Yes, he mentioned you from time to time."

Cook swallowed. "Arthur?" he asked. "Your husband?"

"Yes," she said. "He died in your office."

"He was found dead in my office, yes."

"Ah." She smiled. "Precision. Arthur was that way, too, Mr. Cook. I hope his *being found dead* in your office hasn't inconvenienced you awfully . . . hasn't been overly embarrassing for you." Cook at first took this as haughty and self-pitying, but a glance at the woman's face told him she was genuinely concerned for his position. She seemed to appreciate the way in which he had, in a sense, been compromised.

"It *has* been a little awkward," he said. He noticed that she was not a beautiful woman. Nor was it possible to see traces of an earlier beauty made dim by time. She was merely old and small. Her hair was unkempt and her black dress frayed and wrinkled.

"My condolences," she said, smiling weakly.

Again Cook was suspicious of her meaning, but again she appeared to be serious. "The same here," he said, gesturing offhandedly toward the coffin. They stood together in silence for a moment. The air was very still. In the distance, over the hill, Cook could faintly hear the slamming of doors and the starting of cars as the mourners drove off.

"What was your husband like, Mrs. Stiph?" Cook asked. "I can't say that I knew him very well as a person."

She stared straight ahead at the coffin, thinking. He tried again.

"Mrs. Stiph, I was wondering what your husband was

like." Maybe, he hoped, she liked her questions to be in subordinate clauses.

She stood motionless a while longer before responding. "Mr. Cook, when I walked over here to stand with you I did not do so in the hopes you would ask me questions such as that one." She continued to look straight ahead. Cook waited, not finding it easy. He studied her face. She let him do this, in fact seemed to invite it. She seemed resolved and angry more than anything else. Was she angry because she was alone? Why was there no one to stand by her side at this moment in her life? No one but Cook. Perhaps that was why she was talking with him. Or rather, not talking with him, which was the case right now. But then her eyes changed, taking on a focus that they had lacked.

"Mr. Cook . . . Jeremy—may I call you Jeremy? Yes, I may," she said quickly. "Jeremy, if you were lying in that box instead of my husband, and if I were here at your funeral talking to some friend of yours, let's say that friend you were speaking with just a moment ago, and if I asked him, 'Sir, what was your friend like? What was this fellow Cook like?' what would he say? What would you want him to say?"

She had spoken without once turning to him. She stopped speaking, but her eyes remained brightly focused. She was waiting for an answer. Cook wished she hadn't stopped, at least with that question, for he knew that question well. But he spoke up, trying very hard.

"I would want my friend to say something about me. Something significant."

She stood very still. Then she nodded. "Significant."

"Yes. A story about me. Stories are best. Better than mere words."

"Yes."

Cook sighed a small sigh of relief, feeling stupidly proud of her approval.

"And could he, Jeremy? Could he tell such a story?"

"My friend? The one you just saw?"

"Yes. That one." She looked straight at the coffin, as if she were communicating as much with Arthur as with Jeremy. Her face was determined.

"I don't know," he said softly.

"You don't know. And can you say what story you would want him to tell?"

Cook reached up and rubbed the bridge of his nose under his glasses. "I would have to think about that for a while," he said.

"You would have to think about that for a while," she repeated. "Would you consider it presumptuous of your friend to *try* to—"

"No," he said quickly. "I would definitely want him to try."

She nodded. "I'm afraid I don't have a story to tell you, Jeremy. But I have a story, a written story, to pass on to you. Arthur wrote it when he was an undergraduate at Yale. It tells about a rather . . . unusual and dear man who seeks out certain kinds of people and arranges meetings with them, and then . . . well, I'll let you read it." She paused and tilted her head back and looked at him closely. "I'm giving it to you because it will tell you something important about Arthur and so answer your question, which I take very seriously. This will probably be the last time anyone ever asks me about him. But I'm giving you the story also because it will help you know why he died, or at least why he was where he was when that car struck him. That night, Tuesday night, when he left the house, he said to me, 'Adelle, I'm going out. I've got a backfriend to meet.'"

"A 'backfriend'?"

"Yes. Evidently he had a late-night appointment with someone at Wabash. That was the way he liked to do it."

"But what's a 'backfriend'?"

She smiled. "I'll let Arthur explain it to you. You'll see." She faced the coffin. "Things bothered Arthur, Jeremy. He fought them. He fought hard. I tried to help him where I could." She took a few steps forward, removed a glove from one hand, and reached out and ran a long, bare finger along the top edge of the coffin. Her finger moved slowly, as if she were feeling the wood for imperfections. She turned and looked at Cook. "He had some good years left. He was healthy." She blinked.

For a moment she did not move. Then with an archaic touch of grace, she reached a hand out to Cook. He stepped forward and took it in his own. Together they began the long walk up the grassy hill. Neither of them spoke. Cook was conscious only of isolated sounds in the air—a solitary cardinal high in a tree, in search of a mate, perhaps, a car door slamming somewhere out of sight over the hill as the last of the mourners drove off, a clanking sound from the graveyard toolshed some distance off to the side.

At the top of the hill there were two cars, one just inside the gate, a Volkswagen—Mrs. Stiph's car, apparently—and Cook's Valiant sitting alone far down the main road. Cook walked her to her car. He opened the door for her and she slowly got in.

"Thank you, Jeremy," she said, looking up at him as she reached in her purse for her keys. "I don't need you anymore. You might, though, every now and then, think of an old couple—a couple who were happy for many years." She then said, rather firmly, "I'm glad you turned out the way you are. Goodbye." She waved to him, almost as if he were a great distance away instead of leaning down to the window right beside her.

She drove off. Cook watched the car move down the road and around a turn, and he continued to look long after it had disappeared from view. Then a metallic clank behind him attracted his attention. Curious, he walked back up to the top of the knoll overlooking the graves. In the distance below, two diggers were walking toward Stiph's grave. One of them lazily dragged his shovel behind him, and here and there it banged against a headstone. Cook took one last look at the coffin before turning away.

Not your run-of-the-mill widow, he said to himself as he walked through the cemetery gate. But then Stiph might not have been your run-of-the-mill husband. What about the story she had mentioned? Should he call her about it when he got home? Whom had Stiph planned to meet? Would the story tell him? How could it, if, as she said, he had written it years ago?

He kicked at the gravel along the edge of the road as he walked to his car.

CHAPTER FIVE

NEAR THE WINDSHIELD on the driver's side he bent over to look at it, more curious than upset. There was nothing to indicate what might have caused it. No rocks lying in the area, no young ruffians, no vandalizing squirrels scampering about with oversized acorns. As he frowned and stared at the dent, his scalp suddenly chilled, for some passing quirk of his imagination revealed the contours of Arthur Stiph's head in the depression. But that was impossible. Cook hadn't killed him. Someone else had. Several days ago—Tuesday night. This was Friday.

So where had the dent come from? Had Stiph, seeing the way Cook was carrying on with his widow, reached out from the grave with a bony fist and smashed Cook's car in jealous anger?

No, thought Cook with mounting awareness. There was another explanation—one more conformable to earthly laws.

"Damn!" he said loudly. "What a rotten sonofabitch he must be." He felt the dent, then quickly withdrew his hand. He clenched his fists, feeling more keenly than ever the injustice of what was happening to him. To *him*. Forget about Stiph—he was dead and gone and there was no changing that. But why couldn't he go on with his own life? "What a rotten sonofabitch!" he said again. He examined the rest of the car's exterior and found, to his surprise but not to his great surprise, a tiny piece of fabric, jagged at the edges, hooked on a small piece of chrome in the grill.

He quickly resolved to drive directly to the police station and tell Leaf about it. Thank God the detective had already examined his car, thank God for that. He put the piece of wool into his shirt pocket, choosing not to leave it in its natural state for fear it might blow away in transit. Then, as he drove toward the main road leading back into town, he tried to chase down the thought that threatened to elude him. Whoever put that dent in his car must have known that there existed the possibility of a dent—that "dentedness" was a relevant concept. Which proved, or at least contributed substantially to the view, that there was, after all, a dent in the vehicle that had done the killing.

The Lieutenant was out, Cook was told by a large, white-faced sergeant who gave the appearance of being an excellent bowler. When was he expected back? Cook asked politely, though he felt this information should have been offered along with the report that Leaf was out. Forty-five minutes, give or take. Could he be reached? No, impossible. Could he be informed upon his return that Jeremy Cook was looking for him? Yes, for what it was worth. Would it be profitable for Cook to return at one o'clock, when the Lieutenant was expected back? Perhaps, but no one was making any promises. Would the tight-lipped sergeant enjoy squatting on a hot poker? Perhaps, but no one was making any promises.

As he stood on the sidewalk outside City Hall, Cook wondered why some people were allowed to exist when others weren't. He sighed and consulted his stomach. He wasn't hungry—a rather grunty breakfast had had a concretizing effect on his lower system—but if he didn't eat soon he would become hungry, probably at an inconvenient time. He began to walk the two blocks that separated the police station from his favorite bar and grill. This was the Circus Maximus, also known by some in the area as the Circus, by others as Max's. As he walked he felt a strange sleepiness settle over him. He wondered what he should eat or drink to make it go away, and it suddenly struck him that his whole life was a stupidly futile struggle to be mentally alert.

Inside Max's he found a quiet booth for himself after a quick survey revealed none of his colleagues in the crowd at the bar or at any of the tables. A darkish Mediterranean waitress he knew and liked and whose wedding band should have blackened long ago from the frequent curses he directed at it asked him how he was and took his order. He drummed his fingers softly on the table as he waited for his meal to arrive, trying to look pleasantly occupied with thought, a pose familiar to him from years of dining out alone. All he really thought about, though, was how funny he must look in his black suit. Now and then his booth shook uncomfortably as a large man sitting with his back to Cook's shifted from one position to another, giving a perfect edge to Cook's discomfort.

In time, the waitress returned with his linguine and chicken livers. She set a bottle of beer before him. He admired the dew of condensation on the neck and label. Then, because he was unhappy, tired, and alone, the bottle slipped from his eager grasp and spilled with a loud crash across the table. He lunged forward and caught it, but fully half of his beer was lying in a foamy puddle on the table and dripping into the seat opposite him.

"Hey, buddy, do you have to jerk around so much?"

Cook whirled around in his seat. Over his shoulder the face he saw was red and hostile, and Cook met it with his own, prepared to do battle. Perhaps a fight was the thing to turn the day around. Then the face swam into a familiar focus, as if through trick photography, and Lieutenant Leaf was suddenly grinning at him across the partition.

"Jeremy!" he exclaimed. "How are you? Here, let me join you." Leaf turned and grabbed his goods from his table and stood up, all the while declaring his pleasure in meeting Cook like this, and all the while addressing Cook by his first name, suggesting an intimacy Cook found surprising but not unwelcome. When the Lieutenant started to sit down across the table Cook spoke up.

"Hold it, Lieutenant. That seat's all wet." Leaf recoiled, then bent his large body over the seat as if he intended to sniff at the beer. After a quick cleaning, he settled down across from Cook with a fresh cup of coffee and a cigarette, remarking that Cook looked as if he were on his way to a funeral. Cook wondered anew at Leaf's personality; it seemed to be a perfect mixture of an overweight Jack Webb and Bertie Wooster. He was happy to have Leaf there with him, not only because he wanted to talk to someone, but because he wanted to talk to Leaf. There was nothing nicer, he thought, than speaking when you really had something to say, when you had the power to affect with mere words the body chemistry of your listener, and Cook now sensed he was in such a position with Leaf. He told him about the dent in his car and the man set down his cup of cof0 from his pocket and Leaf banged himself on the forehead and loudly uttered an oath, if the expression "Peas and carrots!" can indeed be considered an oath. Then he examined the material closely under the table lamp. He appeared unwilling to say much about it until Cook reminded him that by mutual agreement they were partners in the investigation. Leaf smiled, then said that he guessed, as Cook had earlier, that it was an attempted frame, and a sloppy one at that.

"It's a little late in the day for this guy to go around denting up cars," he said. He stubbed out his cigarette and signaled to the waitress to pour him more coffee. Cook ordered another beer. "This material will probably match Stiph's pants," Leaf continued after a short fit of coughing. "The ones he was wearing when he got hit. I'll check it out when I get back to the station."

"You still have his pants?" Cook asked.

"Of course. What do you think, that we'd auction them off like a bicycle or something?" He sipped his coffee and then lit another cigarette. "Do you have any idea who did this, Jeremy?"

"The dent in the car, or the hit and run?"

"One and the same, don't you think?"

Cook frowned. Of course he did. Then why had he asked Leaf which one he was talking about? He felt very confused. He sighed, noting to himself that one symptom of exhaustion was to give your listener the impression that you held beliefs that you didn't hold at all.

"No, Lieutenant," he said. "I haven't gotten anywhere on it. I haven't really been thinking about it."

"Har, har, har," responded Leaf. "You haven't really been thinking about it."

"No, honestly," said Cook. "I've had other things on my mind."

"You've had other things on your mind, har har har."

Cook gave up trying to explain, figuring that if he succeeded in convincing Leaf he was serious he would look all the more like a fool. The waitress brought his beer, and he carefully reached for it and took a large swallow from the bottle.

"Do you have any leads, Lieutenant?" he asked.

Leaf raised two hands in front of him and with curled thumb and index finger made two small circles, one in each hand. These he raised to his eyes, forming a little pair of goggles with them. He peered at Cook through his fingers in a way that strongly suggested he had taken complete leave of his senses. Then he removed the circles from his eyes and held them up for Cook to examine.

"Zero, Jeremy," he said by way of explanation. "Double zeros. Nothing. Nothing."

The two men paid their checks and left the restaurant. Cook said he would walk with Leaf back to the station, since he had left his car there. Leaf nodded and said he would like to have a look at it, it being a slow day and all, "knock on wood," he added, reaching up and with a stupid grin on his face knocking hard on the top of his own head. He lit up another cigarette and puffed, not only at the cigarette but for mere air. Cook was awed by the man's health, a feature about him he hadn't noticed before. In plain terms it stank. His entire face was over-red, he hacked throatily every few minutes, and now and then he would scowl around at nothing in particular, as if he labored under the disadvantage of some great internal pain.

Cook asked the Lieutenant if he had already examined the cars belonging to the other people with keys to his building at Wabash. Leaf said that he had, finding nothing. Cook asked him if he had mentioned the possibility of a dent in the hood to anyone besides himself. Leaf thought a moment and shook his head, and then, as he saw in advance where Cook was trying to take the argument, pointed out that the new dent in Cook's car did not necessarily prove the existence of a dent in the culpable vehicle, for the killer, on seeing his car examined by the police, might well have drawn that inference for himself and exploited that official assumption in an attempted frame. Cook thought about this and silently cursed the world for being so complex. He decided he should start at the beginning.

"Just what do you make of Stiph's death, Lieutenant?" he asked as they hurriedly crossed against a red light.

"I make of it exactly what you make of it and what the handful of other people of above-dull intelligence should make of it," he said.

"Do you figure it was an accident? Is that it?"

Leaf snorted to himself. "Let's just say that if I were going to kill someone and wanted to do a good job of it I wouldn't count on running him over in the middle of the night in a place where I couldn't really expect him to be, slamming on my brakes as I did so. Hold it!" Leaf stopped in his tracks. Cook waited eagerly for him to share the insight that must have just leaped into his head. But Leaf, judging from his gaze, had halted because of something he had seen. Cook followed his eyes. They led to an item in the window of a men's clothing store—a purple shirt with little flowers embroidered on the collar.

"Love that shirt," said Leaf with feeling. He moved ahead slowly, reluctantly. Cook stood in place for a moment, looking at the shirt in disbelief, then at Leaf to be sure he was serious, then back at the shirt. He wondered how a man who admired a shirt like that could possibly solve crimes.

"What do you mean when you say that Stiph could not really have been expected to be where he was, Lieutenant?" asked Cook.

Leaf looked at Cook. "Why don't you take that idiotic coat off? You're sweating like an unbaptized hog." Cook, suddenly aware of just how uncomfortable he was, complied and draped his jacket over one shoulder. "Arthur Stiph," Leaf continued, "took frequent and unpredictable walks late at night. In all directions and at all times. According to his widow he was on one such when he was killed."

Cook turned to him. "You talked with her?"

"Of course," said Leaf in a bored tone.

Cook thought a moment. Hadn't Leaf earlier given him the impression that he had never met her? He shook his head, trying to arrive at a clear thought. To his surprise he succeeded, for he hit upon a discrepancy. Leaf apparently thought Stiph's walk was a mere stroll for fresh air.

"She told me he was going to meet someone, Lieutenant."

"Who?"

"She didn't say. Because *he* didn't say. He just said he was going to meet a . . . a something. A backfriend."

"I know. But what the hell does it mean—that they gave back rubs to each other?"

"I don't know." He looked at Leaf. "So she told you, too."

"Of course."

"But you weren't about to tell me."

"No."

Cook cleared his throat. "We have an agreement. I thought we were going to work together. Pool our resources."

"Yeah. Sorry. Listen, now that you mention it, I couldn't

find that word in my dictionary."

"'Backfriend'?"

"Yeah."

"I'll check mine. As I was saying, I was hoping you would see your way clear to be a little more generous with—"

"There's still a problem, you know, with the view that the guy he met had planned to kill him." Leaf spoke not just as if Cook hadn't been speaking but as if he were not even there.

"There is?" asked Cook, his head whirling.

"You said there was a swerve in the skid marks."

"That's right. A little swerve."

"That suggests to me an attempt to avoid the victim."

"Or the effect of a sudden impact with something?"

"Who knows? A look at the skid marks might have cleared that up, but they're gone, aren't they?"

"Yes. They're gone." The two of them walked on in silence for a while, Cook thoughtful and measured, the Lieutenant bustling and coughing at his side. Finally, Cook spoke again.

"Lieutenant, you don't seem to know any more than I do, and I'm just a linguist. Haven't you learned anything besides 'zero, zero'?"

Leaf's large features suddenly condensed themselves into a pout. He turned to Cook, head bent in mock submission, and looked as if he were going to deliver himself of another verbal enigma. But then he simply slapped himself once on the belly. Then, as if unexpectedly pleased with the sound, he slapped himself once more.

Cook reflected silently on this turn of events. He wondered how soon he would reach a point where Leaf ceased to amuse him.

"Jeremy," the detective finally said, "do you know what the best lead in this case is?"

"Yes," said Cook. "The body in the building. The person who stashed the body has a key."

"But there were signs of forced entry," he said with a

rhetorical singsong to his voice, as if he were giving Cook an oral examination.

"About which you felt 'funny,' Lieutenant. You gave me the impression the forced entry was faked."

"Did I?"

"Yes."

"Well, that's because it was."

Cook frowned and wondered where Leaf had learned the art of conversation. "Why do you say that?"

Leaf inhaled deeply, then spoke very quickly. "Because the broken glass was mainly *outside* the building, on the ground, and it wouldn't be there if it had been broken from the outside, and it was done with the wooden end of a hoe that was kept in the basement, and the guy tried to make it look like the body had been dragged through the basement window by sticking a piece of glass in one cuff of the victim's pants, when any moron of a criminal who really didn't have a key would have just entered the basement alone and then opened the door on the first floor to bring Stiph in that way. He overdid it, in other words. Things like that."

Cook thought about this a moment and nodded. "Sounds solid."

"I ain't no dirt eater."

Cook pondered this disclaimer, then pressed on. "This means that the killer wanted to hide the fact that he had a key, which means that he *had* a key, which means that he was one of five people."

"Six."

"What?"

"Six people."

"No. Miss Pristam is out of town."

"Six."

"Mary the Secretary doesn't have a key. And the janitors work days because my boss doesn't trust them with keys."

"Six."

Cook flung his arms out to his sides in exasperation. "What the hell are you talking about?"

"In the eighteenth century a British explorer traveled to Australia and New Zealand. What was his name?"

"Captain Cook."

Leaf grinned at Cook as if he had just walked into the most cunningly set trap in the annals of Indiana detection. "That's right, Cap'n."

Cook suddenly ceased to find the Lieutenant amusing.

"Six is a good number," Leaf continued excitedly, now in a manic phase. "I have six brothers and sisters. I have six cars in my fleet. I like six. It's my favorite number. That there are six suspects in this case has been, for me, the high point of the investigation." He picked at his teeth with a stubby finger.

"All right, Lieutenant. I won't even try to explore my possible guilt with you. I'll leave that to you. Just tell me this. Doesn't anyone have an alibi for Tuesday night? I don't, of course."

"No, you don't, to put it gently. Being at the scene of the crime at the moment of its commission is not normally considered an alibi, har, har. As for the others, only one of them has an alibi, but his wife is the only corroboration and she's a liar."

"How do you know?"

"Parakeets in the living room. People who own parakeets are liars."

Cook laughed. "You're not serious."

"Yes I am. When you're on the force awhile you learn things."

"I take it then that you've talked to all the suspects?"

"Yes."

"Did you learn anything interesting?"

"Yes."

"What did you learn?"

Leaf paused. "I've learned that your language factory or baby farm or whatever it is contains some choice grade-A dicks, let me tell you."

Cook laughed. "You don't have to tell me."

"They're suspicious and creepy . . . nervous-laughter types. Queerbaits all, and cockchafers. Dicks."

"Well, Ed Woeps is a friend of mine. I wouldn't have guessed you would feel that way about him."

"Then you would have gone fish."

"But he—"

"Dicks dicks dicks dicks dicks."

Sensing that this left little room for debate, Cook said, "Is any one of the suspects more of a suspect than the others?"

"No," Leaf said unconvincingly.

"Do you own any parakeets?"

Leaf stopped in his tracks and laughed raucously, uncontrollably. Cook did not enjoy seeing it, for he realized with a shock that this might have been the first genuine thing Leaf had done all afternoon. But even then he could not be sure.

"Let's go look at your car," said Leaf, his face even redder than normal and somewhat wet around the lips. They crossed the parking lot next to the police station. Cook pointed out his Valiant.

"Not bad," said Leaf as he sprawled across the hood. "Not bad. A human head could have made that mark for all I can tell."

"What is the penalty for this sort of thing, Lieutenant? The killing, I mean. Assuming it was accidental. Manslaughter, I guess."

"How would you define 'manslaughter,' Jeremy?" asked Leaf as he heaved himself up on one fender and sat there. Cook watched his car sag severely to one side under the weight.

He sighed. "Lieutenant, do you have to turn everything into a question?"

"Sorry. You needn't be so touchy." Leaf swung his legs back and forth, scissors-like. "Most people think that manslaughter is just accidental killing. But in this state—in most, I guess—there are two kinds, voluntary and involuntary.

If I called you a linguistic dick and you suddenly turned on me and stuck two fingers through my eyeholes into my brain, thereby killing me, you could be found guilty of voluntary manslaughter. It's a kind of murder, actually—in my book, at least—but it's done impulsively. And yet voluntarily. 'In a sudden heat' is how the statute reads." He grinned at Cook for no apparent reason and laughed softly. "But you're probably talking about the other kind. Involuntary manslaughter. That covers accidental deaths committed during the commission of some unlawful act. Like reckless driving. The penalty for that, if recklessness is proved, is two to twenty-one."

Cook raised his eyebrows. "That's pretty serious. For an accident."

Leaf hopped back to his feet and dusted his pants off, as if in silent comment on Cook's maintenance of his car. "Well, the law can't very well let everyone run around rantum scantum." He shrugged. "At any rate you can see why the killer wasn't eager to step forward. Especially since the victim was apparently so likeable and all, at least to hear people talk about him." He paused meaningfully. "But his cover-up seems to have singled you out for some reason."

Cook nodded. "Probably out of simple convenience. My door happened to be open . . . the light was on . . . any idiot could have seen it."

Leaf nodded several times. Then his face took on a doubting look, as if he were debating some private question. When he finally spoke Cook had the feeling that this particular speech had been chosen only after the careful elimination of other quite different speeches.

"Jeremy, I never did tell you what the best lead is in this case. The key to the building is good, very good. But after that it's a question of character. Consider first the accident, again assuming it was an accident. There are two kinds of people—those who are likely to have such an accident and those who are not. That narrows the field already. Then, if you do have such an accident, there are two things to do and two kinds of people to do them. You can hide or you can come forth and seek the mercy of the court. Our man chose to hide, and that narrows the field further. And he chose to hide in a special way. He didn't just run, for example. He was more careful, more deliberate. That's one thing that strikes me about this case. Deliberation after the fact, a sense of, 'Well, what do I do now?' So our man shaves Stiph's head to protect himself, and rounds it off by seating the body at your desk. That took a very special kind of person. And the busted window in the basement. Then put against those things the fact that the guy puked. Whiskey and ice cream. You see, Jeremy, it's a question of character."

"Yes, but for God's sake what *kind* of character?"

Leaf inhaled sharply and scratched his abundant chin. Then he snapped his fingers. "One thing I forgot to tell you, Jeremy, is that Arthur Stiph's wristwatch was on backward."

Cook looked at Leaf and wondered if the fat man was trying to drive him mad.

"Backward?"

"When we found him in your office his wristwatch was on his left wrist, where I suppose he normally wore it, but it faced outward, as if he was always showing other people what time it was. His wife said he never wore it that way. I mean, it would be pretty dumb, wouldn't it? He was a conventional wristwatch wearer." He looked at Cook's watch. "Like you and me, Jeremy." He gave Cook a pleasantly surprised look, as if he had just learned they shared birthdays.

"That's interesting, Lieutenant, but what do we do with it? It's like the goddamn ice cream and whiskey and—"

"Lieutenant! Lieutenant!" The bowling sergeant was suddenly shouting from the back door of the police station. "Sizzle, Lieutenant!" he shouted. "Sizzle!"

Cook did not wonder who Sizzle was, or what "sizzle" meant, because he remembered Leaf using and then explaining the term in an earlier conversation. "Sizzle" was a peculiarly Kinseyan police ejaculation, no doubt coined by Leaf, used in response to exciting developments—things above the ticket-writing routine.

Leaf looked up across the parking lot at the sergeant. "What is it, John?" He spoke softly and patiently, as if the man were his son.

"We've got a shooting. An apparent suicide."

Cook's gaze moved to the ground and his mind became instantly clear with the vision of an old woman waving to him from a short distance away.

The sergeant went on without mercy. "Some old lady, Lieutenant," he called out as Leaf began to hurry to the door. "In a big house near the Baby Wabash. Blew her head off in the living room. A neighbor called in . . . "

Leaf did not allow Cook to accompany him to the scene of the suicide. Nor did he suggest that Cook follow after him, and when Cook suggested this himself, Leaf, rushing to his car with the sergeant, declared the idea "out of the question." Cook thought this a fresh betrayal of their earlier agreement to treat each other as equals (an agreement he had not yet drawn any striking benefit from or for that matter ever fully understood), but he said nothing. He drove home, hesitated at the phone, then went into the bedroom and began to undress to take a shower. But he stopped before removing his pants, and, shirtless and shoeless, returned to the phone, wanting to know the worst rather than merely suspect it.

He looked up the number and then dialed the home of Arthur Stiph. The voice of the sergeant at the other end confirmed it instantly. Mr. and Mrs. Stiph were together once again. Leaf came on the phone and with telling phrases such as "not a pretty sight" gave Cook a vivid idea of the scene in the Stiph living room. Apparently a neighbor was just about to ring the doorbell to see if she could be of any help when Mrs. Stiph pulled the trigger. The neighbor opened the door in time to see her topple forward from the couch across the coffee table.

The rest of Cook's afternoon was rather lacking in focus. He called Ed Woeps to relieve himself of a portion of his burden of news and sorrow, but his friend was out tending to a thumb he had managed to break or sprain while rough-housing with his daughter. So Cook told Woeps's wife the news, but he didn't feel any better when he hung up. He sat by the phone for several minutes trying to think of other friends he could call. Then, inspired in an altogether different direction, he dialed Aaskhugh's number, scratching his bare chest with a certain anticipation. There was no answer. This filled him with an even greater sense of purpose and he called Orffmann's office. When the big-headed, big-throated laugher answered, Cook pressed the phone hotly to his mouth, shoved his chest out, tilted his upper body back, and let out the loudest, foulest, hyena-like bray he could muster. Orffmann did not respond immediately, and Cook hung up the phone.

Then he went into the kitchen, opened a bottle of bourbon, sat down on the couch in the living room, and, with a dirty glass fetched angrily from the kitchen sink, began to drink.

Arthur Stiph and his wife were playing in an old bell tower, childish grins on their old faces. They were pulling two long bell ropes in rapid succession. Mrs. Stiph's rope produced a high-pitched, buglelike *ding,* Arthur's a lower, sleepier *dong,* and they appeared to be having great fun. This vision faded and Cook awoke to hear a final chime of his doorbell, followed by the sound of his screen door banging to a close. Then he heard footsteps on his gravel driveway moving away from the house.

He rolled and lurched into a sitting position. The only light in the room came from a small table lamp beside the couch. It was completely dark outside. He rubbed his hands through his hair, feeling simultaneously drunk and hung over. This feeling was colored by the incurable exhaustion resulting from long, unnecessary sleep. There was a sickening dryness in his mouth, and his bare back itched from its punishing exposure to the rough surface of the couch. He scratched and moaned as he rose to his feet, softly cursing the Creator for having rested on the seventh day instead of patching up all the cruel mistakes He had made on the first six. By the time he had groped his way to the front door, the bell ringer was gone and a police car was pulling away from the house. He opened the door to run out, but a sudden rebellion in his abdomen slowed him to a stop and he stood and watched the car pull onto the road and disappear from view.

At his feet inside the screen door lay a large manila envelope. He gingerly bent down for it, squatting in order to keep his head upright. As he took it into the living room he faintly remembered a tapping sound near his ear occurring with, or just before, the ringing of the doorbell. Lieutenant Leaf, or whoever it was, must have been tapping at his window right over the couch. Cook winced—his sprawling body must have presented quite a sight. And the empty bottle of bourbon was on the coffee table, its label conveniently turned toward the front window. Excellent!

Under the light of the table lamp he read on the outside of the envelope, in a feminine scribble that appeared ugly from mere habit and not from any particular haste or nervousness, "For Jeremy Cook." The envelope had been sealed but the seal was broken. He nodded, recognizing Lieutenant Leaf's brute force approach. Inside were six sheets of paper—Xeroxed pages from some magazine evidently not proud enough of itself to give its title across the top or bottom of the pages. The first of the sheets did contain a title, however: "The Backside of Mankind." The author was Merlin Flexible. In spite of his condition, Cook deciphered the pseudonym instantly. He hoped the rest of it was as easy. A little note attached to the first page read, "Here's that little piece I mentioned, Jeremy. Adelle Stiph."

Cook's stomach churned as he began to read the story, sensing that doing so would plunge him just a little bit deeper into Arthur Stiph's life and death, but he knew that not reading it was impossible. The first few sentences were lost on him because he kept wondering how soon after penning her note Adelle Stiph had shot herself, and what those minutes must have been like for her. But as he read further he soon began to feel that Arthur was speaking to him directly, and his thoughts were far from her.

The story did not and could not contain the name of Stiph's killer. But it narrowed the field of possible names along an entirely new dimension. The story told of an aging professor of philosophy, a Yale graduate teaching in a small New England college, who after devoting fifty years of thought to problems of good and evil concluded that the only real evil that existed in this world was the peculiar by-product of interpersonal loathing: evil was what we imagined we saw in those we hated anyway. There was really no other kind. Having decided that this view raised certain questions not amenable to armchair solution, the hero of the story resolved to grapple with the issue in bodily form, like Jacob wrestling with the angel. That is, he cultivated close personal relationships with people he hated. And, as could be expected from a product of a school with a rich tradition of secret societies, the hero established a club made up exclusively of mated enemies, individuals who in the outside world detested each other to the limits of human capacity. These paired enemies met on a weekly basis "to explore creatively with each other the various hues and shades of personal repulsion." Reconciliation was not a goal. Indeed, it was assumed to be impossible, and from that assumption, curiously enough, the club members drew strength. While mated couples sometimes met with other couples and even claimed to benefit from the experience, the important unit was the couple itself, each member of which was to work at getting in touch with the unique chemistry of antipathy. Club members learned firsthand about loathsomeness and disgust; they learned about the hostile views held by others about them—the range of objections that could be raised against them as people. The chief goal of the club was knowledge—understanding of the mechanics of the hate-spawned dyad. There, the author assured his readers, if we too followed this course, we would find "mysteries of emotion unapproached by literary classics devoted to the sublimest love."

The story went on to show how the Backside Club grew and grew, and it ended with a message about the ultimate, though disguised, unity of all mankind. Plot there was none. The author's chief concern was the constitution (and Constitution, for one was drawn up) of the club, not the adventures of the club members.

A key word in the story was "backfriend"—the word which, according to his wife, Arthur had used that fateful night. In the world of "The Backside of Mankind" this word denoted an enemy-turned-mate. This established a clear direction of inquiry for Cook. Because Stiph still used the word with his wife, the concept must have been a real one for him—even though he had written the story decades ago. In some sense the Backside Club must have still been alive. Stiph had a mate, a backfriend. Now, whoever he was, he had said nothing about planning to meet Stiph—not to Cook and probably not to Lieutenant Leaf either (despite his bizarre behavior about almost everything, Leaf probably wouldn't keep something like this from Cook). Why hadn't Stiph's backfriend said anything about the meeting?

"Because he was the one who killed him," Cook said aloud to himself. Having said it, he could now sit back and examine it. On increasingly sober reflection it appeared to be the likeliest answer to the question.

CHAPTER SIX

COOK AWOKE WITH THE BIRDS Monday morning. He ate a typically heavy and repugnant breakfast and drove to work, arriving at six-thirty, one half hour before the first teachers and children would appear. His floor was silent and peaceful. He passed his office and walked to the end of the hall to check his mailbox. Among those pleasures in life whose peak is in the preliminary steps, Cook ranked fetching his mail right near sex with a complete stranger. This trip yielded some envelopes containing some promise, but nothing that couldn't wait until he had started his morning coffee perking. As he walked back down the hall he remarked to himself that Wach had not left a note of any kind in his mailbox about the grant proposal. This meant that he found it first-rate. Cook knew this as certainly as if Wach had crawled to him on his knees in sobbing gratitude and told him so.

He entered his office for the first time since Wednesday, when Arthur Stiph had occupied it. He stepped inside gingerly, as if he had been forewarned of some undefined practical joke about to take place, and immediately noticed that his typewriter was gone. This had happened once before, and it had turned up in Orffmann's office; the moron had borrowed it without permission or explanation. Perhaps he had done it again. He would have to wait until Mary the Secretary came in with her master key to the offices. Or could the body-stasher have stolen it? But why? His tape recorder and radio were still there. He couldn't remember if the typewriter had been in its place Wednesday or not. Stiph's larger presence had dominated the scene. He shrugged. He would just have to wait.

He went through his mail. It was a typical mixture of niceness (in particular, a brief note from the editor of *The Kartoffel Quarterly* indicating that his "Reply to Hornswith: In Defense of 'Parsimonious Parsing,' " in which he defended an article by Ed Woeps against reckless criticism by some mean flunky named Hornswith, would be published in the "Open Forum" section of the next issue, with Cook's name withheld, as he had requested), nastiness (a journal number containing two articles by two people he knew from national meetings and didn't like at all), and boredom (everything else). He turned his attention to his present brainchild, idiophenomena. He cleared his desk and took five manila file folders out of his top drawer. In these were daily notes, most taken by himself but some by the teachers, on the linguistic behavior of five carefully selected informants at Wabash, age nine months to two years. The notes showed the progress of their humdrum, stop-and-go acquisition of English, but, more importantly for Cook, they showed the stages in their acquisition of a private language doomed to quick extinction. Thus far his most interesting subject had been Ed Woeps's son, Wally, age one year, four months. Cook's notes showed that Wally's vocabulary presently consisted of a number of conventional items, recorded in broad phonetic transcription:

[ma(ma) . . .]	"mama"
[dada]	"daddy"
[bø] (rising)	"toy bird (used in bathtub)"
[tu]	"shoe"
[m:]	"more"
[lalala(la) . . .]	"music"

But Wally also said some unconventional things with fixed meanings. Cook's notes showed this second list:

[ga::] (falling)	"that's amusing"
[f:]	"look at that (and say something about it)"
[ndə] (+ pointing)	"look at that!"
[əpa] (+ palm up)	"give me that"
[mbwi:]	—

The last one puzzled Cook. Wally had been observed using it perhaps two dozen times, but the contexts did not lead to a definite meaning. Several of the utterances seemed to involve nearby people, as if he were pointing at them or calling to them, but Cook did not know what meaning he was expressing. Of course, this disyllabic *m-bwee* could have been mere babbling. (That possibility always complicated things. Why didn't babbling just stop when acquisition of meaning began, the way crawling stopped when serious walking began? Why?)

He studied the files on the four other children and compared them with one another. There were no similarities in the pairing of sounds with meanings, although there were the expected sounds and meanings for this age group. The meanings fell into the categories of requests (or commands) and social expressions. There were no clear statements of immediately unobservable fact ("Uranus is a planet"), prediction ("I'll bet you're going to give me carrots for lunch"), or fantasy ("Let's pretend I'm a duck"). He studied the data, but he couldn't get much more out of it than that. He would have to be patient. Longitudinal studies demanded it.

"Do you have a stapler?"

Cook looked up and saw that it was Paula standing at his open door. He felt momentarily inarticulate, dumb in the oldest sense. Even Wally Woeps's *m-bwee* was beyond him at the moment.

"A stapler?" she asked again, perhaps beginning to think bad thoughts about him.

"Yes!" he shouted ebulliently. He clapped his hands

together once with enthusiasm and instantly felt like a chuckle-head. He began to rummage through a top drawer, his mind racing but empty.

"There's one on your desk. Doesn't it work?"

"Yes!" he said loudly. "Yes!" He reached for the stapler and handed it to her with authority, as if this had been his plan all along—as if, in other words, the best route to one's desk top were through a desk drawer. It was easy to imagine her talking to the other teachers. "Not only is he an asshole," she would say, "but he's a dolt, a clodpate, and a muggins besides."

"I don't believe we've met," she said. "My name is Paula Nouvelles."

"I'm Jeremy Cook," he said, noticing that her jeans were as tight as his voice was. "Please call me Jeremy."

She evened the edges of some sheets of paper against his desk top, standing quite close to him, and stapled them together. "What else would I call you?"

He cleared his throat. "*Dr.* Cook. Too many of the teachers do."

"Why don't you ask them not to?"

"I have."

"But not very forcefully, I'll bet."

"No, honestly, I have."

She studied him without self-consciousness, looking down on him in his chair. "I see that you've quickly identified me as a teacher."

"Yes. I mean . . . aren't you? Someone pointed you out the other day and . . . "

"It just seems rather class-conscious of you, doesn't it? Also the call-me-first-name business. It's a brand of disguised elitism, isn't it?" She said these tags declaratively, the way the British do. Cook swallowed hard and wondered if she was going to box his ears.

"I was just trying to be friendly," he said. The tone of this contained some of the hurt he felt—more, in fact, than he wanted her to know about. Hearing himself speak this way instantly roused him. He would not let her say one more thing like that. He was eager for her to speak again just so he could show his strength.

"I'm sorry," she said softly, giving him a nice smile. "Perhaps you were."

Cook was silent.

"I'll drop a hint to the others about it—about what they should call you. Would that help?"

"That would be nice. But being new here, maybe you—"

"It's no problem. I'll see what I can do. Thanks for the use of the stapler." She set it on his desk and was gone before he could think of anything to keep her there, and he didn't want to anyway. His stomach was in knots. Why did things like this happen to him? What was it about his personality that invited other people to assault it? Unless, in her case, it was just prejudice because of the complete asshole business. If so, had he redeemed himself? She hadn't really given him much of a chance. She seemed friendly in the end, though. Unless she was just pretending, mocking him privately. If so, he dreaded her promised hint to the others: "Get this—the asshole wants to be called Jeremy." Maybe not, though. Yes, *quite* friendly. Tight pants, too. Maybe he should go after her now. Ask her about herself. Yes. He hadn't asked her anything about herself. He stood up, intending hot pursuit. Then he sank back into his chair. He would only make things worse. He had to plan ahead and sort things out before he talked to her again. Like Lieutenant Leaf, she had caught him at a mentally slow moment. He had drunk only two cups of coffee this morning and he wasn't really humming yet. Next time he would make sure he was at a mental peak—though the more he tried to understand his mind and body and nurture and prolong his productive mental states, the shorter they seemed to become. Some days he had only three or four good minutes in him.

He heard footsteps coming down the hall and tensed. He

located the stapler and gripped it tightly. When he saw that it was only Woeps at the door, he felt as if six months had been added to his life.

"Good morning, Jeremy," Woeps said, a smile adding some vitality to his face. "Keeping busy?"

Cook hadn't talked with Woeps for some time, apart from the few words they exchanged at the funeral, so he felt he had several days' worth of conversation for him. He noticed an Ace bandage wrapped around Woeps's thumb and wrist, and he observed his long-standing practice of not asking what had happened, so as not to embarrass him. He told him of the latest developments in the disaster he called his life—his talk with the widow, her subsequent suicide, the dent in his car, and his talk with Leaf. He omitted his recent chat with Paula.

"Helen mentioned you had called with the news about Arthur's wife, Jeremy. What a shame. I tried to call you back a couple of times later that night. Were you out?"

"Yes." In a sense he was, he thought, as he pictured himself lying like Raskolnikov in disarray on his couch. "Did you know her, Ed?"

Woeps shook his head. "I hardly knew Arthur, for that matter." He paused. "You know, Jeremy, maybe you ought to take a leave of absence and devote yourself full time to the case."

Cook laughed, then realized he wasn't sure what Woeps had meant. "What do you mean?" he asked.

"Just that it seems to be forcing itself on you—seeking you out, almost. I don't see how you can get any work done."

Cook was struck by the irony of this. He had wondered the same thing about Woeps many times. How, in the face of one domestic calamity after another, could Woeps continue to be the moderately productive linguist he was?

"Now that you mention it, Ed, I was going over my notes on Wally. This *m-bwee* is still a mystery."

"What have you got?" Woeps set his briefcase down and

walked around Cook's desk to look over his shoulder. Cook pointed to the top of one of the pages.

"See? I've recorded quite a few nonimitative, spontaneous instances of it, but so far—"

"Nonimitative? Wouldn't they always be nonimitative? Who around here is going to say *m-bwee* anyway?"

"Some of the teachers. They think it's cute, and they're mucking up the picture. I've asked them to stop. Now look at the nonverbal contexts. In six of them he's looking at a person, in three of them he's looking at the aquarium, and in one he's looking outside, out the window. The others are obscure. You see, it's not enough. I'm going to spend most of the day with him." He looked up at Woeps. "Did he produce any this weekend, Ed?"

Woeps brought his hand to his face and stroked his chin as he tried to remember. "I recall one. Yesterday. I was giving him a bath. I had just added more water to the tub and he shouted one at me."

"And he looked at you?"

"Yes."

"For a response?"

"I think so."

"And what did you say?"

"I said . . . I don't know, something like 'Yes, *m-bwee.*'"

"What did he do?"

"He kept saying it and looking at me."

"As if you hadn't gotten the message?"

"Maybe."

Cook looked at his notes again. "Damn!" he said. "I haven't been systematic about getting data on the adult response. That's important. Look, Ed." He pointed to one of the examples. "Here I say 'fish' in response to him and he doesn't say *m-bwee* after that. But then here—he pointed to another example—"I don't say anything and he keeps after me with it, as if to say, 'Damn it, Jeremy, *m-bwee* and what do you have to say about it?'"

"I don't know, Jeremy. This stuff is pretty slippery."

"But you don't doubt that it means something to him, do you?" Cook tried to speak without sounding defensive. He had seen that rigid fear of contradiction in others at Wabash when describing work in progress. Milke, the charmboat, was the worst one in this way.

"No, I guess not. But . . . well, with young kids whose grammar is always developing, how can we know the meaning is constant from day to day? You're comparing data stretching over several weeks."

"We can't."

"Or how can we know that we haven't changed the meaning by studying it—say, by means of rewards we are unconscious of?"

"We can't know that, either."

"What does that leave us with?"

"An impure science." Cook shrugged. "I can live with it."

"There isn't even a name for what you're studying."

"Yes there is. I call them 'idiophenomena.'"

Woeps laughed. "Then it's respectable! No question about it!" He smiled. "See you for lunch?"

"Sure, Ed." Whom else could he eat with at this place? It was good of Woeps, who got along with everybody except Aaskhugh and could enjoy lunch with any of them, to reserve his lunch hour on most days for Cook. It was almost as if they had a contract.

Cook heard footsteps and voices and saw Aaskhugh and Milke walk by on the way to their offices. The four linguists all called out "Good morning" at the same time.

"One more thing, Ed," Cook added as Woeps turned to go. "It's about Arthur. Do you know if he had any enemies here?"

Woeps studied the floor and thought a moment. "I doubt it," he said. "But why do you ask? If his death was accidental, how is it relevant?"

Cook gestured for his friend to sit down, and then he introduced him to the world of "The Backside of Mankind." Woeps listened to his summary of the story with frowning wonder.

"And he was coming here to meet one of these guys, these . . ."

"Backfriends. Yes. That's what his wife said."

Woeps was silent a moment. "I can't imagine who it could be. None of us was very close to him, but I think we all more or less liked him, and I guess vice versa."

"Even though the vice versa doesn't follow."

"No, I guess it doesn't," said Woeps as he stood up from his chair. "And that certainly happens sometimes—people being liked without liking in return. Makes things sticky."

Wach's face appeared in Cook's doorway. It was followed by his body. "Jeremy, if you aren't busy I would like to see you in my office."

"Be right there, Walter." Wach nodded and walked on down the hall, evidently just arriving to work. Mary the Secretary, bearing a heavy load of fresh makeup, trotted by about ten steps behind him.

"I'll keep my eyes open and think about it, Jeremy," said Woeps. "That's important evidence."

Cook followed him out the door and closed it behind him. "It's all we've got," he said. He watched Woeps, at the door of his own office, take his keys out of his pocket, drop them, and reach down for them in such a way that he banged his forehead sharply on the doorknob. Cook winced and stepped toward him.

"Are you all right, Ed?"

Woeps smiled with resignation. "Never better," he said as he unlocked his door.

Cook walked down the hall. As he passed Milke's office he glanced in the open door and saw that it was empty. But the smell of his pipe was quite strong. Then he saw Milke standing just inside Aaskhugh's office, chatting with him. All Cook heard as he walked by was "don't see why the sonofabitch doesn't ever" and he assumed with some confidence that Milke was talking about Wach. Milke seemed to prize Wach about as highly as Cook did, the only difference being that Milke talked about it all the time, often with Wach himself. Milke was a generally argumentative sort. How could he also be the charmer he was supposed to be? Maybe he argued just with men and was charming with women. And maybe Stiph was one of the men he argued with.

Cook filed this away as he approached the end of the hall and Mary the Secretary's desk, which he had to pass to reach Wach's office. His last conversation with her had not been entirely pleasant, but he decided not to worry about it. Since she was the one who had behaved like a ninny, the burden was on her to make amends.

"He's expecting you," she said in a transparently forced attempt at her normal dull style. Cook despised her all the more for this. Far better for her to resume the attack or to retreat with apologies than to follow this meaningless middle path. He silently vowed never to speak to her again and passed her desk wordlessly.

Wach was not in his office. Cook was filled with an urge to destroy things. For the first time in his life he understood the roots of vandalism. Where was Wach? What poor devil was he spying on now? What gave him the right to tell people to come to his office and then not be there? He walked around the room in search of things to loathe. He started at Wach's bookshelf and noticed with rising contempt that the spines of the books were all virginally intact. Then his fury momentarily left him and he sat in the chair across from Wach's desk. He realized that if he didn't put himself into a better mood he might say the wrong thing to Wach and do irreparable damage. He sighed and drummed his fingers on the arm of the chair. A toilet flushed and Wach, as if propelled by the noise, flung open his exclusive door to the bathroom and nodded brusquely in Cook's direction. He sat down behind his desk.

"Jeremy, I was at the Stiph funeral Friday." He paused.

Cook looked at him.

"I'm concerned about what is happening."

Cook said nothing. Where was the fool and tyrant going?

"I think we at Wabash have got some retrenching to do." He blinked. "The metaphor is apt. Very apt. *Retrenching.* I want you to give a lecture to the Kinsey Rotary Club."

"*What?*"

"Something light. Something on the bright side, to let the townspeople know that, hey, we're human over here."

"But why?"

"I just told you why. I think we need to reach out to the community a bit more."

"Public relations," Cook said softly, with disgust.

Wach briefly closed his eyes in comment on Cook's naivete.

"You could call it that. I'm concerned about the community perception of the Institute."

"I know you are."

"In these times especially, what with Arthur and all. People out there are talking about us."

"And I'm to be your emissary."

"The Institute's, Jeremy. I would hope you would look at it in that light." His eyes focused sharply on Cook. "Your image could benefit, too."

Cook returned his stare with a blank expression.

"The funeral, Jeremy. The funeral." He looked at Cook. "Damn it, man, do I have to spell it out? You looked like a fool stumbling down that hill."

"I didn't stumble."

"Besides, you're the jack-of-all-trades here. And you're not working on anything at the moment, are you?"

"Of course I am. What do you think?"

"What, then?"

"Idiophenomena."

Wach smiled. "That can wait."

"No, it can't. I've got to observe Ed's son today. And tomorrow. And—"

"*It will have to wait*, Jeremy. We all have to make sacrifices. That's the name of the game. There are a lot of things I would like to do too, but to do this job right . . . I try to do my share, and I would hope that you would want to see things the same way."

Cook wanted to whimper. Why did Wach use "would" like that? Did he speak this press-conference dialect in bed with his wife? Did he go to bed with his wife? Did he go to bed? If he did, did he first address the sheets, commanding them to remain crisp all night?

"I think something on names would have the right flavor."

Cook studied Wach's thin gray Germanic mustache. "Do you mean names of insult?"

"No. I was thinking more along an onomastic line. Proper names. Place names. Nicknames. You know, *nickname* itself is an interesting word. It comes from *ekename,* which—"

"I know."

". . . literally 'also-name,' and the *n* of the preceding article became incorporated into the word."

"I know, Walter."

"Well, good. See? You know a lot about it already. You can whip up something in no time. Or *Hoosier.* There's another one. People here would like to have its etymology explained for them."

"But, Walter, I don't have any interest in this stuff. I don't give a hoot in hell about *Hoosier.*"

"I'm surprised, Jeremy. My own opinion is that there is a wealth of data in this area."

"Data, yes. Theory, no. It's a wasteland."

"Be that as it may, it's for the good of Wabash—hey, there's another one. You could talk about our debt to the Indians. I've taken the liberty of scheduling you for their Sunday meeting of next week."

"*What?*"

Wach raised a hand, palm toward Cook. "That's almost two weeks away, Jeremy. If you get to it I think you can produce a real crackerjack piece."

"Why don't you do it, Walter?"

Wach snorted derisively. "Your question indicates just how little you know about my responsibilities. They are all-consuming." He gave Cook a moment to respond. Then he said, "I've scheduled a meeting of the linguists for ten-thirty this morning. What you could call a retrenching meeting. We've lost some children, you know. The population is down by four since the Stiph thing, what with parents taking their children out of the program. Now I want to be able to tell the others that you've agreed to do this lecture." He looked at Cook.

"So tell them."

"Good. One more thing. When did you last see this reporter fellow, Philpot?"

"Him again? I last saw him on Tuesday, in Mary's office, just about five seconds after you forbade my seeing him."

Wach frowned. "You seem to have a chip on your shoulder this morning, Jeremy."

"Yeah. So where's Philpot? Did he go back to New York?"

"We don't know. He hasn't been here since Tuesday."

"Did you call his motel?"

"No."

"It seems like the logical thing to do."

"It's not my job to go running after reporters. If they want to come here, fine, we'll show them around and be totally above-board. We've got nothing to hide. But I am not about to go chasing after them."

"Fine. Don't call the motel. Keep on wondering where he is."

"*Should* I call the motel? Would you if you were me?"

"The conditional is staggeringly impossible for me to entertain, Walter." Cook stood up from his chair. "Are we done? I've got some *really heavy* research to do on names."

"Perhaps I should call the motel," Wach said to himself as he stood up from his desk and walked Cook to the door.

"Good idea," muttered Cook. He opened the door and found Aaskhugh very close to it on the other side. Mary looked up from her desk expectantly. Her face was very red, as if she had been laughing hard.

"Looks like you've been the victim of a callous prank of some kind, Jay," Aaskhugh said. "I just found this taped to the door of your office." He held up a hand-lettered sign that read, "Cook's Barbershop."

Wach turned to Cook. "See what I mean, Jeremy? See?"

CHAPTER SEVEN

"HE'S GOT LARYNGITIS."

Cook grinned. This was incredibly good news. He had noticed, as he sat down with his colleagues in Wach's office, that Clyde Orffmann was absent, and he had just asked Woeps if he knew where he was. Maybe it would fester into a chronic condition. His neighboring laughter wouldn't be too bad then. He would probably sound like a debarked dog.

"By the way, Jeremy," Woeps continued, "I talked with Clyde Friday about his grant proposal. He said you improved it tremendously."

"He did?"

"Yes. He said that after he looked at your revisions he saw a number of problems that you had cleared up. He says he has hopes of it flying now, and he didn't before."

"You mean after he was done with it, he had no faith in it?"

"Not until you got to it, apparently."

Cook grimaced. "I can't imagine how anyone can work with such little confidence."

"I know what you mean. I think he compares himself with you too much. He's quite in awe of you, you know."

"Really?"

"Oh yes. He told me Friday that he values your friendship highly."

Cook frowned. "But he doesn't have it, Ed. He's a—"

Cook had to cut this sentence short because Wach was

tapping his pencil rhythmically on the desk to begin the meeting. This struck Cook as foolishly parliamentarian of him, seeing that there were only five people in the room. But his thoughts were chiefly on Orffmann. In addition to astonishing him, Woeps's news had pleased him, which showed that one's contempt of others in no way reduced one's desire for their approval, even though people always pretended that it did. But at the same time there was something sad about it all.

"I have called this meeting, gentlemen, to sound you out on ideas about the future of the Wabash Institute." Wach paused. It was one of those pauses that left the listener wondering if he should speak or not.

"So what's the problem?" Milke said boldly.

"I wouldn't call it a problem, Emory," said Wach. "Not yet, anyway."

"Well, when you would," said Milke, "what would it be that you would be calling a problem?"

Wach said, "If we don't watch out, if we don't maintain a steady watch on this thing, we could all be in pretty big trouble."

"What thing?" asked Milke, his voice rising impatiently.

"The . . . aftermath of Arthur Stiph, Emory. I'm suggesting it's time for a kind of, oh, retrenching. I'm sorry. I assumed you knew what I was talking about."

"I know you did."

"Fine. Fine." Wach surveyed the room, looking pleased that peace had been made. Cook wondered if the meeting was now over. "It is no small decision," Wach continued ponderously, "for a parent to entrust a child's care to an institution. That institution must remain above reproach on all counts. Since Arthur died there has been a lot of talk about Wabash. People are asking questions. Our population is down by four children from a week ago. That is bad news."

"Who's doing the talking, Walter?" asked Cook.

"Oh . . . people, I'm sure. People talk, you know."

"But have you yourself heard any talk?"

"Of course. I receive phone calls daily now from the two Kinsey newspapers and WKIN. They're asking some hard questions, too."

"But what about parents? Have they been after you?"

"Parents not so much. Not so much. That's an important point. I want to reassure the parental community of our love for children and our benevolent nature. Jeremy here, I'm proud to announce, shares my feelings to the extent that he is going to address the Kinsey Rotary Club next week at their Sunday morning Prayer and Pancake Breakfast with a talk titled 'Southern Indiana Names.'" Cook sat impassively and endured his colleagues' quizzical stares. "I'd like some further suggestions from the rest of you."

"I suggest we go on doing what we have been doing," said Milke, "and that we do it better. And that we give a little more attention to our stockroom. We've got nothing but seventy-five-millimeter tape for the rest of the month. It's ridiculous."

Wach looked at Milke and nodded, as if to say he was pleased to get this feedback but would not speak to it right away. He awaited further response.

"I don't see that we can do much," said Woeps, "or that we ought to feel we need to. Of the four children who have left Wabash, aren't two of them the McConklin kids?"

"That's right," said Wach.

"They were going to leave anyway. Their father was recently transferred." He spoke softly, like the man of reason he was. Cook loved it. He turned to Wach. How was he going to handle it?

"Technically you're right, Ed," he said.

"Who are the other two?" asked Aaskhugh.

"Emil Bumpers—" Wach began.

Milke laughed. "We're well rid of him. I for one am tired of hearing the kids complain about him."

"Emil?" asked Aaskhugh. "Why?"

"Because he's always kissing them. Boys and girls alike. He is the most despised child at Wabash."

"Emory's right about that," said Woeps.

"—and Buford Wilson," said Wach.

Milke laughed again and leaned forward and loudly banged his pipe into the very clean ashtray on Wach's desk. "Old forceps-face?" he said. "He never said anything anyway. He's got an MLU of point zero zero."

"Any other suggestions?" asked Wach.

Milke chuckled something to Aaskhugh. Wach reddened.

"I've got a suggestion for you, Emory," he said loudly. His short-cropped gray hair seemed to be standing straight up. "Stop teaching the Simpkins twins artificial words. Their mother was on the phone to me last week again. I've warned you about this."

Milke smiled sheepishly. "But I *have* stopped, Walter. Pretty much, anyway. And as a result we're missing a great opportunity to see how twins pass on pieces of a private language to each other. I haven't done anything unethical."

"Well, just watch your step. Cease and desist, as they say." Wach added this last in a spirit of lightening the tone.

Cook looked at Milke. If he was discovered to be Stiph's backfriend and killer, then a conviction would no doubt remove him from the scene, and Cook would be left to wage war against his boss all alone. Milke was certainly useful in that regard. But in other regards—his charm, his beard, his pipe, his sexual aggressiveness—Cook would not mourn his absence.

"I've got a suggestion," said Cook. "Suppose we try to find out who killed Arthur? Swift justice in this matter would have a salutary effect on our reputation, don't you think?"

"Hear, hear," said Milke.

"How would you suggest we go about it?" said Aaskhugh.

"Aren't the police—" began Wach.

"You will all be interested," said Cook, "to learn that the

case is simplified by the fact that one of us probably killed him. Including Clyde in the bunch."

"Emory and I were talking about this on Friday," said Aaskhugh. "We figured the field of suspects was infinitely large."

"You said that, Adam," argued Milke. "I didn't."

Cook shook his head. "Lieutenant Leaf told me that the guy faked the forced entry into the basement." He quickly summarized Leaf's remarks for them. "He had a key to the building and wanted to hide that fact. How many people have keys, Walter?"

Wach cleared his throat. "I'll tell you what I told the police. Each of the staff linguists has a key to the building, and of course I do too. That's all. Unless carelessness somewhere has led to copies being made."

"Any reason to believe that has happened?" asked Cook. "Like a burglary in the past?"

"Not really," said Wach.

"That's an interesting point about Arthur having a key," said Aaskhugh. "If it was in his pocket when he was killed, then the killer could have gotten the key that way. So the field is wide open again."

Cook shook his head. "While the killer could have gotten a key that way, it would mean he was not a regular keyholder, which means that there would be no point in his faking a break-in."

Woeps laughed. "Unless he thought, 'I will now fake a break-in—fake it so sloppily that it will be discovered to be fake and therefore make everyone believe I am a keyholder trying to hide the fact that I am, so they won't know who I really am: some passing Joe who ran into this man and found a key to a nearby building in his pocket.'"

"You lost me," said Aaskhugh.

Cook shook his head again. "Too clever," he said to Woeps. "Few people think that well under normal conditions"—he tried not to look at Aaskhugh—"let alone after accidentally killing someone. And it's unnecessary besides. Merely using the key in the front door would have the same effect as a deliberately clumsy break-in."

"That's true," said Woeps.

A moment of silence passed as the men looked nervously at one another. Cook's eyes locked with Milke's, and for an instant he felt as though the man were trying to look into his soul. Not wanting to be the one to back down, he hardened his stare until Milke frowned and looked away, a hint of an odd smile just showing under his black beard.

Wach broke the silence. "Jeremy, you say you've spoken to Lieutenant Leaf recently?"

"Friday."

"And is he operating under the assumption you just presented to us?"

"He says quite openly that there are six suspects: the five of us and Orffmann."

"Where *is* Clyde, anyway?" said Aaskhugh.

"He's got—"

"I know he's got laryngitis, but that's a stupid thing to stay home for."

"Are you implying fishiness, Adam?" said Woeps.

Aaskhugh smiled his malicious smile—the only one he had. "Well, it's there, isn't it? It's certainly worth talking about."

"You look pretty fishy to me for saying that," said Milke.

"And you to me for that," Cook said to Milke.

Everyone laughed, but to Cook it seemed to echo hollowly off the walls, like the laughter of river pirates in a bare cave.

"I wonder why they haven't been spending more time here then," Wach said, not very loudly and to no one in particular.

"The police?" asked Aaskhugh.

"Yes. If they think one of us did it."

"It's damned awkward, isn't it?" said Milke. "Rubbing elbows daily with a killer. You know, one of us is really an asshole."

Cook suddenly looked from Milke to Wach, then to Aaskhugh and Woeps. "Maybe we ought to have it out—get Clyde in here and all six of us just have it out."

Milke showed his teeth through his beard. "I like that idea. I like it *a lot*."

"Just what are you suggesting, Jeremy?" asked Wach.

"Let's get together and see what happens. Right now I'd like to be able to say a few words to Arthur's hit-and-run killer and be sure he was hearing me."

"And the asshole who did it might slip up and let something out under the pressure," Milke said eagerly.

"Might be interesting," said Aaskhugh. "We could learn a lot about each other."

"It sounds extremely unpleasant to me," said Woeps. "Sorry, Jeremy."

"It's a ridiculous notion," said Wach. "We don't have time for this kind of thing."

Cook said, "We could meet after hours."

"It's uncivilized," said Wach.

"But if you want Arthur's killer to be found out and drummed out—"

Wach fussed with his pencil. "I'm especially surprised to hear this idea from you, Jeremy. You're always the first to complain when I call a meeting."

"This is different."

"He complains about everything," said Milke, smiling at Cook in a friendly way. Cook squirmed in his chair.

Wach shook his head. "You are all free, of course, to do whatever you like. But as Director of the Institute I am not going to sanction this kind of thing on company time. It would look pretty funny if word of such a meeting got out. That could put us in a pretty pickle indeed. We've got enough problems as it is. And I'm afraid I now must tell you about another one." He launched forth another weighty pause, which made Cook all the more eager to ridicule what he was going to say. "This reporter, Henry Philpot, seems to have disappeared. Some of you met him, if I'm not mistaken. I know Jeremy did. He was good enough to show him around Wabash in the morning hours last Tuesday. Did you meet him, Adam?"

"Yes," said Aaskhugh. "A nice fellow, if somewhat unassuming."

"And Ed?"

"No, I saw him, but only briefly."

"Emory?"

"Righto."

"I'm afraid," Wach continued, "that Mr. Philpot hasn't been seen by anyone since Tuesday. That's almost a week now. I of course called his motel. The manager said that Tuesday night was the last he had seen him. And yet he hasn't checked out. So I called his home in New York and talked to his wife this morning. He is not there either. I think I managed to ask her without worrying her. So I have called the police. Don't be surprised if you see them around here later today."

"What do you think happened to him?" asked Woeps.

Wach shook his head. "I can't speak to that, Ed. I really can't."

"There's something odd here," said Aaskhugh. All eyes swung to him. "I know for a fact that this fellow called one of the teachers Thursday or Friday . . . yes, Friday, the day of the funeral, Dorothy Plough. Most of you know her—she's the tall, horse-faced one?"

There were some nods. Cook did not nod. He sat very still.

"She told me he called and asked her some questions about the Institute," Aaskhugh continued. "And she said he called her from the motel."

"He called . . . he called her on Friday?" Wach said, his face puzzled.

"Did he give her any idea why he hasn't been around here?" asked Woeps. "It's strange of him to show up early in the week to interview people and then disappear until Friday, when he made this phone call."

"Yes, it *is* odd," said Aaskhugh. "I don't know if he talked about that or not. We could have her in to tell us." He rose from his seat.

"I don't think she's here today," said Cook.

"Wrong," said Milke. "You and I walked right by her in the hall on our way here, Jeremy."

"My mistake," Cook said equably.

"I'll get her," said Aaskhugh.

While he was gone the other four men sat in silence, with the exception of Woeps, who twice said, "Curious." When Dorothy came into the room with Aaskhugh, Cook tried to hide behind Woeps to discourage any subliminal memories and associations on her part. She spoke nervously, giving a halting description of the phone call that was rich in flashbacks and self-corrections. Cook wondered why she was so afraid. Was it Aaskhugh? No. She had called him a twit. Wach was the one to blame. Under his rule the sense of hierarchy at Wabash bred this kind of fear. Although he felt sorry for Dorothy, Cook was pleased to see that by the time she finished speaking everyone was quite weary of the subject, and only a few token questions were asked.

Wach thanked her, dismissed her, and said that it was "certainly something to think about" and that he would pass it on to the police when he saw them. He appeared to be on the verge of ending the meeting when Woeps spoke.

"There's one more issue I would like to bring up."

"Go ahead, Ed," said Wach.

"I don't like to see a man's work die with him, especially when there are others around who could bring it to a publishable state. I wonder if there's anything we could do along that line. Was Arthur still working on the acquisition of value terms?"

"I don't think so," said Wach. "I think he had set that aside. And, to be honest and frank and totally open about it, I was getting pretty curious about just what he was up to, and was about to question him about it, when—"

"He was looking at linguistic devices associated with esteem," said Milke. "How does a four-year-old talk to someone he likes as compared with the way he talks to someone he doesn't like? How does acquisition of the adult tools for disguising feelings proceed? Are kids really more honest than adults? Questions like that."

"How far along was he?" asked Woeps.

"Not far," said Milke. "He told me he was particularly interested in following up on the work of Ruhig—you know, at the Deutsches Forschungsinstitut für Kindersprache und Entwicklungspsychologie in Munich. Ruhig maintains that kids up to about age two have an instinctive sense of *quality* in people. They gravitate toward good people and shun bad people. Then sometime after their second birthday this innate moral sense gets corrupted by socialization. Arthur evidently believed this and wanted to explore the role of language in this deterioration. But, as I said, he was just beginning."

"Do you think it would be worthwhile to look at his notes?" asked Woeps.

"It sounds pretty screwy to me," said Aaskhugh. "Especially this Rousseauist twaddle. I wouldn't waste my time on it. But then I always found much of Arthur's work suspect."

"Nice of you to say that," Woeps said with a sudden bitterness that surprised Cook. Woeps looked at Aaskhugh as if he were something he had just spit out of his mouth.

"I have more respect for this kind of thing than Adam," said Milke, "but my time is pretty much taken up with my negation project. How about you, Ed?"

Woeps shifted in his seat. "Well . . . I wasn't really thinking of myself for the job. I have several months' work ahead of me on this dialect competition thing, and—"

"It looks as though everybody wants to do his own work," said Wach, laughing mirthlessly. "That's healthy. Very healthy. And these projects have been approved by all of us, whereas Arthur's has not. What Emory has just described is news to me." In the silence that followed, Cook began to feel oppressed by meaningful glances. He was the only one left.

"Jeremy?" said Woeps.

Cook sighed. "I'll look into it. Ill try to work it in."

Wach began to bluster. "But not at the expense—"

"Not to worry, Walter," Cook said with the heartiness of a team man. "*Hoosier* remains top drawer."

Wach smiled uncertainly, surveyed the group for further remarks, and adjourned the meeting. Lieutenant Leaf was talking to Mary the Secretary when Cook and the others stepped out of Wach's office. He turned and watched the linguists file past, smiling and greeting each by name.

". . . and Dr. Aaskhugh and Dr. Woeps and Dr. Cook." He winked at Cook as he addressed him and turned to Wach, who stood in the doorway of his office. "And the good Dr. Wach," he said, stepping toward him. Cook watched the bustling detective pump Wach's hand and guide him back into his office before slamming the door.

Cook and Woeps ate lunch at Max's and discussed onomastics, idiophenomena, centralized dipthongs, and manslaughter. Woeps remarked that their colleagues were still ignorant of the Backside Club and guessed, correctly, that Cook had not shared Stiph's story with them in the hope that someone would declare himself to be an enemy of Stiph's and thereby implicate himself in Stiph's death. Then Woeps apologized again for not being able to support Cook's proposal for a soul-baring meeting of the suspects, saying that he found it "unorthodox and threatening." He said he feared people might say things they would later regret. Cook agreed that the idea was somewhat strange, and said that it had somehow just popped into his head.

As they paid their checks, Woeps asked what expectations Cook was bringing to his talk at the Kinsey Rotary Club, and Cook said, "Fear, nausea, and self-disgust." When Woeps asked if he could help, Cook said no, that it was hopeless, and, as if cued by these words, Paula entered the front door of Max's and stood very erect and surveyed the crowd. Cook, standing nearby at the cash register, studied her closely. Thus it was very easy for him to see Emory Milke enter right behind her and place a gentle, charmingly guiding hand against what was probably a nice part of her back and steer her to a corner table. Milke moved as if he owned the building—not only owned it, but had designed and built it and might level it tomorrow for the fun of it. As they walked he leaned forward and whispered something into Paula's ear. She threw her head back and laughed quietly. Cook saw all of this and felt as if he were watching a bad movie.

"Ah," said Woeps, his eyes following her. "A Cook target."

Cook sighed and nodded and moved to the door. He didn't want Milke to know he had seen him with her.

"It's good that I see you in pain like this now and then, Jeremy. It keeps me from envying you your bachelorhood too much. She's new, isn't she?"

"Yeah. From U.C.L.A. She's doing a doctorate in linguistics." They stepped outside into the parking lot and blinked in the bright sunlight.

"You'll get your chance. Emory can't be too thick with her. She just got here."

"He's quick off the mark."

"So are you."

"Not with her." In fact, before the race someone had stolen his starting blocks, blindfolded him, pointed him in the wrong direction, and tied his shoelaces together. But he wasn't going to give life to that tale by passing it on to his friend.

Back at Wabash, Cook remained faithful to his vow of never speaking to Mary the Secretary again by sneaking her master key out of her desk when she was away from it. As he did this he felt like a man whose life was becoming disturbingly complex. He went to Orffmann's office and found only Orffmann's small portable typewriter and not his own old, large, rackety Royal. He went from office to office, first knocking on the doors of those he knew were occupied, but he failed to find it. He even checked Stiph's office and Sally Good's on the floor below. One more thing to report to Wach, he thought with annoyance. He stealthily returned the key to Mary's desk and missed by seconds being seen in the process by Aaskhugh.

He went to his office and began to leaf through his books in an unimpassioned search for material for his name lecture. He learned that *Hoosier* came either from the question "Who's 'ere?" asked by the typical gruff, inhospitable bumpkin who settled Indiana, or from the question the same gruff bumpkin asked when, upon walking into a bar where other gruff bumpkins had recently been butting heads and gouging eyes, he looked at a certain piece of detached flesh on the grimy floor and said, "Whose ear?" Hence *Hoosier. Quod erat demonstrandum.*

Was this the kind of thing Wach wanted him to talk about? How could he research this crap and lecture on it without his blood actually slowing down to a dead stop? Besides, he already knew what a Hoosier was. In his personal lexicon the entry read, "*Hoosier,* n., etymology obscure and boring: a dumb white man with a fat white wife who eats greens, attaches his muffler to his car with a coat hanger, and leaves refrigerators in his yard for children to suffocate in."

He leaned back in his seat and put his feet up on his desk. He began to think about the morning meeting of the linguists.

He had come away with nothing. Or rather, he had come away with a disrespect for all claims based on inference. It was easy to think, for example, that anyone who resisted his suggestion for a man-to-man, head-butting, eye-gouging meeting did so out of fear that he would expose himself as the killer he was; on the other hand, someone who endorsed the meeting could just as easily be thought suspect—perhaps he was performing a simple-minded reversal (Aaskhugh would do something like that and think it clever) or, being a Stiphian backfriend, perhaps he enjoyed this sort of thing and wanted to take it up with a new group, what with the other half of his repugnant dyad being dead and all. The entire meeting had been full of similar double-sided mirrors. He needed more data. He needed to *listen*. The guilty one knew who he was. He knew what he had done. As a linguist, Cook was aware that every day in almost every sentence people regularly (though often inadvertently) informed their audiences of what they knew. He would have to wait.

He looked at his books. He should do more work on names. He drummed his fingers on the desk, sighed, and then took Wally Woeps's file out of his top drawer. He set up a tape on the tape recorder beside his desk and prepared to listen to it as he followed his notes.

Hoosier will always be with us, he said to himself. *M-bwee* will not.

CHAPTER EIGHT

THEY FOUND HENRY PHILPOT'S BODY in the Baby Wabash, fifty feet downstream from Scopes Bridge. They found Cook's typewriter too. It had been tied to Philpot's body, presumably for weight, but the ropes had worked loose and slipped down to his ankles. As a result, while the typewriter remained on the sandy bottom of the Baby Wabash, Philpot's gas-filled torso rose upward, and his head bobbed up and down at the surface of the water like an anchored buoy. Martha Simpkins, mother of the twins under Milke's scrutiny and forbidden tutelage, arrived early Thursday afternoon to pick up her children, and she chanced to spend a few minutes strolling on the bridge, whose prospect was generally quite pleasant. It was she who first saw Philpot's head.

Cook had left work early that day, dined at home in his usual fashion, and returned to Wabash around six o'clock to take up, for the first time in earnest, the necessary preparation for his lecture on names, which a morning memo from Wach indicated was now to be titled "Highways and Byways of Southern Indiana Names." When he drove up he counted six police cars and one television van in the parking lot. Two policemen stood on the bank of the river and several more were walking in and out of the building. His first thought was for the children, though he would not have been able to specify the nature of his fear. Then he thought of Woeps and hoped he was all right. He learned the truth from a reporter outside the building who did not seem to know or care who he was. The reporter told him that Philpot had been pulled from the river and taken away about an hour earlier.

Cook turned from the building and walked slowly out onto the bridge. He leaned on the railing. The two policemen on the bank looked up at him for a moment and then ignored him. One of them swept an arm out over the water, pointing up and down the river. After a few minutes they left. The crowd of policemen and reporters outside the front entrance thinned out as well. Cook heard the slamming of car doors and the starting of engines as he looked at the water.

He remembered Philpot standing at the playroom door, looking at the children and expressing his regret that he would be missing his daughter's birthday. The image of his young widow in New York trying to explain his death to that girl, whom Cook had never met and never would, now gave him an odd feeling that he finally identified as sorrow mixed with shame for his own life. He took off his glasses and rubbed his eyes with the heels of his palms. He watched the gray, silent water, which held no secrets now but was simply there, dark and oppressive. The light was fading. He stood up from the bench and was about to turn to go when he heard a footstep on the bridge. Startled, he turned quickly to see who it was. Lieutenant Leaf approached him, his hands in his pockets. Behind him, a policeman waited in an unmarked car at the side of the road.

Leaf walked right up to Cook and said without greeting, "I'm getting sick of this. Sick of it."

Cook didn't want to talk to Leaf. He wanted to go home. "Excuse me, Lieutenant. I—"

"Goddamnit," said Leaf. "I'm sick of it."

Cook looked closely at him and saw that he was livid. He actually looked as though he might fall back at any moment clutching his chest in pain.

"Accidents, okay. Cover-up, okay. Suicides, okay. But this." He pointed out to the water. "Jesus *fuck*. What a world."

"I feel the same way," Cook said softly.

"I'll *bet* you do," said Leaf with bitter sarcasm. "You goddamn intellectuals." He glared at Cook. "A family man comes in from the outside and you kill him. Then you just go on with your rooty-toot nonsense, you sonofabitches." He turned and left Cook standing on the bridge, puzzled but without the energy or desire to try to understand what he had meant.

Leaf was his normal self the next time Cook saw him. He paid Cook an unexpected, unannounced visit at his home. It was late Friday afternoon, the day after their meeting on the bridge. Cook had found it impossible to work at Wabash. Police, press, parents—all were there, strident, frightened, outraged. He had escaped for lunch with Woeps and returned with hopes that it would be quieter. It was not. Again the children seemed upset by the commotion, and the older ones were even less civilized than usual. One boy known to Cook only as Dicky and once characterized by Woeps as being "all boy" smashed a toy wooden mallet against a young girl's mouth and made her cry and bleed. Her mother, there to investigate things for herself to decide whether or not to remove her daughter from Wabash, made her decision very easily after that. Panicked, Wach summarily and publicly fired the teacher responsible—somewhat unfairly, everyone thought, seeing that Dicky's blow lacked forewarning. This noise, and more like it, and the reporters knocking on his door to ask him about his typewriter, had driven him away.

He was mowing the lawn when the police car pulled up, driven by the bowler who doubled as Leaf's chauffeur. Cook looked up and then continued to mow the lawn when he saw who it was. Leaf walked up and stood right in the path of the machine, forcing him to stop. He pointed to it.

"Noisy!" he yelled.

Cook understood this as a request and turned it off. Leaf pointed to himself.

"Foolish," he said.

Cook looked at him blankly. Leaf pointed to the left side of his chest.

"Contrite," he said. He pointed to his head. "Bowed."

"Lieutenant," Cook said impatiently, "do you have something to say to me? I've got things to do, and if you're going to talk in adjectives all afternoon you're going to waste my time."

Leaf looked disappointed, as if Cook were denying him an interesting linguistic challenge. "One more, then. Sorry. I'm sorry. Is that an adjective? I lost my head. I was angry. I don't like murder."

"All right. Tell me what you think." Cook gestured to his front porch. The two men began walking. Cook was very glad he had said this before Leaf had said it to him. He wasn't going to let the fat man befuddle his brain this time. He sat down on the porch swing, afraid it might not support Leaf, and pointed to a chair for him. "Sit down."

"I like swings. Scoot over."

Cook held his ground. "No. I was here first. Sit there." He pointed to the chair again. Leaf obeyed.

"What do you know about this Philpot?" asked Leaf.

"No. You tell me first. How long had he been dead when he was discovered? The news reports have been unclear on that point."

Leaf hesitated a moment, then spoke forthrightly. "Maybe a week or more."

"So he could have been killed the same night as Arthur."

"And probably was. And by the same man. Your typewriter is the link."

"What was the cause of death?"

"Choking."

"You mean drowning?"

"No. Strangling. He was throttled. Dead before he hit the water."

Cook did not produce another question right away.

"Evidently the guy we're after threw him down and just choked him with his bare hands," Leaf continued. "He had a busy night of it."

"That would take a lot of strength," said Cook.

"Or motivation."

"In this case . . ."

Leaf shrugged. "Fear of discovery. Philpot must have been a witness."

Cook nodded. He had already gotten this far on his own. "Who was the last to see him?"

"That depends on you. You're the last of the Wabash Six that I have to question on that point. When did you last see him?"

"About noon on Tuesday of last week."

"And what—"

"So who does that make the last to see him?" interrupted Cook.

"Your boss. He dropped him off at his motel about five o'clock."

"So between that time and the time of the accident he met up with one of us."

"Yes. Who?"

"It's hard to say. He could have arranged to meet any of us. In fact he had an appointment with me for a drink late that night."

"You didn't tell me that."

"I haven't had the chance. My point is that he could just as easily have arranged to have dinner or a drink with Emory Milke, or Adam Aaskhugh, or anybody."

". . . who then could have offered to drive him to your office to meet you. Did Philpot know you would be there?"

"Yes. I told him." Cook thought a moment. "That's good. We now have a reason for his being there."

"You know, he would still be alive if you hadn't made that date with him," Leaf said accusingly.

Cook laughed. He was getting a handle on Leaf. He wouldn't ever be bamboozled by him again. "It was pretty reckless of me, Lieutenant. Do I have time to pack before you take me in?"

Leaf said nothing.

"Another thing, Lieutenant. Did that material on my car bumper match the pants?"

"Pants?" Leaf said wonderingly. "Pants?"

"Stiph's pants. You know . . . the piece of wool I found after—"

"Oh. That. Yes, they match. They match, all right. Listen, it's hot and I'm a hot cowboy. What do you have for a working man with a king-size thirst?" He looked around on all sides of him, as if in hopes of finding a spare root beer nearby.

"Lemonade?" asked Cook.

"How about a milkshake?" said Leaf.

Cook frowned. "Well—"

"Don't you have the fixings?"

"The what?"

"The fixings. Ice cream, for example."

"You really want a milkshake?" Cook stood up.

"Do you like ice cream?

"Yes," said Cook, feeling monumentally bored by the question.

"Gimme a bourbon and branch water."

Cook hesitated. "Seriously?" he asked, wondering what new joke or mystery he was walking into.

"Of course."

"What about your man in the car?" Cook looked across the lawn.

"Nah," said Leaf. "Fuck 'im."

As Cook prepared Leaf's drink in the kitchen he resolved to get the upper hand again. Leaf had dominated with the milkshake business. It had put Cook in a weak, domestic position. He knew now how to retaliate, though. Leaf didn't have the answer to one question he knew of—he couldn't. He took a beer out of the refrigerator for himself and returned to the porch, where he found Leaf sitting on the porch swing and smoking a cigarette. Cook handed him his drink and leaned against the porch railing, facing him. Leaf brought the glass to his mouth, sniffed it, and then set it beside him on the swing.

"Lieutenant," said Cook, his breath somewhat short with anticipation, "what do you make of the fact that someone posing as Philpot called one of the teachers on Friday?"

"It puzzles me."

Cook waited for Leaf to elaborate. When he didn't, he said, "Doesn't it rather complicate the case?"

"No." He looked at Cook. "I figure it was just some petty wienie who works there trying to find out what other people think of him." He swung back and forth on the swing, inhaled from his cigarette, and blew smoke up at the porch ceiling—the picture of contentment.

Cook tried to look blank-faced. "So . . . the guy posing as Philpot on the phone isn't necessarily the one who killed him."

"That's right." Leaf continued to swing, his small shoes clicking the porch rhythmically on the backswing. "And yet the profile is the same."

"What do you mean?"

"Fear of judgment. You know, it's a sad thing about this guy. There's a fair chance he wouldn't have been charged with anything. At night that road there is as dark as the inside of a cow, and Stiph was wearing a dark coat. Hell, I could have run over him under those circumstances. Of course the puke in your office suggests the driver was drunk, or had been drinking, but even so, there are ways of hiding that. He definitely overdid it. Or maybe he hadn't been drinking at all before the accident. Maybe he didn't start until afterward, to cheer himself up sort of. Either way, he should have come forth and trusted the judgment of society. Instead he bolts. Digs himself in deeper, even. He won't stop at anything now. You might be next." He began to whistle softly as he swung.

"Me?"

"Sure. In the public eye you are the number-one suspect, so you're showing the greatest desire to find the real killer, right?"

There was no denying it, even though his progress had been nil. "Right."

"If you get too close—*kapowie*!" He smacked his fist against his palm and the force jarred his glass loose from his seat, where it had been swinging, untouched, beside him. The glass bounced on the wooden floor, but it did not break. "They're dropping like flies," said Leaf.

Cook looked at the puddle on the porch floor and said mechanically, "Can I get you another?"

"I think not, Jeremy," said Leaf as he stood up. "I've got to shuffle off to Kokomo."

"Don't you have any other questions for me?"

"Well, one, if you insist. What did you think of that story by Stiph?"

"'The Backside of Mankind'? I don't know—I haven't thought about it much."

"Har, har, har, you haven't thought about it much."

"No, really. I haven't."

"No, really, you haven't, har, har, har."

Apparently Leaf was prepared to go on doing this the rest of the afternoon. "I thought it was all right, I guess. It was cute."

"It was cute, har, har, har."

"Damn it, it *was.*" He paused and looked ahead to where he was going. How did one defend the assertion that a short story was cute? Was that what he now had to do?

"As I understand it—and I'm just a loveable cop, now—he says that evil is just . . . what we imagine about people we don't like. Right?"

"I think so. Something like that. It's an interesting notion, don't you think?"

Leaf grinned at him. It was a grin slow in developing, but it grew quite large. "How much crap do you think it would take to sink a ship, a large ship? Call it the *H.M.S. Philpot.* How much?"

"Quite a bit, I guess," said Cook, beginning to visualize it.

Leaf shook his head and stepped down from the porch. "Arthur Stiph's story could do it all by itself."

Cook sighed and rubbed his hands through his hair. His desk was littered with notes, scraps of paper, and half-open books and journals. He now knew, for what it was worth, that *John, Johann, Jan, Ian, Hans, Hansel, Giovanni, Jean, Juan, Ivan, Vanya, Evan, Sean,* and *Jones* were all ultimately one and the same name; that *Elmer* once was a common greeting name for strangers; that Shakespeare's name was spelled eighty-three different ways in his lifetime; that Lombards were long beards; that Englishmen were crooked fishhooks; and that the folk in Arkansas had turned a certain river named *Purgatoire* into the *Picket Wire*, while American stevedores christened the Norwegian steamer *Björnstjerne Björnson* with the name *Bejesus Be-johnson*. And he finally knew why some people say *uh* for the final vowel of names like *Missouri* and *Cincinnati*, while others say *ee.* This last issue had a special importance to him because he had been asked this very question dozens of times, almost as many times as he had been asked what linguistics was—at parties, at picnics, in bed, at airports, and once, disturbingly, in the restroom of Max's bar. Now, after all these years, he would have an answer.

He took off his glasses and rubbed his eyes. He leaned back in his chair, stretched, and groaned. It was Sunday afternoon, and occasional mysterious squeaks and bangs from elsewhere on the seventh floor told him that he was not the only linguist putting in odd hours. The only incongruity was the contrasting silence from Orffmann's office. Orffmann, like the dormitory roommate you can't stand, was always in. Until recently, at least. His absence worried Cook in that it set up a positive expectation that it might continue, which he knew must someday be crushed. Orffmann's laughter reminded him of carved pumpkins. It suggested a parade of laughing, militaristic pumpkins hell-bent on overthrowing the world. He wondered idly if Orffmann could have been the one to tell Paula he was a complete asshole. It certainly was possible. But Orffmann seemed almost too incompetent, incapable even of slander. And there was that report from Ed that Orffmann considered himself Cook's friend, he just now remembered. No. It was probably Mary the Secretary. Since they were enemies already, he appreciated the economy in thinking she was the one. As guide to new teachers, she had *opportunity*, as a speaker of English (though not a good one), she had *means*, and as someone who probably heard him snicker when he once walked by her desk and saw her empty-headedly playing ticktacktoe with herself, she had *motivation*.

He heard a definitely feminine cough and giggle from the hall. Had Miss Pristam returned to Wabash earlier than expected? If so, he would have to greet her warmly and perpetuate her notion that he was "a nice young man." There it was again. He perked up and leaned forward in his chair, ears straining. It was a giggle. By God . . .

He stood up, opened his door, and stepped out into the hall. To his left, beyond Woeps's office, the door to Milke's office stood open, and out of it came bearded laughter and then Paula Nouvelles, walking toward him, but she called back over her shoulder, "I'll work down here then." She was carrying several books. Cook spun on his heel and went down the hall to his right, hoping he looked like a man on his way to the bathroom. Paula was behind him, following him on her way to wherever she was going. Cook suddenly realized this was foolish and turned to (1) wait for her, (2) greet her, (3) talk to her, and (4) seduce her. None of these, not even the first, was realized. As soon as he turned she too turned—into the central core and out of sight. But not, he noticed, without throwing him a wave and a smile.

He gazed blankly down the empty hall. He turned around. Ahead of him was the bathroom door, perhaps fifty feet away. If he lowered his head and ran full speed into it, the impact might kill him. Of the suicidal options facing him, this was probably the quickest. Had he left junior high school yet? Had he? Then why did this kind of thing make him feel that he hadn't? People said that being single made you feel forever young. Yes, thought Cook, if what they meant was that it made you feel forever foolish.

He stalked back to his office. He was Jeremy Cook, one of the best-known psycholinguists in the country. He gathered up his notes and books on names and dumped them into an unruly pile in one corner. Like Leaf, that stuff fogged up his brain. He took out his notes and tape transcripts, along with a blank yellow legal tablet to help him think.

Thirty minutes later he was as happy, nearly, as he would have been if all four of those things had happened. He dialed Ed Woeps's number. Woeps's wife answered and seemed interested in chatting, but Cook somewhat impolitely urged her to put her husband on the phone.

"Hi, Jeremy," he said. "Any gossip?"

"Not today, Ed. But I think I've figured out Wally's *m-bwee.*"

"Really? Just a second."

Cook heard him asking his wife to take something off his hands. There was some discussion. The something turned out to be Wally, who for some reason remained on Woeps's hands. Cook could hear him intermittently in the background.

"Go ahead, Jeremy."

"I've gone over the occurrences I've got, but I'm going to

need more to verify it. It looks like it's a comment on moving objects, as if to say, 'Something is moving,' or 'Locomotion is going on.' All of my notes show him looking at people or animals walking, or fish swimming—"

"Or water pouring into the bathtub."

"Yes. That's one thing I wanted to ask you. Did he say it about you or about the water?"

"He pointed to the water."

"He did? You didn't mention that."

"I forgot. It's easy to overlook these things. He had two more of them today, Jeremy."

"Good," said Cook, smiling to hear Woeps speak of them as if they were bowel movements. "I'm glad to hear it's still alive. What were they about?"

"One was to our neighbor's cat as she ran by, and the other was at an Indian on TV. I think he was riding a horse at the time."

"Good. Did you take note of the intonation contours?"

"I sure didn't."

"See if you can make sense out of this: I've got distinctly rising contours in his remarks on the four people he said it about—you, me, and two teachers, Sarah and Sally—and on the fish and a wind-up toy that scoots across the floor. But the contour is falling with squirrels and birds. He produced four when I was outside with him one morning last week. All falling—two birds, two squirrels."

"Not much physical similarity, is there?" said Woeps.

"No. It could be that the important thing is that we were outside, so *m-bwee* with a falling intonation might mean 'Locomotion is going on outdoors.' That would be pretty odd, though."

"One thing that strikes me is that he really doesn't like birds or squirrels."

Cook raised his eyebrows. "Really?"

"Yes. He's afraid of them for some reason."

"And he likes you and me and the teachers and fish—"

"Yes. As far as I know."

"Jesus," said Cook, feeling somewhat short of breath. "A window into his personal preferences."

"Maybe. You've got me interested in it now. I'll be more attentive to it."

"Ed, I'm hot to study him. Could I have him for a few hours tonight?"

Woeps hesitated. "Helen's folks are coming up from Louisville, and they'll only be here a—"

"Forget it, then. I'll catch him tomorrow."

Another pause followed. Cook's heart sank. "I'm afraid they're all going for a ride tomorrow, Jeremy. Helen's folks will want the kids along."

"Well, I don't want to press you."

"Tomorrow night would be good. We're going out and we'll have a sitter in for Amy. You could be alone with Wally in his room. He'd like that."

Cook laughed. "And if he doesn't he'll let me know."

"What? Oh . . . yeah, provided you keep moving. What do you think? We'll be out of here about six, and you could keep him up until eight or eight-thirty if you like."

"Fine."

"You know, Jeremy, if his like or dislike is involved, that would explain its relative infrequency. I mean, movement is going on all the time, isn't it? But if *m-bwee* demands the conjunction of movement and strong feeling . . ."

"That's right. But it's pretty unusual. That's why I want more examples." He heard some vocal noises, then a whine.

"I've got to go, Jeremy. He's kicking up a fuss. I'm glad you've made progress. See you tomorrow."

Cook stood up. He walked out the door and down the hall and entered the central core where Paula had vanished. She was in the snack bar near the vending machines, her head buried in a book. She looked up when Cook entered. He rejected a temptation to pretend to be there to get coffee out of one of the machines and boldly approached her.

"What are you reading?"

She showed him the spine of the book without speaking. Rather laconic of her, he thought. In fact, absolutely laconic. Bad sign. But the book—*Presupposition, Reference, and What King of France?*—was a good omen, because this particular work contained two articles by him, one of them perhaps the best thing he had ever written. When he asked her if this was an area of special interest, she explained that she was writing a dissertation on intonation and presupposition.

"You know," she said, "problems like how we can get two readings out of 'It's better than sucking eggs.' With one intonation sucking eggs is no fun at all, and with another there's a presupposition that it's really quite a nice thing to do—hard to beat, in fact."

"Yes," he said. "There are fascinating problems there, especially with stated beliefs, as in 'John thinks that I'm an . . . a drunkard.' Have you thought about sentences like that?"

She set her book down—losing her place, Cook noticed—and leaned back in her chair, looking at him closely.

"Why no, Jeremy, I haven't."

CHAPTER NINE

COOK LOOKED AT WACH, who was surveying the group before him. If ever there was a time for the pretty pickle speech this was it. It was Monday morning, and the impact of the discovery of Philpot's body Thursday evening was now quite clear. Fully half of the children normally enrolled at Wabash had been kept home. Wach's phone had been ringing all morning. Philpot's opening question took on more meaning: considering what Wabash did to its own staff and people dropping in to write a few words about them, what did they do with those babies anyway? Or what might they do?

Wach had called a ten o'clock meeting of the linguists to discuss their predicament. They now sat in his office and waited for Milke, who had stepped out to have Mary the Secretary call Orffmann to see where he was. As they waited, Cook turned to Woeps and asked for and received permission to bring Wally to Wabash that night, since he had decided to tape as well as observe him. Cook arranged to pick Wally up at six. Milke stepped inside in the middle of this and waited (rather politely, thought Cook) until they were finished talking to give the news about Orffmann. But before he could speak, Aaskhugh, whose back was to the door, asked Wach about the enrollment at Wabash.

Like a government economic forecaster, Wach said, "The outlook is not bright." He cleared his throat and glanced down at some papers on his desk. "We have fifty-five percent absentees today. Of those about half are permanent removals—the Simpkins twins are an example. The other half are temporary, judging from what their parents have told me. I believe they have adopted a wait-and-see position." He gestured broadly with his hands at "wait-and-see," as if the expression were newly coined by him and in need of demonstration.

"Is the forty-five percent solid?" asked Cook. "Will they stay here?"

"I think attendance today indicates a sound parental commitment to the Institute," said Wach.

"Until they find something else," said Milke, stepping forward and taking a seat beside Cook. "Or until their neighbors get to them. 'You mean you're still sending your children *there*?' I'm not very optimistic."

"Where's Clyde?" Aaskhugh asked Milke.

"In the hospital. His wife says he has pneumonia. But even more imp—"

"Hah!" said Aaskhugh. "Hah! Pretty fishy."

Woeps laughed. "And if he dies, Adam, does that settle it? Is that as good as a confession?"

"How has Clyde's work been of late, Walter?" Aaskhugh asked, ignoring Woeps and turning to Wach for support.

Wach blinked once. "Normal."

Aaskhugh nodded. "Anyone notice anything unusual about him lately?"

Milke spoke up. "Your line of inquiry amuses me, Adam. I was going to add that Clyde has been officially cleared of all suspicion."

The linguists greeted this news with astonished gasps and undisguised moans of disappointment.

"Evidently," Milke went on, "he had an alibi but was unable, or perhaps reluctant, to produce witnesses in support of it."

"Reluctant?" asked Cook.

Milke smiled. "I was just on the phone to Lieutenant Leaf about it. Clyde's wife suggested I call him. He said some things I didn't quite follow, but I got the impression that our man Clyde was having an affair. Leaf gave me this impression and yet he avoided female pronouns when talking about the alibi. I think he avoided *all* pronouns."

"An affair?" said Woeps. "Clyde? He doesn't seem capable of it."

"It comes as no surprise to me," said Aaskhugh, effortlessly abandoning his old position for a new one. "His wife is a real battle-ax."

"Well, we're moving in on the bastard, aren't we?" Cook said matter-of-factly.

The four men looked at him; then, as they understood what he had meant, at each other. He was about to follow up on this when Wach spoke.

"The purpose of this meeting, gentlemen, is to divert Wabash from its rapidly declining course. I suggest we stick to that for the moment." Cook suppressed a scowl. "I would be pleased to have a little brainstorming from you about how to handle the situation." Wach said this as if their last such session had been a whopping success. Wach Rule Number Eight: people forget things, so people who run things can safely treat past failures as if they had been stupendous triumphs.

In the pause that followed, Milke stroked his beard, Aaskhugh studied his hands, Woeps rubbed at a dark stain covering most of his right pants leg above the knee, and Cook watched all of them doing these things.

"As you know," Wach said encouragingly, "Jeremy here is jumping into the fray with his lecture on names—"

"Walter, while you're on that I'd like to see the title changed to just 'Names.' I've got to deal with more than southern Indiana if I'm to speak for more than twenty seconds."

"Will do, Jeremy."

Milke laughed. "Do you all expect the Rotary Club to jump to our defense just because Jeremy here gives them a bang-up lecture—which I'm sure you can do, Jeremy, don't get me wrong—on this somewhat silly topic?"

"I see it as one small part of a general community relations outreach program," said Wach.

"What are the other parts?" asked Milke.

"We're piecing it together now," said Wach. "All of us."

Milke laughed softly and muttered, "I hadn't noticed."

After another longish pause Wach said, "I'll get the ball rolling then. What would you think of changing the name of the Institute?" Four frowns greeted this.

"To what?" asked Cook.

"I'm not sure," said Wach. "That's not important. What's important is the change."

"But what's the point?" asked Milke.

"Associations," said Wach. "People in the community now associate the name 'The Wabash Institute' with death. They can't do that if we change the name."

Very gently, Woeps said, "I'm afraid that's a little thin, Walter."

"It's not even like a Band-Aid on cancer," said Milke incredulously. "It's like *blowing* on cancer to make it go away."

"Fine, fine," said Wach. "I won't push it. But think about it. Don't dismiss it out of hand. We can come back to it. Now how about some suggestions from you? If the situation does not improve, and it won't unless we come up with something, some cutbacks are inevitable."

"Of the linguists?" Woeps asked nervously

"Yes," said Wach. "This has been in the works for some time, actually, and this is as good a time as any to tell you about it. Some time ago Adam informed me that the Himmelhoch Foundation is cutting back on its funding in linguistics. He has a well-placed source in Washington, isn't that right, Adam?"

"Right."

"They've been so generous," said Milke. "What—"

"They've decided to channel a lot of money into research on alternative sources of energy, or some such nonsense," said Aaskhugh.

"Is that right?" said Milke, confounded. "Jesus. We don't even know how kids learn irregular verbs."

"I know, Emory," said Aaskhugh. "It is pretty sickening."

"Now this will not affect us until next year," said Wach. "And it's hard to predict exactly what the effect will be. But you can see that the daycare enrollment becomes more crucial, not only as a source of income for us but as a justification for six full-time linguists."

Cook spoke up. "I would like to find out how each of you got along with Arthur." He let this sink in before continuing, which he did just as the others were about to ask him why. "This is step one on the way to finding out who killed him, and thereby clearing our name, or names. If you will allow me."

Cook undertook a lengthy presentation of the goals and purposes of the Backside Club, insofar as he understood them. He had finally decided that lurking and eavesdropping were not going to tell him who Stiph's backfriend was. After all, who besides Aaskhugh was going to voluntarily say anything bad about a generally well-liked dead man? A frontal assault on the question was the best approach.

"So," he concluded, "now that I've said this much, I don't really expect any of you to jump forward with avowals of mutual hatred for Arthur, but if you know of anything he might have said about one of us—"

"But we're all *here*, Jeremy," said Woeps.

"That's right. You'll have to say it in the person's presence. Except for Orffmann, and now that—"

"Arthur's contempt for Clyde is a matter of public record," said Aaskhugh, instantly warming to the subject. "I often heard him ridicule him."

"Fine," said Cook. "That's the spirit. But since Clyde is no longer a suspect we don't have to worry about him. Can you say the same thing about anyone else, Adam?"

"I once heard him say that Emory was a loud sonofabitch and that his beard smelled like a tobacco plantation," said Aaskhugh.

Milke frowned and his hand slowly went to his beard. "I must say—"

"Apart from the one famous comment about Ed, that's all," said Aaskhugh, looking around the room innocently.

"And what was that comment, Adam?" asked Cook.

"Well, Ed once showed him an old Indian-head nickel he carries in his wallet as a good-luck piece—is that right, Ed?" Woeps stared at him without answering. "And then after you were gone, Ed, Arthur turned to the rest of us, and there were quite a few of us there, and he said, 'I wonder when it's going to start working.'" He looked at Cook and smiled toothily. "I thought everyone knew about it."

"Go soak your head, Adam," said Woeps.

Aaskhugh looked genuinely surprised. "Now, Ed. *Really.* I didn't say any of these things. I was just going along with Jay's suggestion."

"You can't shoot the messenger for bringing bad news, Ed," said Milke.

"You can if the messenger grins as he brings it. Which is what you do, isn't it, Adam?" Woeps's voice rose. "You're really nothing but a skinny, grinning gossip."

"Well, I—"

"Look, Ed—"

"Listen, everyone, maybe we'd better—"

"Hold it!" shouted Cook. "Just hold it." He inhaled deeply and blew out. "We've got to stick to Arthur. What's important is who *he* didn't like."

"Precisely," said Wach, who had been closely but silently following these proceedings. "I'm beginning to think you're on the right track, Jeremy. Our desperate situation calls for extreme measures now. How about the rest of you? What can we reconstruct of Arthur's opinion of us? From what Jeremy says, the one of us whom he hated the most was the one who killed him."

"It's not certain, Walter," said Cook, happily surprised to have Wach on his side now.

"But very probable?" asked Wach.

"Yes."

Milke opened his mouth as if to speak.

"Yes, Emory?" said Wach, uncharacteristically excited.

"Well, I feel a bit funny about it."

"Go ahead," said Wach. "You're among friends."

"He called you a mental lightweight, Walter," said Milke.

Wach sat straight up in his chair. "Oh?"

"Yes. This wasn't long ago. He said some other things too. He said you were a typical administrator in that you wouldn't pass gas without first considering the budgetary ramifications; he said that your field was no longer linguistics—it was niggardliness; and he said you were as mean as you were dumb."

"My goodness! I—"

"Jesus, he certainly—"

"Old Arthur didn't pull any—"

"I think our format is screwed up," Cook said loudly. Everyone calmed down and looked at him. "You're all telling the person involved. You should be telling the rest of us. It is evidence against him for the rest of us to consider. We're not interested in personal growth here."

"Hear, hear," said Milke.

"That's exactly right," said Wach.

"Jeremy," said Milke, looking at him, "I once heard Arthur say something about you. Or rather," he said quickly, turning away from Cook to the others, "he said it about *him*." He pointed to Cook.

"What was it, Emory?" asked Aaskhugh.

"He said that Jeremy Cook flaunted his good looks."

"That's all? That doesn't even—"

"Rather mild."

"Doesn't amount to a hill of—"

"Quite a letdown."

After a pause of palpable disappointment, Wach said, "Anything else on Jeremy?" Everyone looked around and shrugged. "That's funny. It looks as though the very method of investigation suggested by Jeremy could have the effect of clearing him of suspicion." He suddenly stopped speaking and looked at Cook, as did the others.

Cook stood up. "I'll be right back," he said. He went to his office, where "The Backside of Mankind" was filed in his "Unfinished" folder, along with notes and fragments of manuscripts in progress. He brought it back for the group's perusal. Doing this gave him time to think about what everyone had said thus far. *Listen,* he reminded himself. *Listen.*

"You can ask Lieutenant Leaf about it too," he said. "Arthur's wife also told him, not just me, about his intention to meet his backfriend that night. It's all true."

"Looks it," said Milke, leafing through the pages of the story. He looked up at Cook.

"No hard feelings," said Cook. "This suspicion is useful. It's what we need more of."

Aaskhugh was studying the first page of the story and shaking his head. "I didn't know Arthur very well," he said reflectively, "but I never would have thought he was crazy."

Wach nodded vigorously. "It is something of a shock. I blame myself for not knowing more about him. I hadn't any idea."

"What are you talking about?" said Cook. "I don't think this is odd at all. Arthur had a creative bent and he wrote a story many years ago. So what?"

Wach said, "But he still has these . . . these . . ."

"Yes," said Cook. "That's true. But I see this as just a natural interest in human relationships. This is the stuff of life, isn't it?"

There were several complaints and demurrals to this. Wach found it all "unhealthy," Aaskhugh said Stiph was "making a religion" out of it without specifying the "it," Woeps said the important thing was friends, not enemies, and Milke found the whole idea "wild and wonderful."

"But how about you, Jeremy?" asked Woeps. "Don't you have any kind words from Arthur about any of us?"

Cook shook his head. "I've got absolutely nothing. That's why I'm doing this, which I'm not enjoying much either, by the way."

"How about you, Walter?" asked Woeps.

Wach sighed dramatically. "It is for no small reason that I have said nothing thus far," he said. "What I have to say is unfortunately damning to one of us. I say 'us' because I see our danger and misfortune as a collective problem. No doubt this is the case because of my tendency—perhaps a mistaken tendency but the mistake is pardonable, I believe—to see the fate of Walter Wach and that of the Wabash Institute as one and the same." He paused. "I heard the late Arthur Stiph say a bad thing about just one of us. He said that he loathed this person more than he had ever loathed anyone else—yes, and that he *feared* him, too, and that he feared what he, Arthur, might do to him. He hated him that much. It's not a pretty story, to be sure, but there it is. I'm speaking of Emory Milke."

This speech seemed more earnest and heartfelt than those that had gone before, and a hush followed.

"Emory?" Cook finally said, turning to him.

Milke was taking it quite well, not showing any of his usual brashness. "I don't know what to say. I'm quite hurt. I always liked Arthur, or thought I did . . . I really can't imagine him saying that." As if to console himself, he took his empty pipe from his shirt pocket and began to fondle it.

"I stand by my story," said Wach.

This was a strange thing to say—or rather, it was said with a strange insistence. If Cook understood Milke correctly, he was not really saying he doubted Wach's report. He was saying only that it was hard for him to reconcile it with his impression of, and affection for, Stiph. Milke looked at Wach for a moment as though he were about to clarify his original point, but then for some reason he chose not to. Perhaps, on reconsideration, he thought he *should* have made the challenge Wach thought he had made.

"Ed?" Cook asked, turning to his friend. "We haven't heard from you yet."

"Before we leave this," said Aaskhugh, "I'd like to ask Walter a bit more about what he just said."

"Fine," said Cook. "Go ahead."

"Did he elaborate on this fear, Walter?"

"He did not."

"Did he fear bodily harm?"

"That I do not know."

"You have nothing to add, Walter?" asked Cook.

"That is correct."

"When did he say it?" asked Milke. "And where? And why?"

"Approximately two weeks ago. In this office. We were discussing relationships among personnel at Wabash. It is part of my job to see that things go smoothly in that way."

"Then he must have said something to you about other people too," suggested Milke.

"He chose only to speak of Emory," said Wach, cutting off visual contact with Milke and sweeping his eyes across the rest of the group. Milke sat tensed for a moment, then sighed.

"Ed?" said Cook, sensing this dialogue was over.

Woeps smiled. "I didn't speak with Arthur all that often, and I heard him say nothing bad about any of us." He raised his index finger skyward, then aimed it at Aaskhugh. "Except Adam. He quoted an old Spanish proverb to me once as Adam walked by us in the hall. It's this: 'He who knows little soon repeats it.' He then added that Adam was a classic rumormonger: empty head, empty life, full mouth."

"Ouch!" someone said.

"Pithy, isn't it?"

"A good, clean shot."

Aaskhugh gave what looked at first like a courageous smile, but then Cook realized he found these remarks genuinely amusing. He was untouched personally. Perhaps it was impossible to insult a gossip by calling him a gossip.

"Ed, you're not just saying this to get back at Adam, are you?"

"I'm happy to get back at him, as you put it, but that's not why I said it. What do you think, that I made it up?"

"No," said Cook, "but personal involvement might lead you to exaggerate a story like this, or overlook similar stories about others of us."

"I wouldn't forget, Jeremy, even if it was about you. As far as I'm concerned, there are no saints in this room. Nary a one."

"Fine," said Cook, feeling suddenly depressed. Considering how strongly he liked Woeps, he would never have said what Woeps just said. Was it as nasty as it seemed?

"Of the abuse we have thus far had recapitulated for us," said Wach, "I would say my report of Arthur's about Emory is the most serious."

"I agree," said Aaskhugh.

"Yes," said Woeps.

"But if he *feared* Emory," said Cook, "I would think he would be reluctant to meet him late at night like that."

"Good point," said Aaskhugh.

"I agree," said Milke. "This is all really quite bewildering. And I can't believe we can't get any more dirt on Jeremy." Cook looked at him. "Arthur's ruthlessness seems so general," Milke continued, "that I would expect even as pleasant and likeable a fellow as Jeremy to be scorched by it."

Cook's head began to spin. For five years he had carefully nurtured his dislike of Milke. He had even invented new principles according to which Milke fell short and made them part of his own life. Now here was the man publicly proclaiming something like affection for him. Did Milke actually like him? Why hadn't he shown it sooner? It put Cook in a devilishly awkward position. The fact that no one else in the room, not even Milke, knew this made no difference. What was he supposed to do now—dwell on what was good in Milke, or some such nonsense? No. Milke remained an asshole. Given a few minutes, Cook could easily have remembered and explained the reasons why.

"I must say, I'm somewhat disillusioned about Arthur," said Woeps. "While some of his observations are on the mark"—he looked at Aaskhugh—"the general tenor of his personality seems quite misanthropic."

"Hardly the kindly old linguist he appeared to be," added Milke.

"Hardly," said Woeps.

"This of course doesn't reduce the nature of the crime," said Cook, and as he said it he realized that it did, even though everyone immediately and unthinkingly agreed with him. "And there's Henry Philpot. His death changes everything. I can imagine any of us accidentally killing someone and then covering it up in a panic. But now with Philpot it's a different story."

"You're right," said Milke. "A very pleasant man."

"He was all right," said Aaskhugh. "Nothing special."

"I wonder," said Milke, "if anything in Arthur's office could tell us who he was going to meet that night. His calendar, for example."

"Or his notes," said Wach enthusiastically. "He's beginning to sound stranger all the time. He may have kept notes on his meetings with this backfriend fellow."

Cook said, "I'm going to get in his office this afternoon to check through his work in progress—the stuff Emory told us about last time. I'll keep an eye out for anything interesting along those lines."

"Hmmm," said Milke. "Puts you in a rather privileged position, doesn't it?"

"If I find anything you can be sure that I will show it to you," said Cook.

"And destroy it if it implicates you," said Milke.

"We all ought to go through his stuff," said Aaskhugh. "And at the same time."

"That's right," Milke nodded. "The sooner the better."

"Well . . . it's a bit unorthodox." Wach pursed his lips. "And yet Emory and Adam do have a point. As far as Arthur's personal effects go, his wife was here and took them out the day before she, ah . . . so we don't have to worry about, well, what the family would think and all, and if we—" He looked at his watch. "I've got an appointment with Lieutenant Leaf in forty minutes, and it might look funny if he saw us in there prowling around. We would have to make it snappy." He bit his lower lip and then clapped his hands together once, decisively. "Good. Let's do it."

His impulsiveness was contagious. The five men rose from their chairs as one. They stepped out of Wach's office and waited while he obtained the master key from Mary the Secretary, who looked at the group somewhat warily, as if she feared they had been conspiring to pounce on her. The men hurried down the hall to Stiph's office. As they moved, Cook almost felt as if they formed an unwieldy, homicidal circle of some complexity, each man holding a knife at the throat of the one in front, ready to plunge the dagger at the first hint of steel in his own throat.

The blinds were drawn in Stiph's office, and Wach fumbled for the light switch in the darkness while the linguists slowly entered the room. By the time he found it the others were spread all over the office in ready-to-search positions. Wach warned them not to mess things up. Cook began to work through the top drawer of a filing cabinet, leafing through papers from conferences, some correspondence, and offprints of articles.

"Look!" said Aaskhugh from the desk, where he was rifling the papers in a lower drawer. "Some tit magazines." He held up two of them. Milke joined him and took one from him, idly skimming it a few seconds before becoming conscious of the stares of the others and returning it to the drawer. "And here are some pills," said Aaskhugh. "'Tofranil. Take as directed.'" He looked up. "Anyone know anything about this stuff?"

"Adam, get the hell out of there," Wach yelled from across the room, where he had been looking through a thin black book. "It's obviously irrelevant to what we're doing here."

"You never know," Aaskhugh said somewhat poutishly.

"There's not much here," said Woeps from another filing cabinet, holding up a battered box of Kleenex by way of illustration.

"Nor here," said Milke as he slammed a desk drawer shut.

"Nothing in his appointment book either," said Wach.

"Let me see it, Walter," said Milke. "You can check my work on this side of the desk if you like."

"All right." The two men exchanged places.

"Here are his notes on his work on acquisition of esteem terms," said Cook, lifting a heavy file out of the second drawer of the cabinet. "Some remarks on praise, some more on ridicule . . . here's something on name calling. I'll be taking all of this with me, so the rest of you might want to look through it now too."

Woeps and Aaskhugh drifted over to where he stood. He handed each of them a sheaf of papers. "We'll trade these around," he said. After a few minutes Milke and Wach joined them, and the five men carefully went through the many pages of notes.

"Here's something interesting," said Milke. "I mean just interesting, not important to us. It looks like a table of a sample of the kids here, broken down according to . . . well, it's called 'Love-Hate Chart: Wabash 4-5-Year-Olds.' The initials of about a dozen kids are given along both axes. See, Jeremy?" He showed it to Cook. Next to the names listed vertically was the label "Agent," while above the names listed horizontally was the label "Patient." In the boxes where the names intersected there was an "L," an "H," a blank space, or a dash, the last used where a name intersected itself.

"'L' for 'Love,' Emory? And 'H' for 'Hate'?" Cook asked.

"I guess so. On the left where it says 'Agent' are the lovers and haters, and across the top are the loved and hated ones."

"It was probably something he was developing as a kind of reference source for his observations," said Cook. "You know, if T. T. said to L. W., 'You're a big boogersnatch,' Stiph could check it against this chart to see if T. T. loved or hated L. W."

"Do you think it was just a two-choice system? And how could he know?"

"Maybe the blanks indicate less strong feelings either way. And he could probably tell by watching the kids, or from reports by the teachers, who know the kids better than we do. Besides, it's fairly easy to tell who likes whom. With kids, at least."

Stiph's phone buzzed. The men turned and looked at it as if it were a voice from the grave. Aaskhugh, who was standing closest to it, picked it up and said cheerily, "Backside Club. May I take your reservation?" Then he giggled. He nodded into the phone a few times. "Okay, Mary," he said. He hung up and turned to Wach. "Lieutenant Leaf is here. Mary sent him on down."

"Oh, shit," said Wach. "Let's get out of here. This looks bad. Put those things away, Adam. Jeremy, you can take those notes with you. I think we've all seen them."

"Bit of a bust," muttered Woeps as he opened the door to the hall.

Lieutenant Leaf was leaning against the wall opposite the door, his arms folded against his chest, and again he named the linguists one by one as they filed out of Stiph's office.

CHAPTER TEN

THAT AFTERNOON Cook reviewed his notes in preparation for his evening taping session with Wally Woeps. He had gone over them perhaps forty times before, and he now put them away with an onrushing feeling of ennui. It scared him. He hoped he didn't grow tired of idiophenomena before he found and said something interesting about them. He looked at his watch. He had an hour or so before he would go to Max's, eat heavily and drink lightly, then go to Woeps's to pick up Wally. To pass that time he could work on his name lecture, but the tedium attached to that made him want to crawl under his desk and weep. Arthur Stiph's unfinished work was a cheerier prospect.

He took the heavy file from the top of his filing cabinet and began to sift through it. It quickly became clear that most of the material was of a preliminary, exploratory sort. Because Arthur nowhere spelled out what hypotheses he was testing in the area, Cook had only a dim notion of where the notes were going. He came upon the "Love-Hate Chart: Wabash 4-5-Year-Olds" and looked at it, idly trying to match initials with children's names. "D. M." must have been Daniel Masters, a freckled brute of a boy, and he loved no one and hated—his eyes went up the column to where an "H" was entered—"Z. W." That would be Zebra Whipple. This struck Cook as essentially correct, seeing that Daniel had twice tried to smash Zebra's head with a two-by-four (a bit more forceful a demonstration than the almost daily "you're not my friend anymore" he heard in the central core—or, at another level, the kind of thing that Aaskhugh and apparently even Stiph engaged in).

As he propped his feet up on his desk and turned toward the window, the "Love-Hate Chart" became backlit and harder to read because of some writing on the back of it. At first this annoyed Cook. Then it interested him. He turned the sheet over. On the backside, titled "Love-Hate Chart: Wabash Adult Males," was a grid just like the one he had been studying. But the names were different:

AGENT	PATIENT						
	Aaskhugh	Cook	Milke	Orffmann	Stiph	Wach	Woeps
Aaskhugh	—	L		H			H
Cook	H	—	H	H		H	L
Milke		L	—	H		H	
Orffmann	L	L	L	—		L	L
Stiph					—		
Wach		L	H	H		—	
Woeps	H						—

This interested Cook. Indeed, a personal visit from God—perhaps dropping by to justify bubonic plague or Walter Wach—could not have interested him more. But was this a correct analysis of the Wabash social structure? Cook looked across the row where his own name was entered as "Agent." Yes—it wasn't very pretty, but there you were. He hated them all—all except Stiph, whom he had, well, wondered about but neither hated nor loved. And Woeps? Yes, you could call it love in that he thought about Woeps every day, wondered about his home life a great deal, missed him deeply when he was not at work, worried about him, wanted to help him, and more. Good work, Arthur. Good observation.

Orffmann's profile was striking. As an agent he loved everyone but Stiph, yet as a patient he fared badly in return. Cook thought about this. Orffmann did have a bit of a toadying quality, always expressing indiscriminate awe of everyone. And it was a rare occasion when he was invited to lunch—he generally brown-bagged it alone in his office—and he was rarely spoken of, and if he was, then only dismissively. This meant that there was a fearful asymmetry in Orffmann's life. He was a perfect example of unrequitedness. Cook suddenly found this rather sad. In his memory, Orffmann's solitary laughter now rang hollow, almost pleading.

Cook looked at his own column, blinked with wonder, and looked at it some more. Could this be right? Was he—it made his bowels grumble to think it—loved by Aaskhugh, Milke, Orffmann, and Wach? Why not Woeps? Why was there a blank space where Agent Woeps met Patient Cook? The chart must have been unfinished, or maybe Stiph had made a mistake. He looked for others. Aaskhugh and Woeps—yes, those "H's" seemed to capture the way things stood between them. The same for Milke and Wach. Still, there was something dreadfully wrong about Stiph's perception of Patient Cook.

Stiph's own name was oddly free of emotion, either as giver or receiver. This may have been a gesture of objectivity—perhaps Stiph, as "principal investigator" in this project, felt obliged to make no judgments about himself. And yet there seemed to be a rightness to those blank spaces at his row and column. As an agent he was somewhat aloof in his sleepy way, interacting little with the other linguists, and as a patient he seemed to be the same kind of figure for the others as he was for Cook: a curious object of distant attention and good-natured amusement, but not one of love or hatred. Of course Cook had heard Aaskhugh call Stiph a "lazy turd" some time back, but such words from Aaskhugh's mouth did not signify dislike. Aaskhugh was merely using language in the way he thought it was designed to be used. Even Orffmann, in Stiph's judgment, stopped short of his normal, mindless adoration. It was too bad, though, that the chart was so silent about Stiph. One little "H"—or two, to make it reciprocal—and Cook would know the identity of Stiph's backfriend and killer. He needed something like this, some voice from the outside speaking out and presenting him with a solution to the crimes.

He studied the chart some more and noticed that there were more "H's" than "L's." He wondered if this was true of all groups. Even, say, charitable organizations and churches? He also noticed that while there was reciprocity of hatred (Aaskhugh-Woeps, Milke-Wach), there was none of love. Did this mean there were no true friendships at Wabash? No. Again, Stiph had to be wrong about Woeps. Besides, someone famous once said that a good sign of friendship was two people disliking the same things, and Cook and Woeps both disliked Aaskhugh. Of course Cook and Milke both disliked Wach, and for that matter nearly everyone disliked poor Clyde, all of which proved . . .

Cook stood up and looked out the window and sighed. What did it prove? What was the point of it all? Was there no end to Stiph's perverse idleness? This coldly analytical chart, his general meanness of spirit, his Backside Club—that especially. Cook had thought it was a tantalizing idea at one time. Cute. That was the word he had used in talking about it with Leaf. He looked down from his window to the parking lot, where Clyde Orffmann regularly pulled his weary and disliked bones out of his car and walked to the building where he plied his craft incompetently, and he wondered if Orffmann would find it cute.

When Cook called for Wally, Woeps's wife, Helen, answered the door. As was customary, she leaned forward to be kissed on the mouth by him. He didn't know why she always did this, but because she was nice-looking in a late-forties way, he mildly enjoyed it. Although somewhat high-strung, Helen had to be considered one of the lucky things that had happened to Woeps. And she certainly was nice to

Cook. Only recently she had quite embarrassed him by taking him aside and squeezing his arm and telling him how grateful she was for what he did for her husband at work and elsewhere.

Ed was upstairs with Amy, and when Cook was announced he yelled down something about a car seat. Helen led Cook outside and helped him take one of two seats out of their station wagon and put it in his Valiant. As he was doing this, a man and woman who were no doubt Helen's parents wheeled around the corner of the house. Wally leaned forward in his stroller and pointed at Cook as if identifying him as the man who had stolen his Tommee Tippee cup. Helen introduced Cook to her parents. Wally let Cook take him out of the stroller and put him in the car seat. Amid a thunderclap of bye-byes Cook drove off.

Wally was silent all the way to Wabash, simply smiling in the breeze of the car. Outside the building, he decided to look at a dandelion on the grass. Cook indulged him. Wally picked it and held it out for Cook to take, which he did, thanking him. Judging from the number of repetitions of this that ensued, Wally must have found it richly rewarding. Cook finally pitched a handful of mangled dandelions to the ground behind his back and scooped Wally up in his arms. As he unlocked the front door to the building Wally said, "Uhpah," so Cook gave him his keys to play with as they walked in. He let Wally push the elevator button, and as the light came on Wally said, "Gah," to which Cook agreed.

Upstairs he took Wally to his office and set him up on the floor with his keys and some books on semiotics that he had no intention of ever reading. As Wally began his systematic destruction of the books, Cook unlocked the door to the gym directly across the hall. He turned on the lights and glanced inside, happy to see most of the moveable toys that Woeps had specified as objects of his son's pleasure or displeasure. Unfortunately there was only one of the latter that Woeps knew about—a large, geared contraption on wheels, looking something like a huge watch with its backplate removed. When pulled, its parts moved, and it gave off a hideous thunking sound. Cook didn't much like it either. He hid the experimental objects, for he knew that Wally usually said *m-bwee* only once about an object in a given social situation, and he wanted to be sure he knew which object Wally was talking about.

He stepped across the hall and walked Wally into the gym, closing his office door behind him. He checked the tape in his recorder mounted high on one wall and took down a large clipboard with a blank legal tablet attached to it. He went to where Wally was standing and sucking his thumb, and he sat with him awhile to put him at ease. Wally seemed a bit overwhelmed by the emptiness of the room, since he normally saw it only when filled with many competitive peers. The opportunities for uninterrupted play, for sole possession of each and every piece of equipment, seemed to make him suspicious. This didn't bother Cook. He had even expected it and for that reason hadn't set the tape going right off. He would wait. He spied a *Mother Goose* book on a nearby chair and read to Wally to help him relax. Cook hadn't read the rhymes in a long time, and he now marveled at the cruelty of some of them and at the verb forms of others. Wally lost interest just as Cook finished with "Dr. Fell" and walked to the Creative Playthings slide and began to climb on it. He began babbling, but it wasn't until nearly twenty minutes later that Cook, heavy-lidded and yawning, judged that Wally was his normal sociable self and stood up to turn on the tape recorder.

As he walked across the room Wally looked at him and said *m-bwee* with a clearly rising intonation. Cook told Wally he liked him too. He turned on the recorder and waited a few minutes before producing a wind-up scooting bug, one of Wally's favorites. With almost boring predictability Wally greeted its motion with the same approving *m-bwee* he had just given Cook. A few minutes later Cook produced another favorite toy of Wally's, a duck, and without winding it up he set it out on the floor when Wally wasn't looking. When he finally spied it he squealed, smiled, stood up, and walked to it, banged it around, mouthed it, and did many other things to it, but he did not say *m-bwee* to it. When he set it down Cook quickly wound it up and sent it across the floor. Wally's rising *m-bwee* this time made Cook laugh.

Next came the painful part. He took the disgusting mechanical thing that Wally didn't like from behind a tarp near the door and set it in the middle of the room. He took one end of the long pull cord with him across the room and waited there with it while Wally played, his back turned, with a nondescript plastic block that kept causing him to laugh hysterically every few seconds. As Cook sat there, crouched, he felt like some dumb, bad cowboy in a grade-B film waiting to trip some equally dumb, but good, cowboy by yanking the rope as he rode by. Wally's block spent its power to amuse him and he turned around as if to ask, "What now?" Cook began to pull the toy, slowly and steadily. It sent out one of its *thunk* noises and Wally looked at it, eyes wide open. The accompanying *m-bwee* held a level tone for some time and then began to drop, slowly at first, then quickly all the way to the bottom of Wally's register. He ran to Cook, giving the toy wide berth, and raised his arms to be picked up. Cook obliged him, giving the watch toy a kick that sent it back behind the tarp, and he apologized to the boy.

He decided Wally deserved a break. He stood up and carried him to the tape recorder. As he looked at the counter to see how much playing time was left, Wally's hand squeezed the skin on his neck painfully and the boy's body tensed as he said *m-bwee* again. As just before, the intonation was falling. Cook pried Wally's hand away from his neck and turned around to see what he was looking at. One edge of the watch toy protruded from behind the tarp, and Wally was looking in that direction, his eyes darting back and forth nervously in an arc that included the tarp area and both sides of it as well.

Two things baffled Cook. The watch toy was not moving, and Wally had already said *m-bwee* to it, or about it. He turned the recorder off. Then he began to take Wally out into the hall for a walk, but this meant that they must walk right by the tarp, which lay against the wall next to the door, and this was too much for Wally. He whined and squirmed and clawed at Cook's neck, so Cook turned and left the gym by the door going into the hallway in the central core. This appeared to be fine with Wally. Cook set him down and followed him down this narrow hall to the door opening into the main hall near the bathroom. Cook opened it for him and the two of them moved back down the curving hall toward Cook's office at a torturously slow pace. When they finally reached it, to their right was the open door leading back into the gym—the one that Wally had refused to pass through coming in the other direction. Cook watched Wally strut, with boldness or ignorance, into the gym, oblivious to the tarp and watch toy as he passed by them.

Near the door Cook sat down on a bean bag chair and watched Wally play in the middle of the room. He yawned. He leaned back in the chair and stretched his legs out in front of him. He shook his head quickly when he felt himself dropping off to sleep, and then stood up. He would get a few more positive *m-bwee*'s (the negative ones were too cruel) and then go home. He started the tape recorder and joined Wally on the floor, his knees cracking as he bent down. He said a few friendly words to the boy to put him in good humor.

He heard a scraping sound through the open door that he shouldn't have heard. Or was it his imagination? Wally's sudden alertness—he had turned and looked to the door expectantly—confirmed his suspicion and gave him a chill. The sound seemed to have come from his office across the hall, which he had left unlocked with the door closed. He stood up and walked to it. The realization that he was moving stealthily produced a sinking feeling in his stomach. He reached the door of his office and looked back over his shoulder. Wally was watching with great interest. Very gently, Cook tried the doorknob.

It was locked. His keys were on the floor, inside the office, where Wally had been playing with them. The door could not have locked itself. It took little reasoning to conclude that someone was in there. Who? Should he press the issue? If he did, tomorrow would it be Jeremy Cook sitting in that chair, hairless and muscles taut with death? He should call the police for help. But the other offices were no doubt locked, and so the nearest accessible phone was the pay phone on the first floor. He didn't want whoever was on the other side of the door slipping out while he swapped neologisms with Lieutenant Leaf.

Another scraping sound. A rustle of paper. A squeak.

He knocked sharply on the door. "Who's there?" he said authoritatively. Or so he hoped.

There was no reply.

"I know someone's in there. Open the door."

The silence rebuked him for being a fool.

"For Christ's sake—"

A scraping sound again, as of a chair being moved out of the way. Cook listened carefully. Suddenly a soft, pathetic, frightened whimper came from the other side of the door. Cook's mouth dropped open and he winced to hear it. It was unearthly. He heard it grow slightly in volume and suddenly stop. Heavy footsteps moved away from the door, away from Cook, and a masculine groan of some kind was followed instantly by a loud crash of glass. After a few seconds of horrible silence, there was a faint but unmistakable thud from some distance away.

"Jesus. Oh Jesus."

Cook ran for the stairwell and hurried down the seven

flights, trying to believe in all of the other possible explanations, although none of these was as vivid in his mind as the one he was trying not to believe. Outside, in the dark, the black shape crumpled in the distance proved to be the heavy wooden swivel chair from his office, its back broken and barely connected to the seat. It was otherwise undamaged, for it had landed on soft grass. It was as if the chair had tried to die from the fall much as a human would have died.

Cook looked up to the window of his office. A dark figure leaning out disappeared inside, and an unfamiliar, high-pitched, derisive cackle rained down on him.

Cook thought of Wally and yelled out in reflexive panic. He sprinted to the door and ran up the stairs. When he reached the top he heard Wally screaming and crying loudly from the gym. He ran down the hall. The boy was alone, unhurt, and very frightened, sitting in the middle of the room where Cook had left him. He lifted him up in his arms and comforted him. Wally's thumb went to his mouth, and in the sudden quiet Cook heard running footsteps from the end of the hall near the stairs, then the banging of the stairwell door. He listened but did not give chase. He eased himself down on the mat covering the floor in the center of the gym and sat cross-legged, holding Wally against his shoulder and rocking back and forth.

"Jeremy, I would think by now you would have learned to lock your office."

Lieutenant Leaf, fat and to all appearances uncomfortable behind the wheel of his patrol car, glanced at Cook as he said this and narrowly missed clipping the bumper of a parked car as he turned the corner too sharply. They were returning to Wabash from Woeps's house, where Leaf had driven Cook and Wally. Cook had had to call someone for transportation, because the intruder had taken his keys and locked his office before escaping. Leaf would want to know about the prowler anyway, so Cook had called him from the pay phone downstairs. His first concern was getting Wally home and in bed. When Leaf and his driver arrived at Wabash, Cook found Leaf amiably willing to drive him and Wally to Wally's home. Without ceremony he ordered his driver to wait outside the door of Cook's office until they returned. It was then, as he walked to Leaf's car, that Cook saw that his own car had been stolen. It was turning into a rough night all around. At Woeps's, Cook changed Wally and put him to bed while Leaf, amused, watched from the door of Wally's room. Cook left a message with the babysitter for Woeps to call him at the office or at home when he came in.

"Believe me, Lieutenant," said Cook as Leaf pulled out onto the highway leading to Wabash, "I'll lock it from now on." He looked at Leaf's transmitter on the dashboard. "Can you use that thing to have someone call my boss? His secretary has a master key and they can get us into my office. No point in breaking the door down."

"Right," said Leaf, reaching for his mike. After he was done with this he turned to Cook again. "So . . . as you come out of the stairwell the bathroom is just down the hall to the right."

"Yes."

"And you went down the hall to the left."

"Yes."

"And you figure he was hiding in the bathroom, waiting for you to go in the other direction so he could slip down the stairs."

"Yes."

"Why didn't you check the bathroom? Afraid?"

"No. Wally was crying and I was worried about him."

"But it would have taken just a second—"

"But the kid was screaming. I didn't know what was happening to him."

"Ah." Leaf thought about this. "It's a lot like the way you automatically assumed the guy had jumped out the window."

Cook frowned. "How's that?"

"Why do you think the boy was crying?" asked Leaf, ignoring Cook's question. "Do you think this guy did anything to him?"

"No. He seemed okay to me. Just upset. Maybe because I left him alone. I feel horrible about that."

"No harm done."

Leaf was driving fast on the country highway. Cook glanced at the speedometer. Just over eighty. He reached for the seat belt at the side of the seat next to the door.

"The belt's busted," said Leaf. "Who do you think it was?"

"It could have been any of us but Woeps, I guess."

"Why not him?"

"He's out with his wife and in-laws."

"I'll check that. Did you call any of the others to see if they were home?"

"When? You mean after I—" He slapped himself on the forehead.

"Yes. Just after it happened, just after the guy got away. If they were home and hadn't had time to get home from Wabash, that would tell us something. You didn't do that, did you?"

"No."

Leaf was silent for a while. Then he said, "This fellow Woeps is a friend of yours, isn't he?"

"That's right."

"And you think what happens tonight clears him?"

"In my mind, yes."

"And it's supposed to in mine?"

Cook looked at him. "Slow down, Lieutenant, damn it. You're driving too fast."

Leaf obediently eased back on the accelerator.

"I don't care what you think," said Cook.

"Is there any reason for me to think you didn't make all this up?"

Cook laughed, in frustration and disbelief. "There's no point to it. That's a pretty good reason."

"Except that it could clear your friend. But it won't. It's easy for a desperate man to get his family to lie for him. I want you to know that I plan to ignore what they have to say."

"Where's my car, then?" said Cook, hating himself for allowing Leaf to bait him.

"You tell me."

"I can't."

"Too bad for you."

Cook decided to stop talking. What was he to do next—stick his tongue out at Leaf?

"So," said Leaf in a fresh new tone, as if the conversation were just now beginning, "why do you think this guy was in your office?" He slowed the car and turned into the road following the river up to the building.

"I don't know," Cook said wearily. "Maybe we'll find out when my boss gets here and lets us in."

But they didn't. Wach arrived, dressed as he always was in a tie and long-sleeved shirt, and then Mary the Secretary arrived with her hair in curlers. After Mary let Wach into her desk, he sent her home. Then he opened Cook's office. Except for the absent chair and the glass fragments on the desk and floor, it was to all appearances in the same condition it had been in when Cook had last seen it. He looked through the drawers of the desk and filing cabinet. Nothing seemed to have been disturbed. Wach watched him with concern, but he was taking it well. That is, he did not order Cook to drive immediately to Indianapolis to give a lecture to the Chamber of Commerce on Kickapoo adverbs. His stance was stoic. This was one more cross for him to bear, and bear it he would. He and Wabash both.

When Cook was done examining his office and had turned

to the window, wondering what to do about it, the phone rang.

"That must be Ed," he said to the others. "I wanted to tell him right away." He picked up the phone.

"What's your car doing in my driveway, Jay?" It was, of course, Aaskhugh.

"How long has it been there, Adam?"

"I don't know. I just pulled in and there it was. Keys are in it too. And an infant car seat. I didn't know you had a baby, Jay. What's going on?"

Cook explained, or tried to. He told Aaskhugh he would be over soon to pick it up. He successfully resisted Aaskhugh's efforts to explore the matter further and hung up. He told Leaf and Wach what Aaskhugh had said.

"What a mess," said Leaf. "I'm coming with you, Jeremy. I want to check that car."

"For fingerprints?"

"No. For a bomb."

"Really?"

"Not that I expect to find one, but . . . it's sort of like you and your friend's son. I'd be responsible if anything happened to you. I think we're done here."

The phone rang again. This time it was Woeps. Cook explained what had happened. With Leaf's reminder fresh in his memory, he emphasized that Wally had not been hurt by the experience. Just frightened. Woeps listened without interrupting and told him he would talk to him tomorrow.

In the course of the rest of the week, Cook learned a number of things: (1) that Wach had perversely come up with a still more restrictive title for his ominously approaching lecture on names, (2) that Leaf was somewhat famous, (3) of a miscellaneous nature, that Wach's rules numbered fifteen, with no end in sight; that five—count them, *five*—people did not consider him, Cook, a complete asshole; and that he was going to a party, (4) that Woeps had meant it when he told Cook he would talk to him tomorrow, and (5) what that person was doing in his office.

(1) Wach's title, which greeted Cook in his mailbox the morning after the taping with Wally and all that followed, was "The Lore and Magic of Kinsey County (Indiana) Place Names." Cook quickly informed Wach by memo that the title should be "Names." He wrote this in such a way that it did not clearly call attention to itself as a reminder that Wach had already been so informed; nor did it pose ostentatiously as a first communication of this point, for then Wach, if he remembered Cook's earlier request, would resent being patronized. The memo was no small stylistic achievement.

(2) In the Monday issue of Kinsey's local rag, Cook came across an article praising Lieutenant Leaf for his fine service to the community. The occasion of the article was the twenty-fifth anniversary of Leaf's joining the Kinsey Police Department, feted (as small-town journalists liked to say) the preceding night by Kinsey politicians and policemen in some sort of stag party in the banquet room of a downtown hotel. The article, sandwiched on the front page as if by design between two articles titled "Husband Slays Wife While Children Watch" and "Starving Dog Shot," stated that no "suspicious death" cases and only ninety-three rape cases had gone unsolved since Leaf had come to the Kinsey police force. Leaf was described as "a real go-getter" by the mayor. "He goes and he gets 'em," the mayor was quoted as saying, producing just the kind of joke that Hoosiers laughed at. Cook was skeptical. When would Leaf go and get Arthur Stiph's and Henry Philpot's killer? And how was he going about it?

Unethically, no doubt, judging from subsequent information in the article. Apparently Leaf had a bad reputation among Kinsey judges for violating search-and-seizure laws, as well as other standards of police procedure. The community clearly sided with Leaf on this question (and this explained the inclusion of this background information in the laudatory write-up of the *fete*), so much so that no incumbent judge was ever re-elected. The mulish persistence of every new judge in interpreting the law exactly as his predecessor had (i.e., correctly) must have truly baffled the Kinsey electorate.

(3a) By memo, Cook requested a new typewriter from Wach. By memo, Wach replied with a polite negative. Cook followed this with a polite reaffirmative. Wach responded with a curt denial and a statement that Mary the Secretary's electric typewriter was to be at his disposal. To an outsider this would have looked, if not generous, at least reasonable. But it wasn't. Mary's typewriter, because it was the only electric on the floor (apart from Wach's), was at *everyone's* disposal and had been for years. Wach had thus offered Cook nothing new at all. His gesture was like an apparent counterexample in linguistics (something that at first looks like a counterexample to a claim, but isn't really); it was an *apparent counteroffer*, a disguised way of saying, "Nah." This was at the heart of Wach Rule Fifteen, which Cook had found could be expressed in two ways: offer underlings the status quo as if it were a bold new idea, or, give people nothing, but act as if you were cutting out little pieces of your heart as you did so.

(3b) Cook was able to learn, in one case by telephonic disguise (Mr. Philip Henrypot, credit investigator), in two others by gentle inquiry, and in a fourth by well-timed, pause-at-the-open-door eavesdropping, that four teachers who seemed to him not to like him *did* like him. He was prompted to make these inquiries by the unsolicited, unsought revelation (via a waitress at Max's who got it from a Kinsey League Basketball teammate of Mary the Secretary's ex-boyfriend) that prior to her discovery of Stiph's body in Cook's office Mary "admired" Cook. Cook figured that while some replacement of the lexicon inevitably occurred in the transmission of oral narratives, there was no way to get from "asshole" to "admire" or back again. His chief suspect cleared, he had reluctantly re-opened the investigation.

(3c) In another Paula-related area, Cook received an invitation to a party of the Wabash staff and some neighbors and friends. The invitation came from Milke, but the party was to be "At the Home of Mr. and Mrs. Frank Nouvelles." Cook knew that Nouvelles was Paula's last name. Beyond that, the possibilities were endless—Frank was her husband and she was the Mrs. and both Cook and Milke had been wasting their time; or Frank and the Mrs. were her parents and had overprotectively moved from somewhere to Kinsey to be with their daughter for the duration of her summer job; or ditto and Paula had grown up here (this was supported by the little linguistic evidence he had gotten from his one decent conversation with her: although Paula did not *poosh* her car when it broke down, she did write with a *pin*); or etc. A casual question in Aaskhugh's direction produced a machine-gun volley of facts, among them confirmation of the Paula-a-native-of-Kinsey theory. Nice to know, but what could he do with it? Did the humbleness of her geographical roots make her less attractive (and therefore less painful) to him? No. More attractive (and painful)? No. At any rate the prospect of the party cheered him. Something to look forward to on Saturday night besides linguistics and beef-rice-tomato remnants.

(4) Early Tuesday morning Woeps visited Cook in his office and asked for a recapitulation of the events of the night before. He said he wanted to be sure he understood everything. He also said Wally seemed to be all right—he had awakened him and examined him meticulously right after talking with Cook on the phone. Also, he had given Wally some ipecac to induce vomiting in case he had been poisoned. Cook wondered why Woeps suspected poison, and, when he asked he was told in somewhat impatient language that it was certainly possible that the man who shaved Arthur Stiph and anchored Henry Philpot with a typewriter was the man who had been in Cook's office, and that to such a man poisoning a baby might seem very natural, desirable even, and—here he began

yelling—for that reason it had been unforgivable of Cook to do what he had done. Unforgivable. Hadn't it occurred to Cook, he asked, his face reddening with anger, that the entire event was a scheme to get Wally alone so that something horrible could be done to him? And he had fallen for it like a fool. Didn't he know the importance of care with children? He wasn't quite as perfect as everyone thought he was, was he? Woeps shouted down Cook's attempts to justify himself and forbade him from following him to his office to explain further. His final words as he yanked open the door and almost knocked down two window repairmen standing in the hall with a large pane of glass: "Don't speak to me again until I speak to you."

(5) That same afternoon, after a sad and solitary lunch, Cook looked again at Stiph's notes on acquisition of esteem terms. As he sat in Stiph's chair, which he had taken out of Stiph's office that morning to replace his own, his backside now rubbing where Stiph's had once rubbed, he had an eerie feeling that he was in some sense becoming Arthur Stiph. When he got to the page with the Love-Hate charts, he was a little surprised to see the chart for the adult males at Wabash facing him. When he had finished studying it the day before, he had considered that side the backside and returned the sheet to the folder with the other side up. He looked at the chart closely. The additions were so cleverly forged that he hardly noticed them. Stiph's row and column had been completely blank before, but each now contained one "H." One was in the box where Agent Stiph met Patient Milke, and the other where Agent Milke met Patient Stiph. Cook studied the sheet closely under the light. The ink was slightly different—good evidence that he, Cook, was not going insane. Not so different that you would normally notice, but different nonetheless.

Someone's thinking had duplicated Cook's to a striking degree. One of the suspects had seen this chart (the sheet had been passed around in Stiph's office when they first discovered its frontside; it would have been easy for one of them, without Cook noticing, to see the backside of it and quickly take in its contents); then he had seen the possibilities it presented; then, figuring Cook's office would be accessible that night (Cook had openly—and stupidly, it now turned out—told Woeps about his plans to tape Wally in the gym that night in front of all the others, and it was common practice for the linguists to leave their office doors unlocked when working in the central core with the children), he had acted, picking Milke. The success of the plan hinged crucially on the hope (someone's hope) that Cook had not seen the chart before its alteration. It was not an unreasonable hope either, for Cook had just barely noticed it. And if he hadn't—that is, if he were discovering it for the first time now—how would he view this evidence?

Seriously, he admitted to himself. Seriously indeed. He could easily imagine himself savoring those "H's" and looking forward to life at Wabash without Milke. The choice of those two boxes had been a clever one. He definitely would have acted on it, even though the thought of taking it to Leaf made him smile. First it would confirm Leaf's view that the suspects were a pack of dicklike jackals, or some such, and Cook would have to put up with a kinky speech on that theme. Then Leaf would wonder aloud if Cook himself could have tampered with the chart, or made the whole thing up for that matter, in order to frame Milke and clear himself. But for all that, even as he gave a show of great scorn, Leaf would take the information seriously too.

The image of that fat man mocking him was so striking that Cook decided not to tell him about the attempted frame. He decided not to tell anybody, not even Woeps, despite the fact that being told would put his mind at ease about Wally, for it was now certain that the boy was incidental to the episode. Besides, Woeps had forbidden speech to him, thereby thrusting Cook into a sociolinguistic dilemma he would have found interesting if it had happened to someone else.

The car at Aaskhugh's was another dimension. The intruder probably did not expect to be discovered, so that part must have been spontaneous. Certainly spreading the old guilt around, wasn't he? Since people don't ordinarily frame themselves, did all of this clear Aaskhugh and Milke? Not if you thought like Leaf. In fact he would hang both of them on evidence like this, if only the judiciary would go along with him. The chair-throwing must have been spontaneous too.

Quite a clever man to know how Cook would react.

He seemed to know a lot about Cook. In fact . . . Another thought struck him and made him smile grimly. Maybe the man figured it didn't matter if Cook had already seen the chart or not. Maybe he thought if it failed one way it would work another way, as a *suggestion*, as if to say, "Hey, Jeremy (or Jay), we can really stick it to Emory with this. Think about it."

It gave him a chill. Personal dislike was one thing. This was something altogether different. Maybe there were people in this world who weren't able to draw this distinction, but Cook wasn't one and he wasn't happy about being taken for one, even by a killer.

CHAPTER ELEVEN

"'YOU CAN'T SEE *shit* in there'."

"In that case you're not really talking about shit."

"That's right. Just visibility."

"And the other?"

"No stress on *shit.* Descending intonation to *shit,* then rising. The way you'd say, 'You can't see the Alps from there' if you were a well-traveled snot contradicting someone."

"And with that intonation you *are* talking about shit."

"Right. Or the Alps."

She smiled. "That's really very good. I'll work on it. The trick is to find a general explanatory principle."

"That's the trick all right," said Cook.

Paula studied him a moment. He let her do this and tried to look brilliant and handsome. He also tried very hard to think of something more to say.

"I have really enjoyed talking with you, Jeremy," she finally said.

"Oh? Thanks, but . . . does that mean you're going to leave me now?"

She laughed. "No. In fact, that you would even think that's what I meant confirms what I was beginning to believe about you. Emory will be back with our drinks soon, so I have to speak quickly. Listen carefully. I'm having a little difficulty figuring out exactly what you're interested in when you're with me. This is only the second or third time we've had a chance to talk, so maybe I'm speaking too soon, but it seems that whenever we get together you want to talk about linguistics. That's fine with me, of course, but I can't help thinking something else is going on. Of course linguistics is your life's work, but if you were interested solely in the subject I'd expect that that's all you would talk about with everybody. But I've seen you in the halls and in the playrooms talking with Sally and Ed and the others about just everyday things. Are you trying to appear to be something you are not when you are with me, and if so, why?"

Cook hadn't expected her to stop there and began to panic when she did. He searched for verbal cover. Then he caught himself. This was no time for temporizing, disingenuousness, evasion, or any other of the obsolete weapons in his arsenal—obsolete, at least, in the face of this indomitable wench. He rallied and spoke honestly.

"I want to get to know you," he said, not sure what question he was answering but sure that this explained it all.

"Then you should talk about me. And you."

"But I figured since you're a linguist—"

"That's part of me, but there's more."

"And, to be honest, I wanted to impress you."

"And you have. But why? And why do you want to get to know me?"

"Because you are pretty and you have a nice carriage."

She laughed loudly but good-naturedly. She glanced over Cook's shoulder and said quickly, "Maybe some day I'll give you a ride in it."

Emory Milke suddenly appeared from behind a momentarily speechless Cook, grasping a triangle of two glasses and one bottle between his hands. "A gin and tonic for you, my dear," he said around his pipe as he extended one corner of his triangle to Paula, "and a beer for Jeremy, there you are, and the dealer takes a bourbon, and here's to you, cheers, prosit, and so on." He removed his pipe from his mouth and drank a large swallow. Cook watched a bit of liquid trickle down his beard. Then he looked to Paula to see if she had seen it. Over her glass, her eyes were fixed on Cook. He blushed. She smiled, turned to Milke, and thanked him for getting the drinks.

"No trouble at all, dearest chuck," he said. "The chief inconvenience to me was knowing I was leaving you in, or near, the hands of one Dr. Jeremy Cook of the Wabash Institute. You'll note that I did not dally in the kitchen."

"I noticed even if she didn't," said Cook. On reflection he realized with surprise that he had spoken to Milke without malice, sarcasm, or desire to offend. Perhaps it was the three beers he had had at home before the party that made him so friendly. Or Paula's come-on, if that's what it was.

"Quite a crowd in there," said Milke, looking back to the kitchen. "The place is going to be packed soon. Awfully good of you to throw open your parents' house like this, Paula. And good of them"—here he laughed—"to be in Yugoslavia." He turned to Cook. "Isn't she something, Jeremy? How she just jumps in with both feet? Three weeks on the job and here she is throwing the biggest party in the history of Wabash. Just look at them. They've been absolutely *starving* for something like this. Does Wach think of giving one? Hell, no, the joyless bastard." He laughed. "For that matter, do I think of giving one? Hell, no. But here comes Paula from the far-out Far West, hot to trot and boogie, and she just breathes life into us, doesn't she?" He looked at her affectionately and shook his head. For a moment Cook feared he was going to say, "Oh you kid!" What he did say was nearly as moronic. "Love that spunk." Mike said this with his teeth fiercely gritted, as if in truth he hated Paula. Actually, though, he was just speaking around his pipe again, clenching it firmly between his jaws.

"Pardon me?" said Cook, wanting to call attention to the sentence.

"I said—"

"Oh, stop it, Emory," said Paula in a friendly way.

"Stop what?" asked Aaskhugh, easing into their circle and conversation. Cook had spied him earlier at the far end of the dining room. Aaskhugh's question filled him with a mad temptation to see if he, with the help of others, could keep the "spunk" line under discussion for the rest of the night.

"Emory here," Cook said, "was praising Paula's spontaneity, Adam, and her *joie de vivre*, and he capped it all by saying—"

"Oh now stop it, all of you," laughed Paula. "I'm glad you could make it, Adam."

Without responding to this friendly welcome Aaskhugh went right to work, asking Paula about her exact connection with this house, the precise whereabouts of her parents, her curriculum vitae thus far, and more. Milke and Cook sipped their drinks. Cook half-listened to Aaskhugh and then reminded himself to listen fully and carefully. He resolved to listen to what everyone said.

Milke suddenly turned to him and asked him how his work was going. He added that he was particularly interested in Cook's progress on Stiph's unfinished work. Cook put all his sensory faculties on full alert and told Milke that the work was very complex because Stiph's notes were hard to decipher—so hard that when he came back to them after being away from them he sometimes had to abandon his earlier interpretations, "almost," he said, "as if the notes, believe it or not, had changed while sitting in my office." He packed as much innuendo and meaningful frowning and eyelash-batting into this last part as he could muster, and Milke did look at him a little oddly, but then Milke went on to say quite calmly that if his own notes were any indication he could appreciate how hard it was for one man to decipher another's. This struck Cook as reasonable and apposite and left him with nothing. Milke then wondered out loud just when things were going to settle down at Wabash and if any of their jobs were really in danger, and Aaskhugh turned away from Paula—apparently he was done using her in his own fashion—and addressed himself to Milke's question. He said that his current information on that point was that unless enrollments went back up soon, Ed Woeps would be fired.

"*What?*" asked Cook. "Who told you that?"

Aaskhugh smiled. "I have my sources."

Cook thought, Wach was as tight-lipped as he was tigh-tassed. Who else would know something like this?

"Mary?" he asked. "Did Mary tell you?"

"No fair, Jay," said Aaskhugh, laughing and relishing his power.

"But why Ed?" asked Milke just an instant before Cook was able to.

"I can give you my own opinion on that," said Aaskhugh. "Now that Arthur is dead Ed is the most disposable of us. Clyde is a close second, but Ed is first. His work is the least pioneering, it is the slowest to reach completion, and it is the last to get published. He's not pulling his weight."

"Bullshit," said Cook.

"Adam's right, Jeremy," said Milke. "About Ed relative to the rest of us, at least. Some of his work has been impressive, but compared with you, for example, he falls short."

"Compared with any of us," said Aaskhugh. "You have to admit that, Jay, even though he's your friend. Let's ask Paula. We can use her as a test." He turned to her. "You're a budding psycholinguist, Paula. Who at Wabash had you heard of before you came here?"

She looked at him coolly a moment. "I don't like your question," she finally said.

"But why not?" asked Aaskhugh.

"It promotes invidious comparisons."

"I know," said Aaskhugh, laughing. "That's the whole point. That's what's so wonderful about questions like that. You'll soon learn, Paula, that the first question intellectuals ask about a college or institute is 'Who's there?' Well, when they ask that about Wabash, I just want to know what the answer is.

I would especially like to know what the answer is at a place as prestigious as U.C.L.A."

"Come on, Paula," urged Milke. "I'm kind of curious about this too."

Paula looked at Cook, who said nothing.

"All right," she said, "but I would think you men would have more grown-up things to talk about. I had heard of Jeremy, Emory, and Walter."

"Wach?" asked Milke. "He hasn't done a thing in years."

"I don't know about that. I read something he did some time ago on dichotic listening." She paused. "That's all."

"Just as I thought," said Aaskhugh, though less brashly than before. "But surely you've read my classic work on the syntax of interrogatives."

"I can't say that I have, Adam."

"Well," said Aaskhugh, "if that's what's going on at U.C.L.A. I'll have to think twice about what I think about that place. I sure will." He looked to the floor and clucked his tongue. Paula winked at Cook, making him smile in spite of a certain heaviness in his heart. Aaskhugh just had to be wrong about Woeps. And yet Aaskhugh was seldom wrong. He spied Wach passing through the living room, alone, and he knew from other social gatherings that Wach's departure would be within thirty minutes of his arrival, so he called out to him and waved him over to join their group. He heard Milke mutter some noises of discontent and felt obliged to explain.

"I want to check Adam's story, Emory."

Aaskhugh looked up at him. "That's a bit awkward, Jay. I don't think—"

"You brought it up, Adam. Speech has consequences. You're going to have to learn that."

"What?" he asked, quite puzzled.

Cook turned to see where Wach was. He had responded to Cook's invitation but had been detained by one of the teachers. Cook watched them talk. What, besides business, did people discuss with that man? Was the girl asking him if he had noticed from his newspaper reading that these were hard times for dictators?

"Well, I've argued with Walter at all kinds of social events," said Milke. "Meetings, weddings, funerals . . . I hope I can behave tonight."

"He does bring it out in you, doesn't he?" said Paula.

"Funerals?" asked Cook.

"Yes. After Arthur's funeral," said Milke.

"I remember you mentioning that, Emory," said Aaskhugh.

"*Immediately* after?" asked Cook. His question, supremely pointless to anyone who did not know about the dent in his car, drew puzzled looks.

"Yes," said Milke. "Some rare burst of brotherhood joined me to Walter and we walked back to our cars together. But then our conversation took its normal course."

"What did you argue about?" asked Cook, deliberately asking an irrelevant question.

"Who knows? This and that. The meaning of life. Walter could move a catatonic panda to argument. But why does this interest you so much, Jeremy?"

"I was about to ask the same," said Aaskhugh.

"Did he drive off first, or did you?" asked Cook.

Milke thought. "He did. Why?"

Cook frowned. He saw that Wach was moving toward them again and would save him from having to fabricate an explanation. Milke's story seemed to clear Wach of the crime of dent-making, and by implication it threatened to clear him of the other crimes too. This pleased Cook not a whit. He hoped Milke had made up the story to clear himself. But why would he make up an alibi that cleared other suspects as well?

Wach reached out both hands as he neared the group, and Cook wondered what he was going to do with them. With one he clapped Cook awkwardly on the back, like a man who has vowed to overcome physical disgust with human contact. With the other he reached out to pat Paula on the arm, but he more or less missed her.

"Talking shop, everyone?" he asked. "That's healthy. Very healthy. I don't want to interrupt. Other than to say again, Paula, that it is very good of you to entertain us in your home like this."

"No need to thank me," she said. "I hope to have fun tonight like everyone else." Cook looked at Milke, who appeared pleased to be looked at and gave Cook a salacious grin.

"Adam tells us that Ed might be let go," said Cook. "Is that true, Walter?"

Wach looked from Cook to Aaskhugh, then back to Cook. He deliberated. Finally he said, "I'm afraid so. I spoke with him about it yesterday, so it's all right for the rest of you to know. I wanted to give him a head start in looking for something else. It's a shame, but these decisions have to be made. It's not easy for me, but it's part of the job."

"I think it's just a fraction harder for Ed, though," said Cook.

"You don't have to tell me that, Jeremy," Wach said coldly. "At the same time, I am in the position of knowing that if something isn't done soon Wabash will be in a pretty pickle of a financial crisis. By the way, Jeremy, I can only assume that your lecture is ready."

"Is that all you can do?" asked Cook. "It's ready."

"Bright and early tomorrow" said Wach. "They want you there at eight."

"I know."

"I just wanted to make sure you did."

"What about Ed's work?" asked Cook. "He's right in the middle of it."

"He has all the data he needs. He can take it with him and finish it wherever he goes."

"Provided he lands a job that allows him time to do it,"

said Cook. "Research positions are hard to come by."

"He could teach," suggested Aaskhugh. "He might be good at that."

"Teaching. Jesus," said Milke. "Death."

"It would be improper for us to discuss this further," said Wach. He did not elaborate, and so a silence fell.

"Can I get you a drink, Walter?" asked Paula.

"No. I don't."

"You don't?"

"No."

"I, on the other hand, *do*," said Milke, "and I'm going to do it some more. Refills, anyone?"

Everyone but Wach said yes. Cook gave Milke his empty beer bottle to discard and thought about Wach's sudden termination of the discussion of Woeps. It had made him feel guilty and Aaskhugh-like for treating his friend as conversational fodder. And yet his sole interest in raising the subject had been to find out the truth, out of concern for Woeps. He wanted to return to it, but he wasn't sure how.

"What do you think of Emory's drinking habit, Paula?" asked Aaskhugh as soon as Milke was out of range.

"How do you mean?"

"Doesn't his consumption exceed that of the average American male?"

"I can't speak for him. You'd better ask him." She spoke calmly, as if Aaskhugh's questions were not value-laden. Or, Cook realized with a surge of joy, as if she had no personal stake in the matter.

"He probably drinks daily," said Aaskhugh to no one in particular.

"Do you consider that excessive, Adam?" asked Cook.

"I'm sure I don't know, Jay."

"From the way you asked I thought you had an opinion."

"I sure don't."

Cook decided to leave him alone for the moment and

asked the entire group if Ed was at the party. No one knew. Paula said he had told her the preceding day that he intended to come, but Cook didn't know if that was before or after Wach had given him the bad news about his future. He could have figured it out by asking Paula and Wach more questions, but it wasn't worth it. He looked around the dining room and through the door into the living room but did not see him. He wanted to find him and take him aside and cheer him up or sympathize or do whatever Ed wanted him to do. But his friend had not yet uttered the sentence—any sentence would do—that would lift his ban on Cook's talking to him.

Milke returned, this time with a tray, and he handed drinks around—another bourbon for himself, a beer for Cook, nothing for Wach, and seltzer with lime for Paula and Aaskhugh.

"Adam was asking Paula about your drinking, Emory," said Cook.

"Jay! It wasn't like that at all. What are you trying—"

"It was exactly like that, Adam," said Cook.

"But Emory here is going to think—"

"Relax, Adam," said Milke. "I drink abundantly and daily, Jeremy. How about you?"

"Mmmm, somewhat the same, I'm afraid. At night mainly."

"At all hours for me," said Milke.

"Doesn't it interfere with your work?" asked Cook.

"I guess not. After all, I was one of those Paula had heard of, wasn't I?"

"But maybe you could do even more if you didn't drink."

"Or less. Maybe it helps me."

"How could it?" asked Wach. "It damages the brain—the seat of reason."

"I know, Walter," said Milke, "but it relaxes me, and I'm counting on it to damage just those cells devoted to knowledge of trivial stuff that doesn't affect my work—things like my aunts' birthdays, the Bill of Rights, and so on."

Cook laughed and started to say something friendly, but he caught himself.

"Of course I try not to drink when I'm working at Wabash. That would get in the way."

"I should think so, Emory," said Wach, his jowls shaking in a way that Cook found new and exciting. "I wouldn't want—"

"—people, let's see, from *the community* finding me falling down drunk and buggering some toddler. I know, Walter," said Milke. "Don't pull rank on me here, for Christ's sake."

"I'm glad you are aware of the potential complications," said Wach.

"Unfortunately," said Cook, "drinking can have a chaotic effect on one's memory even if it is confined to after hours." From behind, someone approached and bumped Cook gently on the shoulder blade, but he didn't turn around.

"How's that, Jeremy?" asked Milke.

"It's been my experience," Cook continued, "and I've read of experimental demonstrations of it, that what you forget depends on the state you were in when you first acquired the knowledge and the state you are in when you're trying to remember it. Facts learned when sober are of course best remembered when sober. Sober facts are forgotten in drunkenness, and drunkenly acquired facts are often forgotten in sobriety. None of this is too surprising, really. But this is: knowledge acquired when one is drunk is best remembered in a drunken state. For example, if you take ten people and get them all drunk in the laboratory and teach them a bunch of nonsense words, and then the next day if you divide the group in half and get one half drunk and keep the other half sober, the drunken half will do better on the re-test than the sober half."

"Is that right?" asked Paula.

"People always say the same things over and over at cocktail parties." Cook turned around and found the speaker to be Ed Woeps, who had been standing to his side and just in back of him. Even as he had been speaking Cook had noticed Paula's eyes glancing over his shoulder. Woeps was quite drunk. Cook wondered why he had said what he did. Cook had never given this particular talk before. He hoped Woeps was not so drunk he would embarrass himself.

"What do you mean, Ed?" asked Paula.

"People always say the same things over and over. When they drink. Because they can remember. To say only the things. They have said before. When they were drinking before. State-dependent." He turned and looked at Cook, tilting his head back and raising his eyebrows very high. "Does that make sense, Jeremy?"

Cook sighed with relief. "It sure does, Ed. I think you have nicely placed an accurate observation under the umbrella of a general explanation."

"That's my job," said Woeps.

Cook heard Aaskhugh say something to someone else, and the resulting conversation was loud enough to drown out what he wanted to say to Woeps, so he said it, gripping him by the upper arm: "And I hope it will continue to be, Ed." Woeps nodded slowly several times but looked ahead blankly, and Cook couldn't be sure his meaning had penetrated.

Milke took another request for refills. This time Cook asked for a bourbon on the rocks, to which Milke said, "Now we're cooking with gas." He came back with a tray on which sat a fresh bottle, an ice bucket, and two glasses. He set it on the dining room table and poured drinks for himself and Cook. Wach observed the ceremony coldly—or it seemed so to Cook—and he finally spoke.

"I suppose it hasn't occurred to you that your drinking incriminates you in the death of Arthur."

"How's that?" asked Milke.

"You will recall—I hope you're not that far gone yet, eh, Jeremy?—the vomitus on the floor of Jeremy's office. Whiskey, as I remember."

"Yes," said Aaskhugh enthusiastically. "Bourbon. Which I never touch."

"Oh, horseshit," said Milke.

"Ditto," said Cook. "If it had been me I wouldn't now advertise the fact that I drink bourbon."

"Ditto," said Milke.

"What have *you* been drinking, Ed?" asked Aaskhugh.

Woeps was a little slow to respond. He smiled a dreamy smile, then rocked forward a bit toward Aaskhugh and slurred, "Your blood."

"What?" said Aaskhugh.

"Ed, that's pretty silly," said Cook, laughing. Woeps began to laugh too. Aaskhugh looked at the two of them nervously.

"Along these lines," said Milke, "one could argue, in fact one *will* argue, and I am that one, that because you, Walter, have a master key to the offices, only you could have gotten into Jeremy's office this week to do whatever was done in there.

"Nonsense," said Wach, pressing his narrow lips together in a smile of delight at having caught Milke in a mistake. "First, it is common knowledge that Jeremy left his door unlocked, or have you forgotten?" He looked at the drink in Milke's hand. "Any one of us could have walked in there. Second, I do not have a master key. Mary has the only one. It is kept locked in her desk, to which she has a key, but she lacks a key to her office. One of us must be there for her to have access to the key. Thus no single person, including myself, exclusively controls the master key. The security is impeccable."

"I didn't know it was so well thought out," Milke said sarcastically. "Maybe you're right about the key business, but there must be other incriminating evidence against you. There's got to be. You're such a scoundrel." Milke laughed after saying this, and a stranger to the group would have thought he had spoken lightheartedly.

"I'm afraid there isn't, Emory," said Wach. "On the contrary, the fact that the crime and, in particular, the placing of the body in Jeremy's office call attention to Wabash and cast it into disrepute makes me an unlikely suspect. I would never do anything so damaging to the Institute. You all know of my abiding concern for our reputation in the community."

"Yeah, I heard something about that once," Milke said.

"Rather well prepared with that argument, aren't you, Walter?" said Cook.

"I am of the orientation that one ought always to be prepared," Wach said ponderously. Cook suddenly imagined how horrible it would be to be Wach's son or daughter. The people who would have been his children if he had had any were just as well off not existing.

"What I meant to suggest," Cook went on, "is that only a guilty man would have a defense so well prepared."

Wach did not speak. Cook did not know if he was exercising Wach Rule Four (in dangerous times wise men say nothing), or if he was just "not going to dignify that statement with a response," also a Wach Rule with a number he couldn't remember just now. Preferring drinking and forgetting to abstaining and remembering, he went to the table and poured himself another drink without asking if anyone else wanted one. He sensed it was every man for himself now. When he returned to his place in the circle he noticed that Paula was gone. He spotted her at the foot of the stairs in the living room, just on her way up.

Milke must have noticed Cook looking at her, because he bumped him and said, "Something, eh?" Cook made a face. If the setting had been a gangster movie, and if Milke and he had been discussing their—what was the word? *molls*?—he might have been able to say something. Milke added, "So young. Such a tight body, eh?" He saved Cook the anguish of yet another search for words by suddenly turning to Wach and shouting, "What did you say?"

Wach had been speaking to Aaskhugh and Woeps. He turned to Milke and arched his back. "That you are the primary suspect on my list, Emory."

"Oh? We're even then, because you're front and center on mine. Nothing personal, of course. Or rather, a lot."

"Listen, now—" began Wach, squaring his shoulders.

"Who's first on your list, Jay?" said Aaskhugh.

Cook watched Milke and Wach settle down as he thought about Aaskhugh's question. He gave an honest answer. "Nobody's first. Everyone's in even contention except Ed. He's last. He's not even on the list." He turned and looked at him. Woeps stood rooted in place, staring straight ahead as if he hadn't heard anything. Cook was pleased to see he was not drinking.

"Odd you should say that," said Aaskhugh, "seeing that he's first on my list."

"That's ridiculous," said Cook.

"Arthur's death was an accident, wasn't it?" said Aaskhugh. "That's enough for me."

Aaskhugh, who said bad things about people only in their absence, must have considered that Woeps now was, for all practical purposes, absent. Cook looked at Woeps. He stood there impassively.

"Perhaps. Perhaps not. But Philpot's death was not, Adam," he said, turning back to Aaskhugh. "It was calculated, deliberate, and cruel. Ed is none of those things. He can't speak for himself right now, so I will. You're a shitty judge of character."

"I'm glad you brought up Philpot," said Milke before Aaskhugh could respond. "I can't help wondering if any of us is strong enough to strangle a man."

"Oh, I've seen you wrap yourself around an air conditioner like it was nothing," Aaskhugh said to him. "Jeremy too. He helped me move once. Remember, Jay? We almost lost one out a window, though. It was a fun afternoon. I'm sure either of you could choke a man to death. I doubt that I could, though."

"You shake hands with a strong grip, Adam," said Milke. "I

remember. Here." He stepped forward and reached out his right hand. Aaskhugh took it automatically. They clasped hands. "Oh come on," said Milke, and Aaskhugh rose to the challenge. Milke grinned. "Yes, I was right."

"Let me shake your hand, Walter," said Cook. Wach give him a bone-crunching grip, and Cook's own grip tightened reflexively. After a moment they released simultaneously.

"No point in pretending to be weak," Wach said under his breath. "Weakness is never a good quality." He looked at Milke and Aaskhugh. "Anybody else?" he asked, extending his hand like some champion Indian wrestler taking on all comers.

Milke laughed. "Relax, Walter. Mellow out, if possible. I want to know why I'm number one on your list."

"Because of what Arthur said about you, Emory," said Wach as he took a handkerchief out of his pocket and wiped his hands. "That report that was aired at our last meeting was quite compelling in the way it incriminated you. Also because of your temper. A certain passion would be called for in a man for him to strangle another man."

"I agree," said Milke. "And that is the one weakness in my case against you." He spun on his heel and went to the table for another drink. Wach followed him with his eyes. His lips were pressed tightly closed. Then they parted and his words flew out.

"Oh, yes. You *are* the expert on that, aren't you, Emory. Of one kind, anyway. I ought to know. I'm the one who has to hire teachers to replace the ones you use up and drive away." He had to speak loudly, shout almost, so that Milke could hear him at the table several steps away. This made his words sound even angrier than they were. It also brought the attention of all others in the dining room to the circle of five linguists. A few of the bystanders began to drift away, seeking more of a true party atmosphere in the kitchen or living room.

"That's a fine construction to put on the discontent at Wabash," shouted Milke from the table. He hastily finished pouring his drink and rejoined the group. "The fact of the matter is that human nature craves freedom and sociability, and those are two things your administration discourages. You make people feel like they have to sneak laughs and good fellowship when you're not looking. Which goes with what I said about passion, actually. In my view, better for a man to be guilty of a little excess here and there—ask Jeremy about that, he'll back me up—than to be the emotional cripple you are."

"Why you lush, you bearded, stinking prick, you—" Wach clenched his fists.

"I'm gonna slug me a fishwife," Woeps announced matter-of-factly, as if something had just magically released him from some spell. He stepped toward Aaskhugh, who was observing Milke and Wach intently. Cook reacted too slowly to stop him, and Woeps's roundhouse blow caught Aaskhugh by surprise on the side of his head just behind his left eye. He dropped to the floor as if shot, and Woeps dived or fell on him. Cook tried to part them, and then things became confused. At first Milke appeared to be helping him pull Woeps away, but then someone behind Milke wrapped a hand around his face and Milke was suddenly gone. Then he was back, falling on the pile composed, in order, of Aaskhugh, Woeps, and Cook, and Cook found it hard to breathe and began to gasp, when the pile suddenly flew apart and someone had him down and was trying to hit him in the face. It was Woeps. Cook tried to explain to Woeps what he was doing in his drunken fury, and when it occurred to him that Woeps knew perfectly well what he was doing and was prepared to go on doing it, he threw him off with one angry lunge. He rose to his knees and gasped, panting like a dog. He looked around for Woeps. The last thing he remembered was someone in the midst of the fight, through gritted teeth, saying, "I do not like thee, Dr. Fell."

CHAPTER TWELVE

COOK AWOKE WITH A JOLT and looked at the ceiling. It wasn't his, so it followed that it must be someone else's. This small conclusion cost him so much in the way of energy that he would have felt justified in rolling over and sleeping for another twelve hours.

At least he was in bed. Whose? He looked to the side, where a soft breathing was audible. Unless some very powerful being had played a trick on him, he was now in bed with Paula. She lay on her right side and faced him. The sheet was pulled up to her neck, but a bit of bare shoulder suggested possibilities. Those few square inches of bare skin came close to canceling out the heavy weight of misery and turmoil of the past three weeks. But how did he come to be here? What claim did he have, other than proximity, to those few square inches? After a moment of reflection he communed with his parts and easily determined he was naked. He studied Paula's face for a while, then cast his mind back . . . back to his arrival at the house, his chat with her, especially its highly charged climax—that must have some bearing on his present nakedness and location—then Milke and something about spunk. Aaskhugh and . . . yes, hard news about Woeps. Wach confirming it. Woeps joining them at some point. Very drunk. But then so was he. Some bad-ass accusations and fisticuffs. Then waking up in bed.

Something was missing. His last recollection of the party was a clear image of himself on all fours, panting like an overworked young dog in the desert. That image made his body tense suddenly, and Paula stirred, moaned, sighed, and suddenly opened her brown eyes and looked right at him. For an instant he feared she was going to say, "Get out of my bed, you miserable little turd." Instead, she smiled.

"Feeling all right?" she asked.

"Fine." Except for the headache, sore back, and dry mouth, he thought. "Just a little empty-headed."

She raised herself up on one elbow. Somehow, without her holding on to it, the sheet remained in place over her chest. "Headache, you mean?"

"That, too. What I meant was . . . what happened last night?"

She laughed and stretched. "Starting from when? Your lecture on drink and memory—rather appropriate now, isn't it?—or the brawl, or the police, or the talk afterward, or your final lecture on crime and intonation, or us?"

He fell back on the pillow and gazed at the ceiling. This was serious. "Paula, I don't remember a thing after the fight."

"You're kidding." Her tone told him just how much he had missed.

"No. Can you, er . . ." He rose up on his elbow and looked at her.

"Summarize it?"

"Yes."

She sighed. "Well, you fainted or something . . . do you remember that?"

"Not really. Go ahead."

"You came to right away and we finally settled everybody down. But some idiot had called the police, and they came butting in about five minutes later. They didn't stay long, though one of them sniffed around a lot."

"A fat guy? Imperious? Talks with a funny kind of—"

"That's him. When he saw you he shouted, 'O Captain, my Captain!' "

"Did he talk to me?"

"A little." She stopped and looked at him with concern. "Jeremy, you don't remember a thing, do you? I'm worried. Coupled with your fainting—"

"It's all right," he said, thrilling to hear her say she was worried. Was this what being married was like? Waking to hear a lovely woman tell you she was worried about you? Did it ever grow old? How could it? "It's just the alcohol. And I think I must have hyperventilated during the fight. I'm not used to that kind of thing."

"Oddly enough, you kept drinking after the fight."

He winced and silently swore never to drink to excess again.

"Well, after the police left, you all calmed down and the party sort of broke up. But just as your friends were getting ready to go, saying good night to me and so on, you gave a long and—I'm sorry, Jeremy—largely incoherent speech about how you were going to solve this crime with intonation. You warned everyone that you were listening to all of them and had been for some time, and then you shouted out some of the sentences you and I had discussed, sort of as examples for everyone to consider, but you didn't explain them very well and everyone was quite confused. Then you contradicted everything you had said before by saying that listening for intonation while people were talking to you was impossible because language had evolved for communication, not analysis, and one couldn't do both, and you, for one, were not going to fly in the face of evolution." She paused. "We were kind of confused by that, too. Your friend Ed collapsed on the floor, he was laughing so hard. Which is odd, considering. In the end your speech went unanswered—it was unanswerable, really—and everyone went home."

"Did I really make a fool of myself?"

"A little. It was cute, though."

"Why did you say it was odd about Ed?"

"Well . . . because of what he's been saying about you lately."

"What has he said?"

"Oh, just a lot of moaning and grousing about what a super hotshot you are and how everything always falls in your lap and how his wife is always talking about you. I think he's jealous, Jeremy. That's all."

"Jealous? Of me? He's got two kids, a nice wife, a decent life . . . *my* life's a wreck."

"He probably doesn't see it that way. You had better talk to him about it. I don't want to speak for him."

"When did you hear him talk like this?"

"Oh . . . twice on Friday and once earlier in the week. I'm surprised it's news to you."

Cook was silent. He felt as though someone had carved out part of his past, a good part filled with happy memories, and thrown it away, leaving nothing in its place.

"Anyway, that's why his laughter was so odd. It was very good-natured. He shook your hand afterward and said, 'Well done, Jeremy.' I think it was good that he saw you being, well, ridiculous." She paused. "And then everyone went home."

"Everyone but me."

"That's right."

"What about Milke?"

"Emory? I sent him home."

"How did he like that?"

"He didn't."

"Did he know I was staying? I mean, I assume I stayed. Here I am."

"I don't know if he knew. It doesn't matter." She spoke as of a dead man.

"I thought you and he . . ." His voice trailed off.

"We were, or did. It was brief."

"I won't ask what happened."

"He's an adorable sexist that I got tired of trying to reform."

"I see," said Cook, instantly feeling like an adorable sexist and wondering what he could do to hide it. "As far as that goes, that is, along related lines, did we—er—"

"We started but we didn't finish." She smiled. "One of us was not able to, ummm, meet his or her obligations."

"Well, I hope he or she does better next time." He fell back on the pillow, laughing. It was really marvelous, and so was she. And here he was, still in bed with her. He could make up for last night right away. He shifted and moved toward her. As he did so, he saw her open her mouth just slightly to meet his, but he also saw over her shoulder a large, framed picture of Arthur Stiph staring somberly at him. He shouted out "Aagh" in a seizure of fear and pointed to the night table. "What's that?" he said. "What's Stiph doing in here?"

Paula glanced at the picture. "He's my grandfather. Jesus, you scared me, Jeremy. What's the idea? This is my parents' bed, and my mother has a picture of her father on the night-stand. I swear—if being with you is always this crazy, I'm beginning to have second—"

"I'm sorry," he said. "It's just . . ." He looked at her. "Your grandfather? Why didn't I know that? Is it a secret?"

"Walter was afraid it would look bad. He said if the staff knew, they would make charges of favoritism, or something like that. He made me promise not to tell anyone when he hired me. Of course when he was killed it was even harder, but I stuck with it. The hardest part has been listening to people speculate about his death. Like last night. And Walter was the one who brought it up in front of me—the only man who knew I was his granddaughter."

"Yes. He's a total prick. I'm sorry, Paula. Sorry about Arthur."

"Don't let Walter know you know."

"I won't. Did you . . . were you close to him?"

"No, not really. Neither were my parents. They didn't even come back from Europe for the funeral."

Cook frowned. "That *is* estrangement, isn't it?"

"Like I said, they weren't close. And my parents hated his wife. He married her about ten years ago. She and Grandpa were impossible in many ways. They drove everyone crazy."

"How?"

She sighed. "They couldn't leave things alone. When a relationship went bad they couldn't let it be. That's why they moved back here, where my parents were. Grandpa was delighted to take the job at Wabash just so he could be near the daughter and son-in-law who didn't particularly care for him. My grandpa was obsessed with relationships. Quite the opposite of my parents, who are always getting involved with the rottenest people in political causes, but they put up with the people for the sake of the cause. Grandpa could never do that. He didn't care about anything except being best friends with the man who came to clean the roots out of the sewer."

"That's why Arthur's widow was all alone at the funeral?"

"Yes. I didn't want to be with her. I said a few words to her earlier, and that was all I could manage. The funeral is a perfect example of Grandpa's obsession. Do you remember that taps were played?"

"Yes." No one better, he thought.

"Grandpa wasn't in the service. Ever. But he wanted taps played just so people at the funeral who had been in the service would think he had been too and like him better for it."

Cook looked again at the picture over Paula's shoulder. Stiph stared back at him, his face unrevealing and enigmatic.

"If you and your parents felt that way about him, why is his picture in here?"

"I normally sleep in the other room—my old bedroom—and that's where they keep this picture, but I didn't want it in there so I brought it in here when I first got here this summer."

"Then why are we in here instead of in there?"

"Because you threw up in that bed last night."

Cook moaned. "Perhaps we should stop talking. What other abominations will I uncover?"

"I think that's all of them."

His stomach growled, and he decided to sit up in the bed. He propped his pillow against the headboard and leaned his back against it. Doing this gave him time to think about Paula's connection with Stiph. He thought of something, wondered if he should bring it up, and then went ahead.

"Emory and I are both suspects in his death, Paula. And yet you're friendly with both of us."

"It's not a problem. I know neither of you did it."

"How?"

"Because of who you are. You're both good people."

"Both of us? Him, too?"

"Sure. You're alike in a lot of ways. Your opinions about people. Your enthusiasm for your work. The way you talk to the kids—you two are exactly alike in your concern for them, your respect for them. It doesn't surprise me that you're friends."

"Emory and me? We're not friends."

"He told me you are. He adores you, Jeremy."

Cook steadied himself. He feared that his system could not stand many more surprises this morning. Was she prepared to spend the day watching him foul her beds and then moving to still higher ground with him?

"Of course there are some differences," she continued. "They have to do with what I was talking to you about last night, while Emory was fetching our drinks. But then you probably don't remember."

"I remember that part."

"What I was going to go on to say was that your back-door approach to me was in a sense unnecessary. Besides being confusing to me, I mean. You really had nothing to fear from a more direct approach, something on the order of 'Let's have lunch sometime.' I would have welcomed that, as would most women. But instead you came at me with John thinking I'm a drunkard and not being able to see shit in there, which is all really a kind of apology for talking to me in the first place, isn't it, as if to say, 'I'm sorry to take up your time but I'll try to make it useful for you.' You know, diffidence is not a good quality. It invites, well, attack from some people, but in me it induces other things, like a desire to leave or a desire to put an end to it so that we can get on with other things. That's why I said what I did last night. Your lack of confidence makes no sense to me. And that's where you and Emory differ. Cut his aggressiveness in half and give half to you and you both would be better off." She paused, but just for a moment. "I suppose part of what I'm talking about falls into the category of flirting. When overdone, it's laughable, but in the normal course of things it definitely has its place. You, Jeremy, don't have a flirting bone in your body." She looked at him sympathetically. "You ought to try it. You would be quite a charmer if you did." For a moment he thought she was going to kiss him. She said, "Does your breath always smell this bad?"

He inhaled and moved away from her. "Someday, Paula, I'm going to record your speech—yours and that Lieutenant's—and then I'm going to study it for a monograph to be titled 'Conversation as Agony.' I assume my breath smells this way because it's morning and I drank incontinently last night. Give me a break."

"Sorry. Let's have some breakfast, then. I'll fix you some eggs and pancakes."

"Aagh! Aagh!" he screamed, groping to see the clock on the nightstand and knocking Stiph's picture to the floor. It was twenty minutes to eight. The Grange Hall, where the Annual Rotary Prayer and Pancake Breakfast was to be held, was not far from his house, and if he dashed like a madman he could go home, change, and get his lecture notes—no, his notes were in his coat pocket, hanging in the hall closet downstairs—but he would have to go home and change anyway, and with luck he could make it to the breakfast by eight, or near eight, or not much after nine. He jumped from the bed and began to search the room frantically.

"Where are my clothes? Where are my clothes?" he asked.

"In the other bedroom. Down the hall to the right. What's going on? What's wrong?"

He shot out the door, feeling naked and dumb as he threw the words "Pancake and Prayer" over his shoulder. He found his clothes at various locations in Paula's bedroom, as if they had been placed by a random computer program. Paula came into the room, naked and yawning, as he buttoned his shirt.

"Jesus," he said, looking at her. "Don't go anywhere today, okay? It's Sunday and you don't have to go out, okay? I'll pick up a paper after this thing is over and be back in a couple hours and we'll make some coffee and hang out all day, okay?"

"Fine," she said through her yawn, nodding. "What thing?"

"I'll explain later. It's too absurd. I won't kiss you goodbye. It would be excruciating. Sorry about the bed and my breath and being shy and not flirting and my drunkenness and the fight . . ." He continued the list as he hurried into the hall, down the stairs to the closet, where he grabbed his coat, and out the front door to his car.

"Nice to have you aboard, Sonny."

Cook shook hands with the wizened old man across the table, which was covered with a long sheet of butcher paper secured by thumbtacks. One of these had popped loose, and Cook had been idly playing with it, rolling it back and forth across his empty plate, as he listened to the men around him, responded to their friendly questions about Wabash and himself, and wondered what he was doing there. From the kitchen at the end of the long warehouselike building the smell of pancakes and eggs and bacon produced activity in his torso best described as an intermittent circular swell beginning down low, rising up to his throat, then dropping back down again. He imagined his stomach to be a tetherball tied to his esophagus and swinging around on a swivel anchored somewhere at the back of his mouth. On all sides of him male voices rang out heartily. He wished for three things: aspirin, solitude, and coolness—like cool sheets, or a quiet electric fan blowing in his face. He felt at an intellectual low and wondered where the coffee was. It was his only hope for renewal.

Part of his misery had to do with the size of the crowd. He had anticipated a small band of twenty or thirty local misfits. As it was, over two hundred men were already seated at the long tables, and more were pouring in the doors as if fleeing radioactive contamination outside. Such a large crowd demanded something more theatrical than his modest observations on onomastics. Surely they weren't all there to learn about names.

"Here we are," said the man to his right, who had been assigned the job of looking out for him. His name was Hawkins and he sold farm equipment somewhere. He was showing Cook a program. "I'm afraid you've been saved until the very end, Dr. Cook. Just before the benediction." He handed it to Cook, who saw for the first time that the title of his talk was announced as "From Putnamville to Witch's Pudding: Humorous Anglo-Saxon Place Names of Southern Kinsey County, Indiana." Had Wach totally taken leave of his senses? What was the meaning of his perverse narrowing of the topic to sheer nothingness? More important, for the moment at least, what was Cook going to do about it? "Witch's Pudding"? "Humorous"? The only facts he had that came close to fitting this title were his stories about *Hoosier*, admittedly corny but bound to please this bunch. They would probably be the high point of the lecture. He would have to come up with a way of getting around that title to justify the rest of his material. Something like "No talk on mumble-mumble would be complete without also considering blather-blather." A lame formula, to be sure, but there was no alternative.

His eyes fell on other items on the agenda. Chief among them was the introduction of, and a speech by, basketball star Bud Bumbman, graduating senior of a nearby state college known for its winning basketball team. Bumbman, a key man this past year in generating plenty of what was known in the area as "Hoosier Hysteria," was probably the most powerful man in the state. Cook was to speak right after him. While Cook preferred his own title and subject to Bumbman's ("Jesus Christ at the Foul Line"), he knew as certainly as a breakfasting kamikaze pilot that a fatal dive was part of his day's destiny.

"I wonder if I could have a cup of coffee," Cook said to Hawkins as he returned the program to him. Hawkins sprang to his feet and was gone in an instant, leading Cook to believe that Rotarians took their charges very seriously indeed. But then as he watched him make inquiries at the door of the kitchen, then shake hands and laugh with some friends and perhaps close a few tractor deals, he realized that Hawkins had only welcomed the opportunity to get away from him. Cook shared his feeling. Earlier the two men had devoted nearly fifteen minutes of conversation to those areas of life that can be discussed naturally by complete strangers of unlike dispositions, and after only a few minutes Cook was surprised to feel his brain actually shrinking in size. But knowing that the feeling was mutual did not make being abandoned by Hawkins any less depressing. If it were not for the memory of where he had awakened and the prospect of returning there, he would have been the saddest Hoosier of them all. He looked to his left for possible companionship and saw only a small, dour man scowling straight ahead. Perhaps he was a key figure in a local Klan chapter.

"Like some o.j.?" asked the old man across the table, the one who had called him "Sonny."

"No, thanks."

"Really good o.j.," he said. He held up a large Thermos, apparently his private supply.

"No. Thanks very much though."

"Might help you relax."

"No. I'll just have some coffee."

"Donkey piss."

"Pardon me?"

"The coffee here tastes like donkey piss."

Cook smiled. "Thanks for the warning."

"Really good o.j.," he said again, adding a Bacchanalian smile.

"No, thanks."

"Suit yourself, Sonny."

"I'm fascinated by etymology."

This last sentence was delivered without prelude by the scowling man to his left. Cook could only assume it was meant for him. He said, "Really?"

"I think it's a wonderful thing."

"Good," said Cook, unnerved. The man's expression had not changed as he said this. In fact he barely opened his mouth when he spoke. His face seemed frozen into a permanently mean, unhappy look, somewhat at odds with what he was saying. It was as if he found etymology wonderful as a torture device.

"I learned just the other day that the word *yoga* is akin to *yoke*, that there is an etymological relation between them going back to the ancient Indo-European tongue. That is an interesting fact when you consider that both are concerned with union in a basic sense."

"Yes. That is interesting," said Cook guardedly.

"Also interesting is the fact that common people often alter foreign words in such a way that they become more familiar. *Woodchuck*, for example, comes from the Cree *otchek*, but *otchek* doesn't look or sound like English, so over time it was transformed into the more palatable *woodchuck,* which looks like a good old native compound. The same thing happened to the Algonquian *musquash* when it became *muskrat,* and the Old French *appentis,* which meant 'something attached to something'—you can see the relation with *append, appendix,* and so on—when it became *penthouse.* The transformation always makes the word appear more native: *house, rat, wood, musk* though ironically *musk* is of probable Sanskrit origin. This transforming process is called 'folk etymology.'"

"That's quite right," said Cook.

"The folk make other mistakes with language. I'm thinking of the area of popular explanations for the origins of words. *Yankee* is a good example. There are many fanciful explanations of that word. *Okay* is another. One hears ridiculous stories about these and other expressions."

"Yes. I've heard some of them."

"Or take *Hoosier.* There are those who would have us believe it comes from *who's there,* or even *whose ear,* with silly stories about the occasion for these utterances, when in fact the word is of Cumberland dialect origin, coming from *hoozer,* meaning 'anything unusually large.' Because the truth is less interesting than that other nonsense, the nonsense is forever perpetuated. I can't abide nonsense, and I speak out publicly against it whenever I have the opportunity."

"I share your feelings deeply," said Cook. He turned to the man across the table, who had been watching their conversation as if it were a television quiz show whose rules he didn't understand. "I'll take some of that o.j. now," he said.

"Glad to oblige." The man poured into Cook's cup about five percent more liquid than it could hold. The excess formed a small puddle on the butcher paper. Cook sipped the mixture, which was good o.j. in the sense that it was only about one-quarter o.j. The man grinned at him from across the table. The Grand Dragon to his left seemed oblivious to them and stared straight ahead, perhaps pondering the true origins of words. In a matter of a minute or so Cook emptied his cup and set it on the table in front of him in an ambiguous location just far enough out so that his new friend could fill it if he chose to. He chose to. As Cook brought it to his lips again he thought of a word of his own: splendid. The juice was cool and splendid, and it made him feel splendid, and his headache was splendidly going away, and even the sour etymologizer at his side was splendid, and so was Lieutenant Leaf, old Uncle Rebus himself, who now approached Cook and greeted him and those around him. He looked at Cook closely and told him he wanted a word with him after his "little talk." Cook asked him why he was there—was it just to see him? No, said Leaf. He was there because he believed in the power of prayer. Cook thought that was splendid too, and he set his cup down and lo! it was filled again. He said he hoped Leaf enjoyed his talk. Leaf answered that that was extremely unlikely. He added that he couldn't understand what Cook did with his life. He said he had four children and they learned to say *dog* for *dog* because a dog was a dog and that was that. Cook thought that was just splendid. Suddenly Leaf was gone and that was splendid too. So were the pancakes Hawkins finally set before him. They were splendidly shitty, with burnt edges and splendid uncooked batter in the middle.

After a prayer, an introduction, a speech, a prayer, and an introduction, Bud Bumbman took the podium. Cook realized he was next, and his cool disregard for that was splendid. His brain was emptying by the minute. He could feel the names leaving, one by one, like guests leaving a party. Names—the first thing to go when one is under the influence. But he had his notes. He felt the inside of his coat pocket for the five-by-seven cards. Yes, there they were. And the old-timer was right; he was relaxed. Like Bud Bumbman, he thought, gazing down the length of the table to the stage. If looking angelic, if looking almost androgynous, if looking as though you were not just born again but born last week—if looking this way meant you were relaxed, Bumbman was relaxed. What was that he said? The Trinity was like *what?* Thc three-point play? Did he really say that?

At the same time that names were leaving his head in droves, other things were coming in. Images. Words. Phrases. Adam Aaskhugh's face swam before his eyes, his lips pursed for a *wh,* his favorite sentence-initial digraph, and then Woeps was there, laughing, saying "of all the rotten luck" as if speaking about someone else, then Paula was there, her lips pursed much like Aaskhugh's but in her case for a kiss, but that too was unconsummated, obscured by something the baby-faced dribbler on stage had said, and Cook now saw with concern edging into panic that Bumbman was concluding his cruelly brief speech. No more o.j. for him, he decided. He reached into his coat pocket for his note cards, sweeping his eyes over the crowd as he did so. All eyes were on Bumbman. They were enthralled. The Boy-God could have emptied the floor with an altar call. And Cook was next. From Putnamsomething to Witch's What-was-it? God and onomastics was a *perfect* combination. But why was Leaf, sitting at the head table on one side of Bumbman, not looking at the speaker as the other disciples at the table were? Why was he, in fact, looking directly at Cook? And why did he want to see Cook after the breakfast?

Cook scooted his chair back so that he could set his cards in his lap and skim them unobtrusively. The first one facing him had a large *A* drawn on it. He didn't remember writing that. What could he have intended it to mean? He flipped the card over. The other side was blank. The second card showed an *S*. The next five spelled *S-H-O-L-E,* not an English word, but when it was combined with the first two letters, what resulted was—as the self-made linguist to his left might put it—a good old native compound, one with which Cook was quite familiar. The question of who had effected this substitution, and why, and when, interested him less than the question of what he was now going to do about it. What could he remember? That writers of Old English avoided relative clauses in the middle of sentences. Yes, he could remember that from graduate school, but would it fly in the Kinsey County Grange Hall on this June morning? That Polyphemus was the son of Poseidon. Where had that come from? Undergraduate school? That nine times six was fifty-four. He was going in the wrong direction. He forced his mind back closer to the present, hearing Bumbman ask for questions and gasping with relief to see a hand go up at the next table. Again, visions from the party of the night before tantalized and distracted him. It was no wonder, he realized with dismay. The principle of state-dependent recall doomed him. Because he had been disgustingly sober in all phases of preparation for this lecture, he could not now remember a consonant, vowel, or semivowel of it. The party enslaved his mind.

Again Bumbman asked for questions, and just as it appeared that none were forthcoming, the scowling linguist to his left leaped to his feet and challenged the premises of the Christian faith. Bumbman smiled beatifically and undertook to answer the question with a long locker-room parable. For this reprieve, however short-lived it was to be, Cook wanted to throw the man to the floor and smother him with kisses, and this thought suddenly reminded him of Paula, late at night in her living room—no, upstairs, on a throw rug on the floor of her bedroom—but that was gone and he was still on the floor, this time in the dining room, and so were other people, and some phantom rose up before him and uttered a sentence that immediately reminded him of another sentence, a short one, and he simultaneously hated himself for not having remembered it before and loved himself for remembering it now.

He had to get to Wabash. Nothing else mattered now. He stacked his note cards in order, with the *A* on top, and he handed them to the no-nonsense atheist/linguist/Rotarian to his left, saying, "These are for you." Then he stood up and made for the door, not caring that this august body would remain uninformed about names from Puckey Huddle to Witch's Pussy, not caring that Bumbman was now saying; "Jesus Christ gave one hundred and ten percent on the cross," not caring.

CHAPTER THIRTEEN

THUNK.

"*M-bwee.*" (falling tone)

(running steps; kicking of toy)

"I'm sorry for scaring you, Wally. Let's take a break."

(walking steps)

"*M-bwee.*" (falling tone)

(recorder turned off)

(recorder turned on)

"Okay, Wally. Here we go again."

(pause of fifteen seconds; walking steps; pause of eighteen seconds; knocking on door)

"Who's there?"

"I know someone's in there. Open the door."

"For Christ's sake—"

(pause of twelve seconds; groan; glass breaking)

"Jesus. Oh Jesus."

(running steps; pause of fifty-eight seconds; high-pitched laughter; door opening, being locked)

"*M-bwee.*" (falling tone)

(hissing noise; Wally cries; running steps; pause of one minute, seven seconds; running steps)

"It's all right, Wally. It's all right."

(comforting sounds; tape runs out)

Cook slammed his hand down on the desk with finality.

He grabbed himself by the hair and pulled—not in drunkenness, for he was quite sober now—but in triumph and self-reproach. How could he have forgotten the importance of that unexplained *m-bwee*? How could he have forgotten that the tape recorder was running during the entire episode?

As he had played the tape and roughed out a transcript of it, he had reconstructed the events of that Monday night. The thunking watch toy had scared Wally and elicited a negative *m-bwee* from him. He had run to Cook, who kicked the toy aside and apologized to him for using him so callously for the advancement of science. Then Wally evidently saw the intruder going into Cook's office and gave *him* a negative *m-bwee* while Cook fussed with the recorder, his back to the door. Cook now remembered puzzling over that one *m-bwee*, but then he had forgotten about it, his forgetting aided by his natural discomfort in the face of anomalous data. After a short break and walk down the hall they had resumed. Cook heard a noise from his office, walked to the door, knocked on it, and uttered some normal, banal sentences at it. The chair was then thrown through the window, and he—the fool—ran downstairs and outside, only to be insulted with laughter from above. The culprit left his office, locking the door behind him, and received another negative *m-bwee* from Wally, forever observant and consistent in his judgments. Then the intruder, or maybe Wally, produced an odd hissing noise. Then he ran off. Cook returned upstairs to calm the boy, and the tape continued to play for a minute or so until it ran out. The recorder shut off automatically and the tape had sat there untouched for almost a week. Several other machines were mounted on the wall, and if any of his colleagues had done any taping in the gym that week they had simply used one of those.

He leaned back in his chair and wondered if, in the annals of crime, a sixteen-month-old toddler had ever identified a suspect from a lineup. All that remained was for Cook to choreograph it. Perhaps Leaf could help him there. But any man who thought a dog was a dog and that was that might balk at the notion that *m-bwee* means "locomotion is in progress and I like/ don't like that which is doing it." Cook would be better off making the plans by himself. But what to do with the killer once Wally had singled him out? He would just have to figure that out when the time came.

The phone rang. He hesitated, wondered why he was doing that, and then answered it.

"Jeremy, Lieutenant Leaf is looking for you. He says it's urgent." It was Paula.

"Where is he? What does he want?"

"He's on his way to Wabash. I don't know what he wants you for. He had three patrol cars with him. It was like the goddamn Gestapo in here, the way they stomped all through the house. The last of them just left."

"Come out with your hands up." It was Lieutenant Leaf, amplified.

"Excuse me just a second, Paula," Cook said as evenly as possible. He walked to the window and looked out. Five or six rifles or shotguns or bazookas were presently pointing upward, trained on his head. At the other end of them crouched flunkies under Leaf's command. He was to be seen leaning heavily on the roof of his car, using it for protection against any pencils or erasers Cook might be tempted to throw at him, and he was bellowing into a megaphone.

"The building is surrounded," he went on predictably. *"Come out."*

Cook stepped back and tried not to panic. He understood what Leaf was doing because he wanted to do exactly the same thing. Also, his belief in justice and the American way, though presently shaken, remained strong enough to give him confidence. He picked up the phone and told Paula everything was all right. He would be with her later, he said. She began to protest and asked for an explanation of the voice she had heard, but he simply repeated that it was all right and hung up. He locked his office and took the elevator downstairs. He walked boldly out the front door and waved. The policemen were still gazing up at the seventh floor and aiming their guns there.

"Resistance is futile," Leaf droned on.

"Hi, Lieutenant," Cook called out. "Save me any pancakes?"

Leaf turned and stared at him a long moment. Then he lowered the megaphone and put a grin on his face. "Jeremy!" he said. "I didn't know you were here. How very good to see you. We're on maneuvers. We must have given you quite a scare. I thought the building was empty."

Cook pointed to his Valiant, conspicuous in the parking lot. "You think I store it here on weekends and walk home?" he asked.

"Silly goose that I am! Silly goose!" said Leaf, broadening his grin. "I get so caught up in these things, making sure these young bucks don't shoot their toes off, that I sometimes overlook the obvious." He turned to his troops. "Okay, men," he shouted. "Duck squat to the river and wait there for orders." As if motorized, Kinsey's finest dropped to their haunches and waddled across the parking lot and out of sight down the hill. Leaf watched them critically and lit a cigarette. Then he turned to Cook and said, "I must say, Jeremy, I enjoyed your talk this morning much more than I expected to. I thought it was just the right length, har, har, har."

Cook barely heard him. His mind was racing. He hadn't expected Leaf to abandon his plan so quickly. And yet it made sense. Once Leaf had seen it was not working, he had to give up on it immediately. What struck Cook was that if he had been guilty it would have worked. Leaf's large, unyielding presence could have a telling effect. He could use Leaf now, but he would have to be careful.

"Lieutenant, could you muster this kind of force if I produced the killer of Stiph and Philpot for you?"

Leaf frowned deeply. "It wouldn't take this many men to bring in one of you twirpy eggheads, no offense I'm sure."

"I don't need it for that. I mean to scare him into bolting. His running away will be a confession."

"*Hey!* I like that! What a fresh idea. Boy, that's a head you've got on your shoulders, even if it isn't as pasty white and perfectly round as mine. That just may be worth a shot."

"Could we plan it for tomorrow? Here at work?"

"Sure. These young bucks will be out in the country on more maneuvers, but I've got some old uniforms kicking around and I can deputize some of the locals. But how will you know?"

"I'd rather not say. You'll think I'm silly."

"Trust me."

Cook laughed hard at that, and Leaf joined in. Cook sensed it was a rare, human moment for the Lieutenant. "I'll tell you afterward," he said. "But it's solid. It's a linguistic cue."

"A what? Oh. That. I wouldn't want to hear it anyway. That crap bores me."

The two men made plans for the next day. Cook was surprised at Leaf's cooperativeness. It seemed that for the first time since Stiph's death Cook was free of suspicion, or at least as free as anyone could be with Leaf. Free enough, at any rate, to be listened to and taken seriously. And Leaf was desperate. Tactics like his present one must have been part of his last-resort arsenal. But most important of all, Leaf must have been grateful to Cook for participating in the maneuvers pretense. To maintain that pretense Cook did not ask Leaf what he had wanted to see him about, either after the Pancake and Prayer Breakfast or at Paula's. Nice touches, those. Especially the one after the other, with the alerting, terror-promoting phone call from Paula a safe assumption.

"I'll see you tomorrow, then," Leaf said in parting. "I may be able to make a little contribution to your plan. The old hair trick. I'll be by first thing in the morning for samples from all of you, to set it up. We'll talk then." He walked toward the river. Cook looked after him and heard him call out to his men, "Okay, you shitheads. Let's go back to the station and have some Spam."

After the policemen had piled into their cars and driven away, Cook walked out onto the footbridge and thought. Then he returned to his office and listened to the tape once more, just to be sure. As he was locking the tape in a desk drawer, the phone rang. It was Paula, worried about him. He gave her a brief account of his meeting with Leaf and told her he had more to tell her too, but he would save it until he saw her. She said she had some things to pick up at the store for dinner. He looked at his watch and was surprised to see it was almost four o'clock. He hadn't eaten breakfast or lunch, and he had had only three or four hours of sleep the night before. He told her he felt like a nap. She said she would leave the door unlocked and he could let himself in. She closed by saying she was very, very eager to see him again.

Talking with Paula reminded him of what she had said that morning about Woeps. He decided to call him.

"Ed, how are you feeling?" he asked.

"Worse. It will be better soon, though. I hope."

"Can we talk? I've learned something—a couple of things—that make it rather important that I see you."

"Yes. I'm glad you called, Jeremy. I was going to call you later, when my head cleared. It appears that that is not going to happen, so this is as good a time as any. Why don't you come over? I've got an explanation or two to give you, and a peace offering to make. Maybe a bit of the hair of the dog—"

"No! Not that! But I *will* be over, right away."

The phone rang again as soon as he hung up.

"I demand an explanation." It was, of course, Wach.

"You're referring to my lecture, Walter?" asked Cook. Word travels fast, he thought.

"I am."

Cook sighed and decided he should know only half the reason for its nondelivery. "It would have been a bust, Walter. Maybe biblical onomastics would have done it, or basketball onomastics, but I'm not even sure of that. They're all fundamentalists."

"I don't see how the religious orientation of the audience permits you to just walk out on an assignment I have long viewed with some gravity. What were you thinking, man?"

"You don't understand, Walter. I would have bored their pants off. The best thing I ever did for Wabash was to not give that talk. Besides, I've got a little bone to pick with you. The title on that program had nothing to do—"

"Are you complaining about the way I execute my responsibilities?"

"Well, in this instance—"

"I do my job as I see fit."

"I'm sure you do, but—"

"I was elected from the staff to serve, was I not?"

"That's right. Of course nobody else wanted the job, but—"

"And I have delivered, have I not?"

"Well, sure, I mean—"

"If you have reservations about the way things are going, Jeremy, it might be better for you to consider your options elsewhere."

"I don't have options elsewhere, Walter, and I love my work here."

"Ed could stay on if you left. He's got a family and less flexibility. He's a friend of yours and that puts you under a certain obligation to him. You see, Jeremy, I feel I can approach things with a greater sense of fairness than you can. I think my moral sense is keener than yours. That's my opinion."

"Well, you're entitled to it, of course."

"Don't be offended. In my position I try to remain above personal acrimony."

"I'm sure you do, Walter."

"Think about your job. We'll talk about it tomorrow. Meanwhile, I'll make apologies to the good people in the Rotary Club." He hung up.

"So you're suggesting a kind of contract, Ed?" Cook squinted against the sunshine. They were sitting in lawn chairs in Woeps's backyard, watching Wally chase a neighbor's cat and say things to it.

"You could call it that, but I don't think it does justice to the trust we place in each other. And don't look so downcast. We're still friends."

"Why doesn't it feel like it?"

"Because I've popped one of your balloons, I guess. But you've really got to start thinking about these things, Jeremy. You're too isolated. My main point is that you're going to have to start devoting as much energy to your friendships as you do to your . . . your enemyships. Is there a word for that?"

Cook thought about it. "Backfriendships?"

"Good enough," said Woeps.

"Run through it again, Ed. What do you want me to do?"

"First, stop complaining to me about other people. I'm sick of it, and it makes me feel insecure too. Besides, it's hypocritical. You make fun of Emory and Clyde and then you chat with them daily. It's quite cruel, really—saying good and friendly things to them and then bad things about them."

"I don't know how else to get along."

Woeps suddenly jumped to his feet to see what Wally was putting into his mouth. Nothing, apparently, for after examining him he returned to his chair.

"Try liking people," said Woeps as he sat down. "Your objections to them are really quite trivial. Clyde's laughter in his office, for example. I mean really."

"There's more, somehow."

"But that's all you talk about, so whatever else there is it couldn't be too substantial. I really don't care if you like them or not, but I do want you to stop complaining to me about them."

"But I'm not alone in doing this," said Cook, taking the offensive for a change. "You've been saying things about me, haven't you?"

"Yes, I have."

"So what's the difference? You're friendly to me—up until last night, that is—and yet you say bad things behind my backside."

"But I caught myself and resolved to speak man-to-man with you. I didn't keep on doing it the way you do."

"So it's just recently that you've been talking about me?"

"Yes."

"So you didn't call me a complete asshole about three weeks ago?"

"No. Why?"

"I have reason to believe someone did. It's haunting me."

"Ignore it."

"I can't."

"Then look for good things that people have said about you, for the sake of balance."

"Those don't impress me. My own bad thoughts about myself meet them on their way in and annihilate them."

Woeps laughed. "I really don't know how to help you with that, and we're drifting far afield. Speaking of help, I want you to stop trying to help me. You're always looking for ways to improve my life. Don't. I can manage."

"You've never mentioned this before."

"No. But it's a big problem. And here's another one. Stop being so successful. Just stop it. It makes me mad. You don't have to take that one seriously, of course, but I'm serious in saying it. It's something I've wanted to say for a long time, and lately I've learned the importance of speaking my mind. I am resolved to face my problems head-on now, and to stop bowing and suffering. Speaking up to Adam has helped me there. Maybe this kind of approach will turn my luck around." He paused and looked off into the distance, as if in dreamy contemplation. "Anyway, I can sum up all these things under one injunction: forget about perfection. In me, in others, in yourself. Forget about it."

As Cook puzzled over this, Woeps's wife opened the screen door and yelled something to her husband. Woeps jumped to his feet.

"What is it, Ed?"

"Long-distance call. The Director of the Center for Applied Linguistics. Adam knows him and put me on to him. They have an opening. My chances are nil, but I've got to try for it. Can you watch Wally for a moment?"

"Sure."

"Stay for dinner." Woeps hurried toward the house.

"No, I'll go," said Cook. "I've got other plans."

"I'll be there early tomorrow with Wally," Woeps called back over his shoulder. "This thing had better work or we'll all look pretty silly."

"It will," Cook called after him. Then he added, "I'm surprised that nincompoop knows anyone important. Is there anything I can do to help you get the job?"

Woeps frowned over his shoulder and hurried on to the house, shaking his head.

"*M-bwee,*" said Wally, looking at his father.

"I like him too, Wally," said Cook. "But damn the complications of friendship."

Paula was still out when Cook finally got back to her house. He went upstairs and collapsed on the bed. When he awoke it was dark in the room. She was beside him, asleep. He looked at the clock. It was two in the morning. He looked at her a moment and wondered what he should do. He decided to let her sleep. He slipped out of bed and went downstairs, where a nice note told him where the lasagna was and suggested they get together sometime. He found the lasagna in the refrigerator and put it in the oven to reheat it. Then he sat down at the kitchen table and thought about the day ahead of him.

"Adam, this is Jeremy. Could you come down to my office for a moment? In going through Arthur's files more carefully I've come upon transcripts of some sex counseling sessions involving Ed and his wife. Also some notes on Walter's recent psychoanalysis, and something that suggests that Emory, Clyde, and Mary the Secretary have a weekly thing going. Some diagrams too. I don't know how Arthur came by this stuff, and it's not really all that interesting, but I would be honored if you could find time to come down here and go over it with me."

"Jay, I'm on my way," and he was. Cook could hear him opening his office door even as he hung up his own phone. Cook hurried out of his office and looked into the open door of the gym, where Wally Woeps sat with his father, facing the door some twenty feet from it. Woeps gave Cook an "okay" sign, and Cook took up a position in the hall about five feet from the door. He and Woeps, using little-understood principles of body space, had established this as the optimal location to cause an approaching pedestrian from the other side of the door to slow down as he passed Wally's field of vision. Aaskhugh bustled toward him, his fingers twitching. Cook gestured to him to come close, and, being human, Aaskhugh behaved as planned, slowing his walk as he passed the open door and pulling up to a stop in front of Cook just beyond it. Cook raised a finger to his lips and listened. Aaskhugh frowned at him.

"M-bwee," said Wally. The rising tone pronounced

Aaskhugh not guilty. Part of Cook was saddened by this. He stepped to the door and looked in.

"I heard it, Ed. Real good."

"He's being very cooperative," said Woeps.

"Jay, what is this?" Aaskhugh whispered to him. "Does Ed know you're going to show me this stuff?"

"There's no stuff, Adam. You have been an unwitting subject in a little experiment on idiophenomena. I just wanted you to walk down here. Thanks for your help. You can go back to your office now. I'll share the results of the study with you when I'm finished." He smiled to hear himself utter this standard palliative to experimental subjects. Nobody ever honored it.

"Jay! This is quite a disappointment. I must say . . ." Aaskhugh went on in this vein, a model of frustration, as he turned and walked back down the hall.

"Ready for the next one?" Cook asked Woeps.

"Ready. Call him."

Cook went to his phone and dialed the intercom. "Emory, there's a young divorcée down here with her tits hanging all over the place who says she's going to name you in a paternity suit. Would you know anything about it?"

"God, Jeremy, tell her I'm out. I'll try to sneak out the back way through Walter's office and the bathroom."

"She knows you're here, Emory. I think maybe you can talk her out of it. It's the best way. Come on down to my office."

Milke moaned a bit. "All right," he finally said. When he appeared in the hall he was biting his thumbnail and looking nervously toward Cook. When he passed the open door, in spite of his beard, aggressiveness, tobacco smell, sexism, etc., he received a positive recommendation from Wally. For some reason, Cook was not surprised. At the same time, he suddenly feared that his reasoning about *m-bwee* was all wrong. What if Wally gave Wach a rising intonation too? Where would he be then?

"Sorry to scare you, Emory, but it's for a good cause," said Cook. Drawing a distinction between Milke and Aaskhugh, he went on to explain to him exactly what they were doing. As he did so, one of the teachers began bringing several children into the gym, and Woeps chased them off, asking for a few more minutes of privacy.

"Incredible, Jeremy," said Milke. "And the prick is the only one left. If you're right about this business it's got to be him."

Cook nodded. "We have to hear the falling intonation from Wally."

"Let's get him down here and ice it, the bastard," said Milke.

"Wait in here out of sight," said Cook, directing him to stand behind the open door. "It's good you're here. We can use one more witness."

Cook went to his office and called Mary the Secretary, with whom Wach insulated himself. When she answered he said, "Walter? Walter?" He knew very well that it was Mary, but pretending to be thinking he was addressing Wach was the only way he could make good his vow never to speak to her again.

"I'll ring him. Is this Dr. Cook?"

"Walter? This is Jeremy."

"I'll *ring* him. Hold your horses."

"Yes?" Wach said in his unfriendly way.

"Walter, this is Jeremy. I've got someone from an outfit called Videohype here in my office, and he's pushing a closed circuit camera system. He says they're having a promotional campaign and he's willing to give us free installation, maintenance, and rent of the equipment for two years. You know—a camera in every playroom, even in every office, if you like, all hooked up to monitors in a convenient central location such as your office. Ideal for staying on top of things. Would you like to come down and meet this guy or should I send him packing?"

Wach tried not to sound too interested. He said, "That's not an unattractive concept, Jeremy. I'll be there presently. Afterward, we can address ourselves to that other matter."

"I look forward to that, Walter."

Cook took up his position beyond the door and waited nervously. Wach finally appeared, stepping toward him like some Prussian parade marshal. He passed the door and Cook again raised a hushing finger to his lips and listened. He heard a giggle and scampering noises, but no *m-bwee.* Wally suddenly appeared at the door and turned and began to walk with his propulsive, precipitate gait down the hall in the opposite direction. Wach, who had been looking at Cook as if about to demand an explanation, turned and saw Wally.

He hissed, and the sound of it made Cook's skin crawl. "That child should not be in the hall," he said. "Where are those teachers?"

Wally halted at the sound of Wach's voice and turned around. Wach took three steps to the door to look into the gym, and Wally watched him move and then said it, with an intonation that went down, down, down. He stood rooted in place. Then, as if he knew more than he could possibly know, he raised a stubby finger at Wach and pointed at him.

"*Ecce homo*," said Cook under his breath.

"What's going on here?" said Wach, looking from Woeps to Cook.

Woeps stepped out into the hall. "All of a sudden he decided to play Chase-the-Baby, Jeremy. Sorry."

"It's okay, Ed. He said it."

"Did he say it?" said Milke, stepping out from behind the gym door.

Wach looked at him, bewildered. "I demand an explanation," he said loudly.

Cook looked at Wach. For five years the sonofabitch had kept him hopping. His relief in knowing that this period of his life was over was nearly as great as that in knowing who killed Stiph and Philpot. He began to whistle "Sweethearts on Parade."

As arranged, Lieutenant Leaf stepped boldly out from the nook near the stairwell with what looked like the Third Army behind him. It was an intimidating show of force. They moved down the hall with plenty of noise, if not precision. Leaf looked at Cook, Woeps, Milke, Wach, and then Aaskhugh, who was coming down the hall inquisitively from the other direction, and then he looked at Cook again. Cook did not stroke an imaginary beard or purse his lips into a *wh.* Instead, he stiffened his back and pointed to his watch. Leaf nodded.

"Dr. Wach," he said loudly. "You are under arrest. The lab shows traces of your hair under Henry Philpot's fingernails." He shrugged and grinned at Wach. "These things happen," he said in a friendly way.

Wach bolted. He blurted out something inarticulate and bumped Woeps to one side as he began to run down the hall toward his office.

"Stop him!" Cook yelled to Aaskhugh, who, his mouth open in wonder, watched Wach give him a stiff-arm to the face that banged his head back against the wall and sent him to his knees. His subsequent groveling on the floor of the hall slowed pursuit. Wach shot into his office. Behind him, Cook led Woeps, Milke, Leaf, and the Kinsey Police Department to the door. Mary the Secretary looked up from her empty desk and began to scream to no purpose. Wach's door was locked, and Cook kicked at it angrily.

"The bathroom!" he shouted. "Some of you stay here." He forced his way through the crowd of confused policemen and began to sprint down the curving hallway, hurdling Aaskhugh's still struggling body on the floor, and clenching his fists as he approached the bathroom. Behind him trailed the others. They packed into the bathroom, only to find the connecting door to Wach's office locked.

"Some of you stay here and watch this door," he shouted.

"There's another way out." He led a smaller group back into the hall and into the central core. The door from Wach's office leading into the core was wide open. Cook ran into the gym. Milke had apparently anticipated Wach's escape by that route and had turned into the gym as the others were running to the bathroom. He had struggled with Wach and lost. He lay on his back next to a tipped-over changing table, dazed and moaning. A spilled diaper pail lay next to him, the liquid forming a puddle all around his shaggy head. Paula and another teacher had just discovered him and were trying to help him.

"He got Wally," he was saying over and over. "He got Wally. He got Wally."

Cook cursed and ran to the stairwell with Woeps right behind him. They stopped at the top to listen. Wach was several floors below, running. They ran down after him. Farther upstairs, Leaf and the others followed. By the time Cook and Woeps reached the ground floor and ran out to the parking lot, Wach was nearly to the footbridge. He was carrying Wally like a football under his right arm. Cook and Woeps gave chase. When Wach reached the center of the bridge he raised Wally at arm's length above his head with both hands, one at his feet and one at his neck. He turned and looked back to the parking lot. Wally, no doubt dazed and overwhelmed, was silent.

"Keep him looking this way," said Woeps. He veered off to the right, crouching, hidden from Wach's view by the parked cars. Cook looked at Woeps. He was making for the river, upstream from the bridge. Cook began to walk to the bridge slowly. Behind him, he heard Leaf order his troops to stop.

"Take it easy, Walter," Cook shouted.

Wach glared at him, his eyes wild. Wally began to wriggle above his head, and Wach tightened his grip on the boy's feet and neck. Wally began crying then.

"Don't hurt him," Cook shouted. "There's no point." He watched Wach carefully to see how he reacted. He felt helpless to say the right thing. He glanced to his right. Woeps had just reached the water. Wally began to cry loudly now, and Wach shook him over his head.

"The boy has nothing to do with this," Cook yelled, beginning to panic. He wanted to run out there and throttle him. But Wach could throw Wally into the water or dash him against the floor of the bridge. Wally began to scream now and Wach shook him harder.

"For God's sake, Walter," he shouted.

"Put up that rifle, Hawkins," he heard Leaf say behind him. "Better yet, give it to me."

Woeps was floating to the bridge now. His son's cries grew louder and more frantic. When he reached the bridge he stretched one hand up and just caught the edge of the floor. He struggled against the current to pull himself up. Wally's crying seemed to enrage Wach, and he lowered the boy to his eye level, stood him on the railing of the bridge, and began to choke him with both hands. Cook ran for the bridge then. He saw Woeps lose his grip on the bridge and fall back into the water. The current swept him under the bridge. Cook heard a shot and saw Wach's head snap back. He stopped running and watched. Wally fell into the water, almost landing on his father. Woeps fished for him and caught him, supporting him with both hands as he kicked awkwardly for shore. His son's screaming was a welcome sound now.

"Thank God," Cook heard someone behind him say.

"There he goes," said another, and Cook saw Wach teeter for a long moment on the railing and then splash into the water. He ran to the shore and waded out to help Woeps. Wally clung to his father and kept looking back to the bridge as if fearful of pursuit. He was sobbing hysterically now, gasping for air, and his father tried in vain to soothe him as he carried him to land and held him. Whichever way Woeps held him, Wally spun and looked back to the bridge. Then he saw what he was looking for. Wach's body had caught on a snag, and now it spun free and floated close to the shore. His face rolled up, streaked with watery blood, as he floated slowly past. Cook heard Leaf give an order for someone to go after him.

"M-bwee," said Wally, his intonation going down as he watched the water carry Wach's body downstream and away from him. He became calmer then, and his sobs grew fainter.

CHAPTER FOURTEEN

"I THINK HE PLANNED on the lecture being a disaster, Jeremy," said Woeps as he took an armload of books from his shelf and stacked them on a cart. "It would have given him an excuse to fire you."

"But why would he want to fire me?"

"Because he probably saw you as a threat—as the person most likely to crack the case. Turns out he was right, though my boy did his share too, didn't he? And even if by some miracle your lecture didn't bomb, the preparation for it had your attention for a few weeks. He probably wanted to keep your mind occupied."

"So you don't think there was any sincerity in his claim that it might have important p.r. value for Wabash?"

"Not an ounce. He was just looking out for himself."

Cook shook his head. "That bastard. I worked like a dog on that stupid thing."

Woeps emptied one shelf and began on another one. "He had all of us hopping. He told me he wanted a preliminary report on my dialect competition work in two months—an impossible deadline, particularly because it wasn't going anywhere at all. He did the same thing to Emory and Adam, too."

"What thing?" asked Aaskhugh, who had just arrived, or at least now showed himself, at the door of Woeps's office. Woeps smiled thinly and told him what he had just told Cook.

Aaskhugh looked at the empty shelves. "Moving already?" he asked.

"That's right," said Woeps.

"Are you that power-hungry?"

"Nothing of the sort. You don't want the ship of state to drift without a rudder, do you?"

It was like Woeps to compare himself to a rudder rather than, say, a brave helmsman, in referring to his new position as Director of the Wabash Institute, a position to which he had been nearly unanimously elected by the other linguists the day after his predecessor and justice encountered each other for the first time.

"Can I help move this stuff down the hall, Ed?" asked Aaskhugh.

"No, thanks. Jeremy's been helping me and we're nearly finished. Once I'm settled, though, I'll be needing your help. I'll be needing everyone's help."

"Hell, Ed. You can count on me."

"Good." For a microsecond, the two men smiled warmly at each other.

Milke appeared at the door and greeted everyone. "Lovely morning, isn't it? Just lovely. The birds. The trees."

"Emory," said Cook, "it's hotter than hell, and the humidity turned my shirt into a hot washrag before I could finish breakfast." He paused. "And yet . . ."

"Ah," said Milke. "You take my meaning."

"I do. I do."

"Walter's palpable absence almost makes up for a setback in another arena of my life, Jeremy. *Almost*. Do you take my meaning once again? Do you?"

Cook swallowed. "Yes, Emory. I'm awfully sorry—"

Milke reached out and put a hand over Cook's mouth. It was a very gentle touch. "Not a word more, lad. All's fair in love, etc., other fish in the sea, etc., probably better off anyway, etc. You see, I can cope. The three of us must have lunch sometime, though. Maybe I'll manage to spill a bowl of soup on your head, ha, ha. Today, maybe?"

"I'd like that," said Cook, "but hold the soup. I think tomorrow would be better. I'm meeting Clyde for lunch today."

"Orffmann?" said Aaskhugh with disbelief.

"That's right. The poor guy's been in the hospital for two weeks now and no one's been to see him."

Milke nodded and said, "Jeremy's right. It didn't even occur to us to consult him about Ed's election."

"You're welcome to join me," Cook said to him. "You're all welcome."

"I'll try to make it," said Woeps. "We have to talk to him and see if Wednesday nights are okay with him."

"Right," said Milke. "With Walter gone Clyde's essential."

"I'll bring a copy of the story for him," said Cook. He turned to Aaskhugh. "Adam? Lunch with Clyde?"

"If I don't go you'll probably talk about me." Everyone laughed.

"How's Wally, Ed?" said Milke.

"He's fine, Emory." Woeps turned to Cook. "You know, *m-bwee* is dead."

"*What*?"

"He doesn't say it anymore. He's had several opportunities since Monday and he just hasn't said it."

"I'll be damned," said Cook.

"Got room for a fat man?"

They all turned to the door. It was Lieutenant Leaf. Once he stepped inside his question seemed apt, for there was just barely room for him. Everyone negotiated around the boxes and carts to accommodate him.

"The place seems busy this morning," he said. "A lot of cars pulling up with little cherubs in them."

"That's right, Lieutenant," said Woeps. "Enrollment is climbing back up already." He looked at everyone sternly and attempted an imitation of Wach. "I need not remind you of the importance of maintaining this trend or of the dangers of over-optimism." The linguists laughed at this while Leaf watched.

"I always thought it was Walter," said Aaskhugh. "He was a bad one, wasn't he?"

This met with several nods and a hearty "Hear, hear" from Milke.

Leaf laughed. "I'm glad to see you all getting along so famously. It wasn't long ago, you know, that you were pointing fingers every which way." He folded his arms across his chest, index fingers extended, pointing to both sides at once.

Everyone muttered disclaimers and shifted uneasily.

"I bring this up only because I am here to say, with some sadness, that I have reason to believe that Walter Wach had an accomplice." He looked from one linguist to the next, and as he watched their jaws drop and their eyes go to their neighbors with the old suspicion, he guffawed. "Just kidding, har, har, har. Human nature kills me. How about you, Jeremy?

Cook smiled weakly.

Mary the Secretary appeared at the door. "Dr. Woeps? WKIN is on line three. They want to send a team over for an interview."

"Thanks, Mary," said Woeps, reaching for his phone. "Let's look sharp when they get here, men," he said to his colleagues as they began to move toward the door. This time it was hard to tell whether or not he was kidding.

Milke said it for all of them. "Don't turn into a jerk, Ed."

Woeps laughed and pushed a button on his phone. "No chance," he said cockily.

"We'll make sure," Aaskhugh said as he stepped into the hall.

"Oh?" Woeps called after him. "Physician heal thyself, Adam."

"Save it, guys," said Cook. He and Leaf followed Aaskhugh out the door and closed it behind him. Aaskhugh swallowed his rejoinder—he looked as if he had one ready—and began to walk down the hall with Milke. Milke said something to him about a problem that had come up in his work and asked him to come to his office. Watching the two of them talk like this gave Cook a sudden sense that workaday life at Wabash was back to normal. His mind began to drift back to his own unfinished research projects.

"Well, old pal," said Leaf, "I hate to make apologies—who knows, the day after I apologize to someone he may give me a good reason to arrest him or shoot him in the head, and then where am I?—but one is in order here. Until Monday I thought you were the one."

"You mean I was first on your list?"

"You were the *only* one on my list."

"Jesus, Lieutenant. Do I really strike you as the kind of person who could do those things?"

Leaf sighed. "That did give me pause. My only hope was that you were good at hiding your true nature. I should have seen earlier that no one could be that good at it. All along I was thumpin' on the wrong watermelon. So it's time for me to say I'm sorry about the dent."

"The dent?"

"Yes. The dent I made in your car."

"You did that?"

"Yes. After the funeral."

"Why?"

"I wanted to spook you, see how you would react. Anything less than pure outrage at being framed would have sent you to the gallows."

"And my reaction?"

"Pure outrage at being framed."

"And still . . ."

"Still I suspected you. Your calling that girl who works here, pretending to be Philpot, confounded me. It looked like an obvious attempt to confuse the investigation. Come to think of it, just why did—"

"How did you know about that?"

"I put a tap on your phone the day after the killings," he said matter-of-factly.

"Did you get a court order?"

"Nah. Nobody cares about that stuff. The important thing is to catch killers. So, like I said, I'm sorry about the dent."

"That's all you're sorry about?"

"Sure. What else is there?"

"Well, apart from your illegal activities, there's your suspicion of me. I deserve an apology for that."

"I don't see why. There was nothing personal about it. The personal element does not exist in my line of work."

"Why didn't you suspect Wach? *He*'s the type."

Leaf shrugged. "I didn't know him. But you did. Why didn't you suspect him?"

Cook blinked and felt his mind go blank. "I don't know," he said slowly.

Leaf looked down the hall toward the elevator. Cook began walking with him.

"He was quite a case," said Leaf. "Drank like hell. Alone at night. That's what his wife said. She's been really burning our ears about him, as if she's been saving it up for years."

"He pretended not to drink," said Cook.

"Doesn't surprise me," said Leaf. "He pretended a lot of things. I checked his record. He was arrested on a child molesting charge back in 1946. He was a teenager then, and the charge didn't hold up, but from what his wife says . . . well, without being active he was still chronically inclined in that direction. People like that dedicate their lives to hiding things. The watch is a good example. I figured Stiph's watch broke when he was run over, and then—get this—he was afraid people would think of his name, *Wach*, when the watch was discovered broken, so he goes home and gets an old watch from somewhere for Stiph, but then he puts the damn thing on backward. Now isn't that a crazy sonofabitch who does something like that? All he did was call even more attention to the watch, and in spite of that no one thought of his name in connection with it, which shows how far-gone his thinking was in the first place. Did you know he was going to change his name, too?"

"Really?"

"Yes. That's what his wife told us. After you and I had arranged our signals Monday morning I thought about it. While I was cooped up trying to keep my men quiet, I thought of the watch being on backward and its connection with his name. So at that moment, without having any idea how you were going to crack it, I was convinced I had, too. If he hadn't bolted I would have gotten it out of him anyway. Once I'm sure, I can get it out of people."

"I don't doubt that." They reached the elevator and Cook pushed the button for him.

"Considering he was basically a hider of things, these meetings with Stiph are a real puzzle—you know, this childish club. How could such a secretive man open himself up to an enemy? It doesn't make sense. And yet we have to figure that Stiph was on his way to meet Wach that night, since we have to assume that the killer is the man Stiph met. Like you once said to me, why else would this man not step forward and say, 'Yes, I'm the one Arthur Stiph planned to meet'?"

"Unless that person didn't know," said Cook, surprised that he hadn't thought of this before. "Maybe this was their first meeting, and Stiph was going to surprise him with it. It could have been any one of the linguists. It could have been *me.*" Cook laughed at the idea.

"What's so funny about that? Why couldn't it have been you?"

"No, no."

"Why not?"

"I just have the feeling that . . . he liked me."

Leaf snorted. "What's not to like, eh?"

The elevator doors opened and Leaf stepped inside and turned the toggle switch to "Off." It apparently did not concern him that someone on the ground floor might want to ride up.

"I assume I will be compensated for the dent, Lieutenant. Should I get estimates from some body shops?"

Leaf laughed loudly. "Are you kidding? For that piece-of-shit car?" He coughed and reached for a cigarette in his shirt pocket. "Well, keep your nose clean, and don't let your nose hairs grow too long. But don't pull them out, either. That can cause an infection. Bye." He flipped the switch to "On" and stepped back and leaned against the back wall of the elevator. The doors closed on his smiling, round face.

Cook walked to his office. He thought about Leaf's suspicion of him and, more keenly, his own insufficient suspicion of Wach. He saw now that he had reasoned badly, or rather that he had not reasoned at all. Distracted by the other suspects, he had not stopped to ask himself if it followed that being disliked by Jeremy Cook made one capable of murder. Aaskhugh, Milke, Orffmann—it was easy to draw from his lexicon of disparagement in talking about these men, but that did not make them murderers. To think otherwise was to commit the classic Stiphian blunder. It suddenly struck him that the world was made up of two kinds of people—those who believed in good and evil, and those who fussed over friends and enemies. The second type made lousy detectives. Not one of his gang—not even Milke, whose suspicion of Wach was personal—had stopped to ask this question in its pure form: who among us is evil?

He took out the file of Stiph's notes on love and hate. Then he went to Mary's office, first locking his door behind him—no telling but that if he left it unlocked the ghost of Geronimo or Ramses II might wander in—and he asked Mary for the master key to the offices and thanked her when she gave it to him, speaking words right to her. Then he walked down the long hall to Stiph's office and deposited the file in the drawer where he had found it, not caring if posterity produced a temperament more suitable than his own for carrying on Stiph's research.

"But what reminded you to go back to the tape?" Paula held the bottle of wine over his glass and looked at him. He shook his head.

"I've had enough, thanks. It was a *Mother Goose* rhyme. 'I do not like thee, Dr. Fell . . .'"

"I know it:

The reason why, I cannot tell.
Yet this I know, and know full well,
I do not like thee, Dr. Fell.

I like to read it to the four-year-olds. It's one of their favorites."

"Well, somebody said it, or a fragment of it, at the party, during the slugfest," Cook continued. "It lodged somewhere in my bleary brain and then a nice man with some orange juice brought it out again at the Pancake and Prayer Breakfast. I suddenly realized that Wally Woeps, whom most people regard as almost prelinguistic, was capable of making such a declaration, that he had in fact made such a declaration at a crucial moment, and that he was capable of making it again." He reached for a piece of French bread and began to butter it. He planned to use it to shovel the rest of the excellent salad Paula had made onto his fork. No more Grunt Meals for him.

"How does he say it?"

"*M-bwee*," said Cook, giving it a downward tone. "An important sentence, it turned out."

He looked at her a moment and set his fork down. The one nagging mystery in his life could be solved in a matter of seconds. All he had to do was ask her. But he felt a new Cook emerging, one for whom it was distasteful to dwell on such things. So he wouldn't ask her. He picked his fork up. Then he set it down again. Well . . . at least asking about it was now distasteful. That was something, wasn't it?

"There's another one I would like to take up with you, Paula, now that I know you."

"Another sentence?"

"Yes. Let me start by asking you how you first formed your impressions of people at Wabash. Before starting work, I mean. Did anyone brief you?"

"Well, Walter told me a few things about people, but not much. Grandpa told me a lot. He went down the staff of linguists one by one and summed up his views for me. It was quite tedious. Remember, I told you he was consumed by petty likes and dislikes—a trait I've seen evidence of in you, by the way."

"Well I can't help it," he said impatiently. "Especially when people are running around saying bad things about me all the time."

"About you? Are you crazy? If you don't know just how well liked you are, and how highly—"

"Listen to this, then." He described in fanatical detail the scene, time of day, parties present, and general atmosphere of the occasion of her utterance. "'This fellow Cook is supposed to be a complete asshole.' That's what you said. You bitch." He said this last jokingly, but he was surprised at how much he enjoyed saying it.

She laughed. "I did? I'm sure I don't . . ." She frowned and looked away from him, as if trying to remember. Her eyes danced back and forth, and he couldn't be sure she was taking him seriously. "Oh!" she said enthusiastically. "Yes, I remember. I remember it very well now. We weren't talking about you at all. We were talking about a guy I know at, ah, Max's. Jane, the girl I was talking with, has a friend who works as a cook there, and one day he was telling me what a creep this other guy who cooks there was, and I didn't know if Jane knew that about the other cook, so I said to her, 'This fellow cook—that is, this cooking colleague—is supposed to be—'"

Cook exploded with laughter. He slapped himself on the side of the head and banged his fist on the table. What a relief! He was free!

Paula laughed too, harder and longer than he did. In fact, to his mild surprise she spontaneously burst into laughter several times as the evening wore on, well after they had left that subject and had begun to talk about more important things.